THIS SIGNED EDITION OF

FINDING IT

by

cora carmack

HAS BEEN SPECIALLY BOUND BY THE PUBLISHER

LIMITED SIGNED EDITION FOR TARGET

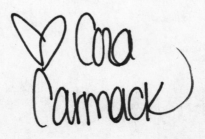

Dear Target Reader,

Five years ago, you could have found me in a Target store; not on the back of a book, but wearing red and khaki and working at the fitting rooms. It was one of two jobs I held during college, and I used to wander the book section on my breaks contemplating how many books I could afford on my poor-college-student budget. While I hung up clothes or straightened shelves, I would plot out the story of whatever book I was writing at the time, but I don't think I ever had the confidence (or the audacity) to dream about a day when my books might be on the Target shelves. Traditional bookstores, sure; I thought about and hoped for that all the time. But Target only ever carried the best of the best, the bestsellers. Now, five years later, it is still so surreal to me to walk into the place where I used to work and see one of my books. I swing by the book section on every visit expecting them to have disappeared because this was all a dream.

If you're picking up one of my books for the first time, I write about characters in their early twenties who fall under the label "adult," but don't necessarily have any idea what that actually means. There are so many huge, life-changing decisions to be made in your twenties, all while you're dealing with college classes, student loans, living on your own, working full time, and/or worrying how you're going to pay your bills. It's a lot to juggle. And if you get it wrong, the consequences aren't just far-reaching, they affect the entire trajectory of your life. Couple that with all the fun times of college, and you have a really exciting life stage about which to write.

As a writer, I always start with characters first. I figure out who my characters are and what they want the most, and that in turn allows me to flesh out their lives and the plot of their book. This book was different, though. I threw that out the window and decided to focus on a very real theme that many people face in the early years of adulthood: What if I don't *know* what I want? It was difficult, not only because it challenged my process, but also because I've always been a very focused, motivated person. The first time I went on record saying I wanted to be an author was in kindergarten. I had to really work to put myself in the mind of a character who was well and truly lost. I asked myself: What happens if what you desire most is to want something so completely, so intensely, that you could base your life around that thing? *Finding It* was born out of that endeavor. The book is set in Europe and based loosely on my own time backpacking after a semester studying abroad.

I hope you'll enjoy Kelsey's adventure, and you'll be inspired to take a few leaps of your own.

Cora Carmack

FINDING IT

ALSO BY CORA CARMACK

Keeping Her (novella)

Faking It

Losing It

FINDING IT

CORA CARMACK

WILLIAM MORROW
An Imprint of HarperCollins*Publishers*

FINDING IT. Copyright © 2013 by Cora Carmack. All rights reserved. Printed in the United States of America. No part of this book may be used or reproduced in any manner whatsoever without written permission except in the case of brief quotations embodied in critical articles and reviews. For information address HarperCollins Publishers, 10 East 53rd Street, New York, NY 10022.

HarperCollins books may be purchased for educational, business, or sales promotional use. For information please e-mail the Special Markets Department at SPsales@harpercollins.com.

FIRST EDITION

Designed by Diahann Sturge

Library of Congress Cataloging-in-Publication Data has been applied for.

ISBN 978-0-06-231662-2

13 14 15 16 17   OV/RRD   10 9 8 7 6 5 4 3 2 1

To Kristin, my eerily perceptive travel buddy.

Remember that time we were stuck in a train station overnight?
And taking a cab from Germany to the Netherlands?
And that microwave I ruined in Spain before I almost died?

Thanks for being there for all of that and more.

1

Everyone deserves one grand adventure, that one time in life that we always get to point back to and say, "Then . . . *then* I was really living."

Adventures don't happen when you're worried about the future or tied down by the past. They only exist in the now. And they always, *always* come at the most unexpected time, in the least likely of packages. An adventure is an open window; and an adventurer is the person willing to crawl out on the ledge and leap.

I told my parents I was going to Europe to see the world and grow as a person (not that Dad listened beyond the second or third word, which is when I slipped in that I was also going to spend his money and piss him off as much as possible. He didn't notice). I told my professors that I was going to collect experiences to make me a better actor. I told my friends I was going to party.

In reality, it was a little of all of those things. Or maybe none of them.

Sometimes, I just got that strange niggling sensation at the back of my mind, like the insistent buzz of a mosquito, that I was missing something.

I wanted to experience something extraordinary, something *more*. I refused to believe that my best years were all behind me now that I'd graduated from college. And if adventures only existed in the now, that was the only place I wanted to exist, too.

After nearly two weeks of backpacking around Eastern Europe, I was becoming an expert at just that.

I trekked down the dark city street, my stiletto heels sticking in between the cobblestones. I kept a tight hold on the two Hungarian men that I'd met earlier in the evening, and we followed the other two in our group. I guess, technically, I had met them last night, since we were now into the early hours of morning.

For the life of me, I couldn't keep their names straight. And I wasn't even drunk yet.

Okay . . . so maybe I was a *little* drunk.

I kept calling Tamás, István. Or was that András? Oh well. They were all hot with dark hair and eyes, and they knew four words in English as far as I could tell.

American. Beautiful. Drink. Dance.

As far as I was concerned, those were the only words they needed to know. At least I remembered Katalin's name. I'd met her a few days ago, and we'd hung out almost every night since. It was a mutually beneficial arrangement. She showed me around Budapest, and I charged most of our fun on Daddy's credit card. Not like he would notice or care. And if he did, he'd always said that if money didn't buy happiness, then people were spending it wrong.

Thanks for the life lessons, Daddy.

"Kelsey," Katalin said, her accent thick and exotic. Damn, why couldn't I have one of those? I'd had a slight Texas twang when I was younger, but my years in theatre had all but beat that out of me. She said, "Welcome to the ruin bars."

Ruin bars.

I paused in ruffling István's hair (or the one I called István anyway) to take in where we were. We stood on an empty street filled with dilapidated buildings. I knew the whole don't-judge-a-book-by-its-cover thing; but in the dark, this place was straight out of a zombie apocalypse. I wondered how to say *brains* in Hungarian.

The old Jewish quarter. *That's* where Katalin said we were going.

Oy vey.

It sure as hell didn't look to me like there were any bars around here. I took in the sketchy neighborhood, and thought at least I'd gotten laid last night. If I was going to get chopped into tiny pieces, *at least* I'd go out with a bang. Literally.

I laughed and almost recounted my thoughts to my companions, but I was pretty sure it would get lost in translation.

Especially because I was starting to question even Katalin's grip on the English language, if this was what "bar" meant to her.

I pointed to a grungy building devoid of any signs or address and said, "Drink?" Then mimed the action just to be safe.

One of the guys said, "*Igen*. Drink." The word sounded like *ee-gan,* and I'd picked up just enough to know it meant yes.

Whoo-hoo. I was practically fluent already.

I followed Katalin and András (I was seventy-five percent sure that her guy was András). They stepped into the dark-end doorway of one derelict building that gave me the heebiest of jeebies. The taller of my Hungarian hotties slipped an arm around my shoulders. I took a guess and said, "Tamás?" His teeth were pearly white when he smiled. I would take that as a yes. Tamás equaled tall. And drop-dead sexy. Noted.

One of his hands came up and brushed back the blond hair from my face. I tilted my head back to look at him, and excitement sparked in my belly. What did language matter when dark eyes locked on mine, strong hands pressed into my skin, and heat filled the space between us?

Not a whole hell of a lot.

Tonight was going to be a good night. I could feel it.

We followed the rest of the group into the building, and I felt the low thrum of techno music vibrating the floor beneath my feet.

Interesting.

We traveled deeper into the building and came out into a large room. Walls had been knocked down, and no one had bothered to move the pieces of concrete. Christmas lights and lanterns lit the space. Mismatched furniture was scattered around the bar. There was even an old car that had been repurposed into a dining booth. It was easily the weirdest, most confusing place I'd ever been in.

"You like?" Katalin asked.

I pressed myself closer to Tamás and said, "I *love*."

He led me to the bar where drinks were dirt cheap. I pulled out a two thousand forint note. For less than the equivalent of ten U.S. dollars, I bought all five of us shots.

Amazing. Maybe I should stay in Eastern Europe forever.

And I would totally consider it . . . except there was one downside to Europe. For some reason that made no sense to me, they gave lemon slices with tequila instead of lime. The bartenders always looked at me like I'd just ordered elephant sweat in a glass. They just didn't understand the magical properties of my favorite drink. If my accent didn't give me away as a tourist, my drink of choice always did.

Lime or not, tequila is my bestie, so I took it eagerly.

Next, Tamás bought me a gin bitter lemon, a drink I'd been introduced to a few weeks ago. It almost made the absence of margaritas in this part of the world bearable. I downed it like it was lemonade on a blistering Texas day. His eyes went wide, and I licked my lips. István bought me another, and the acidity and sweetness rolled across my tongue.

Tamás gestured for me to down it again. It wasn't really that kind of drink, but who was I to deny him? I threw it back to a round of applause.

God, I love when people love me.

I took hold of Tamás's and István's arms and pulled them away from the bar. There was a room that had one wall knocked out in lieu of a door, and it overflowed with dancing bodies.

That was where I wanted to be.

I tugged my boys in that direction, and Katalin and András followed close behind. We had to step over a small pile of concrete rubble if we wanted to get into the room. I took one look at my turquoise heels, and knew there was no way in hell I was managing that with my sex appeal intact. I turned to István and Tamás—sizing them up. István was the beefier of the two, so I put an arm around his neck. We didn't need to speak the same language for him to understand what I wanted. He swept an arm underneath my legs and pulled me up to his chest. It was a good thing I wore skinny jeans instead of a skirt.

"*Köszönöm,*" I said, even though he probably should have been thanking *me*, based on the way he was openly ogling my chest.

Ah well. I didn't mind ogling. I was still pleasantly warm from the alcohol, and the music drowned out the world. My shitty parents and uncertain future were thousands of miles away across an ocean. My problems might as well have been drowning at the bottom of said ocean for how much they mattered to me in that moment.

The only expectations here were ones that I had encouraged and I was all too willing to follow through on. So, maybe, my new "friends" only wanted me for money and sex. It was better than not being wanted at all. Besides . . . everyone wants something from someone else. I just preferred to be up front about it.

István's arms flexed around me, and I melted into him. My father liked to talk, or yell rather, about how I didn't appreciate anything. But the male body was one thing I had no issue appreciating. István played soccer, and he was all hard muscles and angles beneath my hands. And those girls were definitely a-wandering.

By the time he'd set my feet on the dance floor, my hands had found those delicious muscles that angled down from his hips. I bit my lip and met his gaze from beneath lowered lashes. If his expression was any indication, I had found Boardwalk and had the all clear to proceed to Go and collect my two hundred dollars.

Or forint. Whatever.

Tamás pressed his chest against my back, and I gave myself up to the alcohol and the music and the sensation of being stuck between two gorgeous specimens of man.

Time started to disappear between frenzied hands and drips of sweat. There were more drinks and more dances. Each song faded into the next. Colors danced behind my closed eyes. And it was almost enough.

For a while, I got to be blank. A brand-new canvas. Untouched snow.

I'd checked my baggage at the door, and *just was*.

And it was perfect.

There was no room for unhappiness when squeezed between two sets of washboard abs.

New life motto, right there.

I gave István a couple notes and sent him to get more drinks. In the meantime, I turned to face Tamás. He'd been pressed against my back for God knows how long, and I'd forgotten how tall he was. I leaned back to meet his gaze, and his hands smoothed down my back to my ass.

I smirked and said, "Someone is happy to have me all to himself."

He pulled my hips into his, his arousal pressing low against my stomach, and said, "Beautiful American."

Right. No point expending energy on cheeky banter that he couldn't even understand. I had a pretty good idea how to better use my energy. I slipped my arms around his neck and tilted my head in the universal sign of "kiss me."

Tamás didn't waste any time. Like, really . . . *no* time. The dude went zero to sixty in seconds. His tongue was so far down my throat, it was like being kissed by the love child of a lizard and Gene Simmons.

We were both pretty drunk. Maybe he didn't realize that he was in danger of engaging my gag reflex with his Guinness record-worthy tongue. I eased back and his tongue assault ended, only for his teeth to clamp down on my bottom lip.

I was all for a little biting, but he pulled my lip out until I had one half of a fish mouth. And he stood there, sucking on my bottom lip for so long that I actually started counting to see how long it would last.

When I got to fifteen (FIFTEEN!) seconds, my eyes settled on a guy across the bar watching my dilemma with a huge smile. Was *shit-eating grin* in the dictionary? If not, I should snap a picture for Merriam-Webster.

I braced myself and pulled my poor, abused lip from Tamás's teeth with a *pop*. My mouth felt like it had been stuck in a vacuum cleaner. While I pressed my fingers to my numb lip, Tamás started placing sloppy kisses from the corner of my lips across my cheek to my jaw.

His tongue slithered over my skin like a snail, and all the blissful alcohol-induced haze that I'd worked so hard for disappeared.

I was painfully aware that I was standing in an abandoned-building-turned-bar with a trail of drool across my cheek, and that a guy across the room was now openly laughing at me.

And he was fucking gorgeous, which made it so much worse.

Sometimes . . . the *now* sucked.

2

My amused stalker had olive-toned skin, dark eyes, and hair cut close to his head. He had that muscled, military look about him, which sparked half a dozen dirty puns in my head about him invading my territories. Plus, he was tall with a permanent smolder that would have made Tyra Banks stop the crazy train and stare.

Unfortunately, the only staring happening was on his part. Why did it have to be someone so hot who witnessed my face sucking of shame? And as if he could read my thoughts through my gaze, he laughed *harder*.

I tore myself away from Tamás and put my hand up to keep him from following me.

"Bathroom!" I blurted.

The word meant nothing to him, so he reached for me again.

"Eh-eh!" I gave him the Heisman and tried, "Toilet?"

His brow furrowed, and he held a hand to his ear. So I yelled louder, "Toilet!"

The volume didn't help, but it did make a dozen or so people around us who obviously spoke English stop and gawk at me. And my traitorous eyes found the guy across the room. If he laughed any harder, he was going to pop a lung.

Damn it.

I guessed he didn't have any issues understanding my English.

I turned and fled, probably only exponentially increasing the size of the scene I'd just made, but I was only focused on washing away the embarrassment with another drink.

I tried to walk over the rubble pile that led back to the bar, but the ground kept moving, and I felt a million miles tall in these heels. Tipsier than I realized, I blinked, trying to bring the world back into focus. I had to bend and balance my hand on a chunk of concrete to keep from toppling over.

"What? No more locals around to carry you?"

I turned my head to the side, and my worst fears came true.

Soldier Smolder. He was even more gorgeous up close, which was only magnified by his deep voice. And from the sound of it, he was American, too. The look on his face was part teasing—part condescending, but his eyes still had my organs doing somersaults.

Or . . . that could have been the alcohol.

Both. Let's go with both.

"I don't need anyone to carry me. I'm perfectly—whoa."

I tried to straighten up, but my ankle twisted and the world went a little topsy-turvy. In what seemed like fast-forward, I went from standing to sitting on the rubble in the blink of an eye, the heels of my hands scraped raw from the rough concrete. I was still trying to figure out if I was moving at lightning speed, or if the world was moving really slowly, when suddenly—I was flying.

My vision filled with a strong jaw that gave way to soft, full lips. And then eyes so piercing, they reminded me of growing up in church and feeling certain that somewhere out there was a God that was watching, and could see everything I didn't want him to see.

"You remind me of God," I mumbled, then immediately wished I could suck those words back into my mouth.

He laughed. "Well, that's a new one for me."

"I meant . . ." I don't know what I meant. God, I was drunk. "Let me down. I don't need anyone to carry me."

He spoke, and I felt his low voice vibrate from his chest into mine. "I don't care what you think you need."

Story of my life. I loved men as much as the next girl, but why was it that they always seemed to think they knew better?

I rolled my eyes and said, "Fine, carry me all night. Works for me."

I leaned my head on his shoulder and snuggled up against his chest to get comfortable. I was just curling my hand around the back of his neck when he plopped my feet down on the ground, on the other side of the rubble. I winced, pain jolting up from my ankles to my knees from the hard landing.

Sigh. I should have kept my smart mouth shut. I pre-

tended like I wasn't disappointed, shrugged, and turned toward the bar. He appeared in front of me so fast, and my
reflexes were so slow, that I barely managed to keep from
face-planting into his pecs.

Wait . . . Why was I trying to keep from doing that?

He said, "What? No thank-you?"

I leveled him with a stare, feeling more sober than I had
a few moments ago. "I'm not in the habit of thanking people
who do things to me against my will. So, if you don't mind—"

I pushed past him and flagged down the bartender, who
thankfully spoke English. I asked for tequila and took a seat
on a barstool.

"Give her a water, too," my stalker added, sitting down
beside me.

I eyed him. Hot, he was definitely hot. But I'd never met
a guy in a bar who tried to get me *less* drunk. That somehow
made it harder to trust him.

Twisted, I know. But I had learned a long time ago that if
you didn't figure out what people wanted from you at the beginning, it would come back to bite you in the ass later. Plus,
if I was reading the tension in his jaw correctly, he was angry,
and for the life of me I couldn't figure out why he was sitting
there beside me if I annoyed him so much.

I said, "You're awfully pushy, stranger."

And kind of dangerous. Who knew stranger-danger
could be so hot?

"You're awfully drunk, princess."

I laughed. "Honey, I'm barely getting started. When I
start talking about how I can't feel my cheeks and get a little
touchy-feely, then you'll know I'm *awfully drunk*."

His eyebrow raised when I said touchy-feely, but he didn't comment. My shot arrived, along with a cup of water. I glared at the latter, pushing it away from me, then grabbed my shot.

This trip was about adventure, about living life with no baggage and no strings and no thought. Only *now*. It definitely wasn't about drinking *water*.

I tipped back the shot.

Now.

For a few seconds, the warmth settled in my middle, grounding me. I was beginning to get used to the lemon slices, sweeter than limes, but the sour taste still gave a tiny jolt on my tongue. I signaled for another, but my tagalong's deep voice sliced through the lovely haze I was building.

"If you're trying to drink away the memory of that kiss on the dance floor, I doubt it will work. That's the kind of kiss that sticks with you."

Cringing, I said, "You don't have to tell me that."

I wiped at my cheek again even though the slobber was long gone.

The cup of water slid back in front of me, pushed by his forefinger. I squinted up at him. His dark eyes were steel gray, hardened. But there was a hint of a smile in his gaze that was nowhere to be found on his mouth.

And a fascinating mouth it was.

I said, "You know, you could always help me find another way to erase the memory of that bad kiss." He turned and leaned his back against the bar. His arm brushed mine, and I shivered. So, he was a bit on the aggravating side, but he was also big and warm and masculine, and, hell, I didn't need to list anything else. I was already sold. My body didn't so much care about what kind of tension was between us. Tension was tension.

He kept his eyes fixed coolly on the dance floor across the room. With that strong, stubbled jaw and those delicious muscles, he was the epitome of tall, dark, and dangerous.

My vocabulary narrowed to one word: *yum.*

He said, "I *could* do that . . . ," glancing sideways at me.

Oh, please. Let's *please* do that.

"But it's so much more fun to keep picturing the look on your face as it was happening."

Damn it.

His shoulders bounced in a silent chuckle. Great. Now he was laughing at me again.

I let my arm brush his and said, "I can think of a few things that would be *more* fun."

He stopped laughing. His eyes broke away from the dance floor and trailed up my body, starting with my heels. I knew there was a reason I braved these stilettos. When his gaze reached my hips, he dragged a thumb across his bottom lip, and I was ready to jump him right then. I pushed my shoulders back, and like a charm his eyes settled on my chest.

Bingo!

Thanks for keeping my secrets, Victoria. The grin of victory was already climbing onto my face, and then he returned his gaze to the dance floor without a comment.

What the hell?

He didn't look at my face. He didn't even look at my body for that long.

I was kind of offended. My girls, Marilyn and Monroe, were *definitely* offended.

See! This was what I meant about not trusting a guy who wanted me sober. I'd been awake too long and had too many drinks to figure out what he wanted. And though he was gorgeous (of the drop-dead variety), he was also killing my buzz. Not to mention that alcohol and insecurity were a very bad combination.

I said, "Well, this has been *interesting*. I better get back—"

"To the dementor out on the dance floor? Really?"

I took a few steps and threw a smile over my shoulder.

"You got a better offer?"

I'd expected the same cool once-over. Instead, his eyes blazed, and his jaw tensed. He leaned away from the bar like he was going to follow me. My steps stuttered, and something fluttered in my belly. I almost threw myself at him. *Almost.*

He wasn't nearly as uninterested as he wanted me to believe, and *that* was what made *him* interesting. I bit my lip and had the satisfaction of watching his eyes zone in on my mouth.

Smiling, I stepped back toward him and leaned in until our chests brushed. His head tipped down toward mine, and though his expression was carefully blank, I saw his Adam's apple bob once and then again as he swallowed.

I braced a hand on his hard chest as I reached for the forgotten cup of water behind him. I bit my lip to keep from smiling too wide as I pulled the cup between us. Tilting my head to the side, I looked up at him as I wrapped my lips around the straw and took a long drink.

He cleared his throat, his gaze fixed on my mouth. Excitement seized low in my belly. "Let me know if you change your mind," I said.

I turned and flounced back to the dance floor, my hips

swinging a little more than usual. I made it over the rubble alone this time, though I had to be very cautious and careful about where I put my feet. It wasn't until I was standing back on the dance floor and saw Tamás, the terrible kisser, that I regretted my killer exit.

So when I spotted István, I made a beeline.

Tamás was officially no longer on my to-do list.

I looped my arms around István's neck and spun so that he was stationed between me and droolboy. I didn't even make it a few seconds before I found my thoughts once again drawn to my friend at the bar. His eyes lanced through me.

Yeah, he was definitely interested.

I smiled and took another sip of my water.

Time for a little show.

With my eyes on Dark and Dangerous, I ran a hand down István's chest. I shook out my fair curls and pressed myself closer to him. I twisted and wound my body around his, putting a little extra intensity into my movement for my audience.

From here, I could see the way his fist clenched on the bar.

I leaned my back against István's chest and faced my real target. Running a hand down my body, I shot him a sly smile.

This was going to be a piece of cake.

One of István's hands slid around my waist to my abdomen, and I dropped my head back on his shoulder. My eyes fluttered closed, and my lids were almost too heavy to lift again. My muscles tingled pleasantly.

There was that buzz again. Hallelujah. The tequila was kicking in.

This . . . this was how I wanted to feel all the time. Set adrift, no longer tethered to the earth and her demands and troubles. I wanted to float out to sea, drift out to space, forget who I was.

It was perfect.

But I could think of one way it could be better. I opened my eyes, and had to blink away the blur before I could focus on the bar.

Dark and Dangerous wasn't there.

I looked back to the wall where I'd first spotted him, but he wasn't there either. I searched for his broad shoulders and his olive skin, but couldn't see him anywhere. He'd vanished into the crowd, taking tonight's most interesting option with him.

Damn it. I'd played too hard to get. I should have just jumped him as soon as I saw his interest at the bar.

I frowned and fought off my disappointment. I tried to settle back against István, but suddenly the heat from his hands on my hips and his breath against my shoulder felt much less exciting. I took a deep breath, stretched my neck, and turned to face him.

He must have thought that was the go-ahead to make a move because he leaned in to kiss me. I pulled back and his lips grazed my chin instead.

I stepped back and shook my head. What was wrong with me?

I looked at the cup of water still in my hand and decided that maybe I just needed another drink.

Traveling alone wasn't easy. There was too much quiet, too much time spent in my head. Sometimes it felt a lot like work. And the antidote to work was more play.

When István and I reached the bar, he smiled and said, "Drink, beautiful American."

Right. Maybe it would have been nice if he knew a *few* more words in English.

I ordered another round of shots. At any other time—hell, *yesterday*—I would have made things interesting with the lemon wedge or some salt, but I wasn't up to it at the moment. That would take too much effort.

I knew the minute I put the glass to my mouth that it wasn't a good idea. My mouth was watering, and my stomach felt like it was residing somewhere up in my rib cage. But I took it anyway.

I'd stop after this one, ride it out for a while. I had it totally under control.

Or I thought I had anyway.

Five minutes later, that shot didn't just hit me. It *bulldozed* me, backed up, and flattened me again. Just trying to walk made me feel like one of those lame inflatable flailing-tube guys. The ground kept bending up toward me, no matter how carefully I walked. The air seemed to ripple with each thump of the base. Neon lights bounced around the space. With the dancing people, the trippy décor of this place, and the noise, the inside of my head made the Harlem Shake look like a garden party.

"I think . . . I think I need some air."

"Dance?" István asked.

God, no.

"No dancing. I just need . . ." I pushed back through the crowd to the hallway that we'd arrived through. I ping-ponged between drifts of people and the walls like a pinball before reaching the exit. I burst out into the cool night air, and took a huge gulp of fresh air.

That was my downfall.

I balanced myself with a hand on the building, and then was atrociously, epically, *mortifyingly* sick on the street. The quiet, empty, not-yet-zombie-infested street.

Footsteps came up behind me, and warm hands pulled back the hair that was hanging on both sides of my face.

Okay, so not entirely empty.

Eyes watery and my throat sore, I looked over my shoulder expecting to see István or maybe Katalin.

Instead, I found the guy who'd disappeared on me earlier reappearing at the absolute *worst* moment. And that trace of a smile I'd seen in his eyes was long gone.

Kill me now.

3

was scared that if I opened my mouth, I would hurl again . . . from the alcohol and the embarrassment.

The world was spinning, but his face—the straight nose and chiseled jawbone—that was still and clear, almost as if the universe wanted this moment imprinted on my brain forever.

"You okay?" he asked, his voice gruff.

No. I was so very far from okay (though still very much in four-letter-word territory).

"I'm fine." I pushed off the wall where I'd been bracing myself and tottered out into the street.

"Where are you going?"

"Away." Just . . . away.

The night air was cool, and it felt exquisite against my sweat-dotted skin.

"Hold on," he said, trailing behind me.

"Seriously?"

He should be running right now. That's what you *do* when someone makes a supreme asshat out of themselves. You look the other way and keep walking.

He stopped before me, his face cast in shadows from the street lamps. "I'm not letting you walk around by yourself."

Oh. He was one of *those*.

Couldn't he take a hint? My head was spinning, and my mouth tasted like something too disgusting for me to name. I never thought there would be a moment where I *wanted* a hot guy to leave me alone, but it appeared there was a first time for everything.

"I told you, I'm fine."

"Bad things happen to people who are fine every day."

So, Dark and Dangerous was really just a Prince Charming with a buzz cut. That shouldn't have been appealing. Normally, I couldn't stand that kind of thing. But against all odds, I could feel myself softening, the edges of my will blurring.

I blamed the stubble. I never could resist the scruffy look.

"Listen, I get the whole protective thing. It's what guys like you do. And don't get me wrong, it's kinda hot. But I don't need a babysitter. So put the knight-in-shining-armor fantasies on hold for the night."

I thought I sounded firm and very adult (but then again, I was drunk). The roll of his eyes told me that he wasn't taking me very seriously.

"And I already told *you* that I don't care what you think you need."

"So, *what*? You're going to follow me whether I want you to or not?"

His lips pulled together, and I could see the mirth written in the curve of his mouth. Such a tempting mouth.

"That's exactly what I'm going to do. Someone needs to get you home."

Not even a measly one percent of me managed to believe that "get you home" meant anything other than dropping the pitiful drunk girl off at her hostel to wallow in her nausea and misery.

We couldn't have that now, could we?

I sidestepped him. "I'm not going home yet. So run along and find yourself another damsel."

He smiled, but there was an edge to it. He ran a hand over his short hair, and I made myself walk away.

He called after me, "You're a real piece of work."

That made *me* smile. I stopped and spun, walking backward. I stretched out my hands and yelled, the sound echoing through the street, "You bet I am."

If there was a museum filled with people who were a "piece of work," I'd be the main fucking exhibit. I would have said as much, but the whole walking backward thing wasn't the best idea in my current state. I stumbled, just barely managing to catch myself, but my stomach felt like it had plopped down to the ground anyway. I didn't look at him, knowing I probably looked twice as foolish as I felt, which was a lot.

I took a steadying breath, afraid I might be sick again.

The funny thing about alcohol . . . when it makes you feel

good, you feel amazing. But when it makes you feel bad, you've never felt worse. Not just the nausea, but all of it. I might be a piece of work, but I knew myself well enough to know that if I went back to my dingy hostel—mattress springs pricking at my back, the cacophony of snoring roommates, the threadbare blankets—it was a recipe for hitting rock bottom.

Most hostels were devised so that you met other people, and yet they were the loneliest damn places in the world. Everything there is temporary—the residents, the relationships, the hot water. I felt like a flower trying to plant roots into concrete.

Nope. I needed to walk off the alcohol before I went home if I wanted to avoid a breakdown of child-star proportions. And this time, I should walk facing the right direction.

After only a few steps, my tagalong was right at my side. I scowled and tried to walk faster, but my stilettos weren't having that. And I didn't trust myself not to face-plant into the cobblestone with the kind of night I was having.

And though I wouldn't admit it to anyone, I was a little glad for the company.

"What's your name?" I asked.

He arched one dark eyebrow.

"You waited long enough to ask that."

I shrugged. "Names aren't exactly the important bit in places like this." I gestured behind us to the bar we'd just left. "And, honestly, I couldn't care less."

Or that's what I was telling myself. And him.

"So, then why ask? If names aren't important and you don't care?"

"Well, first, we're no longer in said bar. And second,

you're following me, and I'm asking questions to fill the silence because otherwise things will get awkward. And talking keeps me from thinking about how you're probably a serial killer, hence the whole following thing."

"From a knight in shining armor to a serial killer."

"The nice-guy bit could be an act. And you definitely look like you could be dangerous."

"Are you always this honest?"

"Not even close. It's the alcohol talking. Totally powers down my filter."

The smile was back in his eyes, and maybe it was because I was drunk, but this guy didn't make a lick of sense. That should have worried me. Maybe there really *was* something off about him. But at the moment, my brain was full just trying to stay upright and breathe.

He said, "I'll tell you my name if you'll tell me something about yourself."

"Like what?" My pin number?

"It doesn't matter. Something else honest."

I couldn't seem to walk in a straight line. My path kept veering toward his. Probably because I was drunk. Or his muscles were magnetic. Both completely plausible options.

My arm brushed his, and the sensation went straight to my head, electric and fuzzy, so I said the first thing I thought of.

"Honestly? I'm *tired*."

He laughed once. "That's because it's almost dawn."

"Not that kind of tired."

"What kind of tired, then?"

"The bone-deep kind. The kind of tired that sleep doesn't fix. Just tired of . . . being."

He stayed quiet for one, two, three steps down the narrow, echoing street. Then his pace slowed, and I could feel his eyes on me. I strained my peripheral vision to see more of him. He said, "You don't show it."

"I don't show much of anything."

Three more silent steps.

He said, "I bet that gets tiring, too."

What was I doing telling him this shit?

I looked over at him. My stilettos apparently weren't safe unless I was watching them, because they slipped between two stones on the street. My ankle turned for the second time that night, and I teetered sideways. I reached out to try to balance myself on his shoulder, but I was falling away from him, and I was too slow. Luckily, he was faster. He turned and caught my elbow with one hand and wrapped the other around my waist. He pulled me upright, and I could feel a stubborn blush creeping up my neck. I had no problem playing the ditzy blonde to get what I wanted, but I hated that I was living the stereotype unintentionally at the moment.

"How are your cheeks?" he asked.

I blinked, hyperaware of his hand around my waist and the long fingers that could easily have skated farther down my body. Just thinking this had my heart racing to catch up with my thoughts.

"Can you feel them?" he added.

Oh, *those* cheeks. Disappointment doused the longing flame in me.

The hand that had been tucked around my elbow came up and grazed the curve of my cheek in reminder. And the flame was back.

"They, um," I swallowed, "just feel a bit heavy is all."

His eyes pinned me in place for a few seconds. There was so much behind that stare, more than there should be from a guy I'd just met tonight (if vomiting in front of him counted as meeting, since I still hadn't even gotten his name).

He righted me, and his warm hands left my skin.

Resisting the urge to pull him back, I said, "Your turn."

"My cheeks feel fine."

I smiled. "I meant your name."

He nodded and started walking again. I followed, more careful now of where I placed my feet.

"Most people call me Hunt."

I took a few quick steps and caught up to him.

"Should I call you that? Am I most people?"

He pushed his fists into his pocket, and his strides grew even longer. He glanced back at me once before focusing on the narrow stone street ahead of us.

"Honestly, I have no idea what you are."

What did that mean? He didn't know what kind of girl I was? (Because I would *totally* tell him what kind of girl I was.)

Based on the set of his shoulders and the fact that he barely looked at me, I was guessing he meant something a bit more serious.

I didn't know how to answer, so I didn't try. I'd spilled enough to him already.

Together, we walked. I didn't really know where we were going, and he stayed silent, following me when I chose to turn at random. I let my mind wander from the brooding gothic architecture to where I might travel next to home and then back to the man next to me.

Hunt.

What kind of name was that?

Predatory. That's what kind.

I really should be scared, walking around a dark, unfamiliar city with a complete stranger. But there were a lot of things that I *should* be and wasn't. And when I looked over at him, I couldn't seem to conjure an ounce of the fear I knew I should have. Dad always accused me of having a death wish. Maybe he was right.

A glow began to creep across the sky, and we exited a narrow street into open air. A winding river bisected the city, and the sunrise peeked its head above it.

There was too much to see, and I slowed to a stop to take it all in. The sky breathed in pink and purple, and a soft gold glinted off the river. I couldn't remember the name, but it was the same river that was only a block or two from my hostel. Despite my wandering, we'd ended up fairly close to the home to which Hunt was supposed to be taking me.

I swallowed, still feeling antsy at the idea of returning to the hostel. So, rather than walking north toward bed, I pointed south. "There's a club a little ways that way that's open until six."

He gave me a hard look. "I think you've partied enough tonight."

The judgment in his tone made me squirm, mostly because I knew he was right. If another drop of alcohol passed my lips, I'd be sick again in no time.

But that buzzing was there at the back of my mind, telling me I needed to do *something*. It was always safer to do than to think. I turned away from Hunt and jogged into the street toward the riverbank.

"Where are you going?" Hunt called after me.

I turned, walking backward again, and said, "Absolutely no idea."

I was raising my shoulders in a shrug and my lips in a smile when he darted out into the street and grabbed me by the elbow. With a forceful tug, he turned me around and pulled me up onto the sidewalk on the other side of the road.

"Are you crazy? Don't walk across a fucking road without looking where you're going!"

I pulled my elbow out of his grasp and stepped away from him. "*Relax*. I'm fine. There's no one out this time of morning anyway."

Then the universe one-upped me as a sports car zoomed past, wind rushing around us in its wake. Hunt raised his eyebrows at me. His jaw was tense with anger, and I couldn't tell whether I wanted to push it away or press my lips to it.

"You don't have to say it," I said, turning before he could say, I told you so. "I'm a piece of work. Got it." I jogged ahead toward the river. "But you know what? I'm *so* good at it."

I reached down and slipped off one heel, and then the other. My feet ached against the flat, cool stone, but I didn't mind. I held both of my shoes in one hand and skipped toward the river, Hunt following behind.

I screamed just to hear the sound echo out over the water.

"You're ridiculous," he said.

I didn't like the way he said it. Like he pitied me.

"Correction: I'm *fun*."

I left him behind, running for the water. I thought briefly of just diving in or perhaps skinny-dipping in the river, but decided people would be coming out soon, and there was no telling what was in that water.

Dark and deep, like a bruise, the river had a quiet energy that made me slow down and stare. It was beautiful and silent and solemn with just a dab of pain written in the current. Even the rising sun only broke through the first layer, the light swallowed by the dark just a few inches below the surface.

A little ways down the riverside, small dark shapes lined the edge of the walkway, and I moved toward them, curious. But when I got there, I didn't understand any more by seeing them up close.

There were shoes. Dozens of them. Black and cast in iron, lining the river's edge. Empty shoes.

It was a sculpture of some kind, but I was at a loss for what it meant. The shoes ranged in size and shape, belonging to both men and women. Some were small, made for the tiny feet of children. Some were simple and others elaborate. I took a step forward to walk among them, but something held me back. If the river was a bruise, these were grief. Loss. There were no feet in them, but they were far from empty.

"It's a holocaust memorial," Hunt said from behind me.

I sucked in a breath, the cold air was slightly tangy on my tongue. All those shoes. I knew they were just replicas, just pieces of metal, but they *spoke*. They sang.

You don't realize how small you really are until you're faced with something like that. We live our lives as if we're at the center of our own universe, but we're just tiny pieces of a shattered whole. Here I was . . . worried about how I was going to survive life post-college. God, it didn't even seem right anymore to think of it as surviving, not with this reminder of all the people that hadn't. I pushed my fingers back through my hair, lacing them behind my neck.

I knew I was lucky. Blessed, even. But it was a lot of pressure . . . trying not to waste what you've been given. I wanted to accomplish something. To love something. To *be* something. But I didn't know how. I didn't know what.

All of my friends were off chasing their dreams, moving into their futures, and I just wanted to want something with that kind of desperation, that kind of fire. I was an actress. I'd spent nearly half my life stepping into a character, searching out her desires, finding what drives her. But for the life of me, I couldn't do the same for myself. It had been a long, long time since I'd let myself want something enough for it to matter.

I felt like such a failure. Every shoe before me represented a dream that would never be lived, a life that would never be loved. I'd never faced that kind of oppression or struggle.

This place bled with history and tragedy, and in comparison it made the wounds of my past seem like scratches.

4

"Are you okay?"

Hunt stood right next to me. On instinct, I turned my back to him. I was glad for it as I wiped my cheeks and my hands came back wet.

I cleared my throat.

"Yeah, I'm fine. Just yawned. Maybe I'm a little tired after all."

"You mean I finally get to walk you home?"

I composed my face into a smile and turned. "Come on, then, Prince Charming. Let's see what this chivalry stuff is all about. I hear good things."

His lips tipped in a smile. "I haven't been called chivalrous in a *long* time."

I raised an eyebrow as we crossed the road back to the other sidewalk. "Fine by me. Chivalry sounded pretty boring anyway." I was much more intrigued by the not-so-nice side of him.

He laughed, and I took a moment to get my bearings. We weren't far from my hostel at all. I was pretty sure it was just a block or two north. Once we'd set off walking again, I looked at Hunt. "Tell me something. If you're not walking me home because it's the gentlemanly thing to do, why *are* you here?"

We crossed over another side street and he said, "Back on the serial-killer bent, are we?"

I surveyed him for a second. In my sobering state, he wasn't any less muscular or intimidating, but he didn't seem dangerous. He could be, definitely. His hands were probably big enough to crush someone's skull, but all that power seemed dormant, locked under multiple layers of control.

"Nah, you're not a serial killer. Too soft for that."

"Soft?"

I grinned, and turned the corner. There was my hostel, tucked inconspicuously between a tourist shop and a restaurant.

"Hold on, now," Hunt said. "Did you just call me *soft*?"

He took hold of my shoulder and spun me around to face him. I braced a hand against his stomach and— Holy mother of washboard abs! I looked up at him, at those penetrating eyes.

"Well, I wouldn't call *this* part of you soft."

His playful expression turned dark, the tension creeping back along his jaw.

His tone full of warning, he said," Kelsey."

I wasn't sure what he was warning me against, nor did I particularly care. I tilted my head to look up at him, the colorful early morning sky still painting itself behind him.

"How did you know my name?"

"That girl said it. The one you came to the bar with."

Katalin.

I smiled, and touched my free hand to his shoulder. "Well, then. You know my name, and I know yours. How *else* could we get to know each other?"

I let the hand on his stomach slide up until his chest arced outward. God, if his body looked half as perfect as it felt, I wanted to use it as a dinner table.

He swayed toward me, and the scent of him, woodsy and masculine, meshed perfectly with the morning air. His fingers touched my rib cage, and I shivered. Long and strong, those fingers could play me like a piano, and it would be a masterpiece.

He exhaled a heavy breath, and I nearly groaned at the way his muscles moved beneath his skin. I gripped the back of his neck, and a low rumble resonated in his chest.

I lifted myself up on my toes, my lips level with his chin, and said, "Feel free to keep showing me how *not* soft you are."

The hand on my ribs flexed, and my shirt bunched in his fingers.

"Goddamn it." He groaned, and tipped his head back away from mine.

Was that a good sign?

I resisted the urge to crawl up his body, and settled instead for wrapping my arms more fully around his shoulders.

I tipped his head back down toward mine, and his breath puffed across my lips, warm and sweet. I pulled myself closer, and I felt the start of something pressing against my stomach.

I let out a breathy sigh at the same time that he pulled away.

He put several feet between us, and then in a low voice said, "You should go. Get some sleep."

I blinked. "What?"

"You've had a long night."

I blinked again. I had *hoped* it would become an even longer night.

"That sounds an awful lot like chivalry to me. *Boring* chivalry."

He took another step away from me. "This is you, right?" He pointed to the hostel at my back.

"Uh, yeah, it is, but—"

"Good. Then I'll leave you alone."

But what if I didn't *want* to be left alone?

He took a few more steps backward, until he stood in the sunlight that washed the main street.

"Good night, Kelsey. Or Good morning."

Then he left, leaving me alone, still a little drunk, and mind-numbingly turned on.

"What the fuck?" I said aloud, my words echoing through the small street just as a tiny old lady opened up a second-floor window on the building across from me. I waved a hand at her, and called out an apology before heading to the hostel entrance.

What had just happened? He wanted me. I'd felt that

much, and there was no way *that* was a cell phone or something else in his pocket. Unless they'd started making pockets in a very awkward spot.

I rubbed my hands over my eyes and up into my hair.

Well, that made it official. Tonight sucked balls.

After a pitiful few hours tossing on my hostel bed, I gave up and rose as the rest of my room was waking. I dressed quickly before Creeper Chris could wake up and watch. He'd been staying in this hostel for several months already when I arrived, like a bad case of bed bugs they couldn't seem to shake. And after the night I'd had, I might end up punching him if he looked at me longer than two seconds.

I grabbed my toothbrush and headed for the communal bathroom down the hall. I used my elbow to push open the door, and then immediately wished I hadn't. Someone must have had even more to drink than I'd had the night before because the bathroom smelled *atrocious*. No wonder I'd seen that Canadian girl brushing her teeth back in our room.

I took a deep breath, and ran into the bathroom just long enough to wet my toothbrush, and then I bolted back to the hallway.

I leaned against the wall with a groan and set to brushing. For what must have been the hundredth time, I assured myself that Hunt had only blown me off because I'd been sick. This hadn't occurred to me when I was pressed against him because, well . . . my mind had had a singular focus then. But when I got into my room, I realized how ridiculous it was to think he would kiss me after seeing me lose the contents of my stomach in the middle of the street. Not exactly sexy.

That was the reason. It had to be. It was the only one that made sense, really.

I did another speed run into the bathroom to wash out my mouth, and then went to grab my things.

Maybe it was time to suck it up and start staying in a hotel. I'd chosen hostels not because of the cheaper price, but to meet people (and to piss off my father as much as possible). And sure . . . both tactics had worked out well. I met some fellow travelers, some of whom I'd become *intimately* acquainted with, and my dad had blown a gasket, saying I was going to end up sold as a sex slave or bleeding in an alley.

That was Dad. Never one to sugarcoat his feelings.

But without being able to see his red, angry face in person, the hostel was proving not worth the trouble.

I'd look into some hotels this afternoon.

I stepped outside, savoring the fresh air. I made myself look away from the spot where Hunt and I had stood that morning and rounded the corner straight into the beauty of Budapest. The Paris of the east, that's what people called it. It was a gorgeous mix of old and new, nature and architecture. The sight was almost enough to dull the headache forming just over my right eye. Either it was a hangover coming on or that bathroom had been filled with biohazardous materials.

Whatever the reason . . . I needed a pick-me-up. Bad. And coffee just wasn't going to be enough.

I walked a few blocks to the nearest Internet café, and paid cash for fifteen minutes on the computer. I didn't bother checking my e-mail. The only person who ever wrote was Dad's secretary. He didn't even care enough to write me himself, so I didn't bother caring enough to answer. I logged on to Facebook, and had one new message.

Bliss Edwards
Keeeeeelllseeeeey. Where are you? I haven't heard from you since you landed in the Ukraine. I don't mean to go all mommy on you, but how am I supposed to live vicariously through you if I don't even know you're actually still living?! (Should I have tagged skank or whore onto the end of that? Would it have made it less mom-like?) Anyway, I need you to talk me out of a panic attack of epic proportions. I leave for Philly on Saturday. I've already sent most of my stuff up ahead of me. Can you believe it? ME. LIVING WITH A GUY. I keep waiting for pigs to fly . . . or you know, for the universe to implode. Or maybe I'm going to wake up and still be in my government class, and this was all just the product of the most boring lecture in the history of the universe. Seriously, though. Write me back, whore. (See how I did that?) I need you to give me something else to think about! I *know* you've got stories.

I hit reply.

Kelsey Summers
Oh, I do have stories. I think we've somehow managed to switch lives because I'm currently suffering the slings and arrows of outrageous awkward.

Prepare yourself . . . what I'm about to tell you in-
volves bodily fluids, one horrifying make out ses-
sion, and the most mortifying/depressing moment
of my life.

As I relayed the story of last night, it was almost worse
reliving it for Bliss than it was experiencing it the first time
around. I was wholly unaccustomed to this kind of embarrassment. When you came from a family of piranhas like I
did, you didn't get into mortifying situations. And if you did,
you made damn sure no one witnessed it. I'd perfected the
art of the bribe at the tender age of seven by following Daddy's example. And let's just say I got all my acting skills from
Mom. Starting with breakfast every morning, she got drunk
faster than a pint of beer on St. Patrick's Day, but she always
managed to hide it well around guests.

Laughing about the humiliation and rejection of last
night made it feel like it was farther in the past than it was.
And even though it was just words on a screen, I could picture
Bliss's face as she was reading. I could imagine her reassuring
me that she'd been through worse and telling me stories.

It made me feel less alone.

I had hoped maybe Bliss would be online, so that she
could tell me more about her move, but as I stared at the
screen waiting for a response, my time ran out. I could have
bought more time, but one thing I'd learned—contact with
friends back home made me feel better for a little while, but
twice as worse afterward.

Of course . . . I *could* go home now.

Nothing was keeping me here. Well, nothing except for

the fact that home was a prison. My life was all mapped out for me there. Charity functions and internships and dates with pompous ass-rich guys my mother picked out. I could argue with my father all I wanted, but he always managed to get his way by one method or another. But here . . . I had freedom. I had choice.

If I wanted to sleep with a different guy every night, I could. If I wanted to get messy drunk every night, I could. If I wanted to hop on the next train leaving the station with no thought to where it was heading or when it would get there, I could.

I wanted to make every choice—the good and the bad. I wanted to fill myself up with decisions and consequences, pleasure and pain, so that maybe when I returned to the States . . . maybe I'd have enough life in me to survive living in my own home.

I grabbed my bag and headed for the door.

Now for that coffee. Bliss and caffeine—the perfect one-two punch to put all thoughts of last night to rest.

It felt like cheating to go to the Starbucks up the block since I was in another country and all, but I couldn't bring myself to care. I compromised by taking my drink to-go and finding a park to relax in. Near the center of a green space that covered a couple blocks, I found a fountain adorned with statues. I settled onto a park bench and let my eyes trace over the figures depicted—a man at the top of the fountain, barely clothed and rising out of the water, reminded me of Posei-don. Then below him were three women, soft and beauti-ful, lounging nearly naked above the water. The sky was a rich blue above them, and I made myself still in their image, soaking up the sun.

I sipped at my coffee and watched the people around me. There were a few other obvious tourists, but for the most part it was locals, and I listened to the way the complicated language rolled off their tongues with such ease. Maybe I would learn another language while I was here. That would be something *more*. Something better. But would it be *enough*?

I tried repeating a phrase that I heard an older woman say near me, but the words mashed together in my mouth. I didn't try again for fear of what offensive thing I might say by accident.

When I was close to finishing my coffee, a group of kids raced past me, laughing. That sound, at least, was the same in every language. They were dressed in matching uniforms, a school group I guessed. The one in the front was around twelve, maybe thirteen, and the biggest of the lot. He held up a sketchbook over the fountain, and a few of the kids around him egged him on, in English. So, I guessed, they were from some kind of international school.

Another smaller boy came running up to the group then, his hair in disarray and his glasses askew on his face.

"Give it back!" he demanded.

The bigger kid pretended to fumble the sketch pad, catching it only a foot above the water.

"Give me a reason, Cricket."

Without really thinking it through, I stood and walked in their direction. I pulled out my map of Budapest and stopped when I was close to the bigger kid. "Excuse me, do you speak English?"

I thought he was going to ignore me at first, too enamored with his bullying, but after a few seconds he turned, and like any pubescent little boy, his eyes went from my face to my chest in two seconds flat.

While he stared, I repeated, "English? Can you help me?"

He smiled back at the other boys and said, "Of course."

I moved closer and tried not to be repulsed by the way his eyes stuck on me as I bent over the map.

"Can you tell me where I am?" I asked, dumb-blonde mode powered up to full. "I'm trying to get to this metro stop, and I just keep going in circles."

While he leaned close to me, simultaneously searching the map and me, my eyes darted to the other boy. His eyes were on the sketchbook grasped in the bully's free hand, and I could see him contemplating making a grab for it.

"Here," I said, pushing the map completely into the kid's hands. "I just can't find it for the life of me."

He struggled to open the map with the sketchbook still in his other hand, and I dove for my opportunity.

"Let me help."

I snatched the sketchbook out of his hand before he could argue, and took in the sketch on the first page.

Immediately, it pulled a smile to my face.

It was a sketch of the fountain, the lines of the sculptures captured almost perfectly in highlights and shadows. I can only imagine what an average little boy's drawing of half-naked statues would look like, but I was certain that it wouldn't be like this. This was mature. Realistic. The boy had found a way to capture the reflection of the sun on the water too, giving it all a three-dimensional feel. It was fantastic, really. I never would have guessed that a kid his age could do this.

For the most part, the sketch focused on the fountain, and I could tell he'd put in a lot of time working on the details of the figures. But in the corner, he'd begun work on another part of the sketch. The lines of the park bench were drawn quickly without too much detail, and on the bench was a girl. It wasn't as detailed as the fountain, not yet, but the face and the hair were finished enough for me to think that the girl might be me. The swoop of my sundress around my knees made me fairly certain.

"Is this yours?" I asked the bully.

He paused, torn between impressing me and his friends.

He glanced at two of the guys closest to him and then said, "No. No way."

A small hand went up at the back of the group, and I was smiling before he even spoke.

"It's mine!"

I took a step in that direction and the group of boys parted for me. In my heels, the boy had to crane his head backward to look at me, and his face was splotched red and white.

"You drew this?"

He hesitated, and for a moment looked like he wanted to run. But then he nodded.

"It's wonderful!"

The silence from the boys behind me was almost palpable, and a few of them shifted, trying to actually get a look at what was on the paper.

"Really?"

"Really. You're very talented." I pointed to the girl in the corner and said, "Is this me?"

Now he *really* looked like he was going to run. Or perhaps

take a page out of my book and be sick on the street. I decided to put him out of his misery, and held the sketchbook out to him without requiring an answer.

"It's beautiful. Keep drawing like that and you won't be able to keep the girls away from you."

Then . . . because I couldn't resist, I swooped down and placed a kiss on his cheek.

His pink face exploded into hues of red and almost purple, and as I walked away the boys around him were cheering and asking to see the sketch. A quick glance over my shoulder revealed that the group had shifted to encircle the boy with the sketch pad, leaving the bully standing alone and dumbfounded, still holding my map.

He could keep it. Let it serve as a reminder not to be an asshole.

I sent one last smile at the artist, and then headed for the street.

I couldn't keep the grin off my face. Who knew all it took to cheer me up was to put some punk-ass kid in his place?

I glanced down the street, contemplating where I should go next, when I caught sight of a familiar buzzed head.

Hunt.

My heart skyrocketed up into my throat, and I took a step in his direction before a touch at my elbow pulled my attention. I stared at the guy that I thought was Hunt for a second longer before glancing behind me.

It was the little artist.

Before I could even open my mouth to ask what he wanted, he shoved a paper into my hands and ran. I looked down, and my heart melted back down into my chest at the sight of his fountain sketch, torn from the pages of his book. I turned to watch him join the group of boys, this time to a high five and cheers.

I held the sketch close to my chest and waved at him. He must have been braver for the distance because he waved back enthusiastically.

When I turned in the other direction, my phantom Hunt was nowhere to be seen. I sighed. It probably wasn't him anyway. The odds of seeing him again, and on the street no less, had to be minuscule.

Maybe I should hold off on going to that hotel and stay in the hostel a little while longer. Because if Hunt did try to find me, that's where he would go. I mean . . . he probably wouldn't. Not after the ass I'd made out of myself, but just in case. It wouldn't kill me to stay a few more days.

Hopefully, I could keep myself from killing Creeper Chris in the meantime.

5

Hunt didn't find me that day.

Not that I was broken up over it or anything.

He was *one* guy. Hardly the first guy to catch my attention here, and definitely not the last.

I didn't see Katalin or the guys again either. I wasn't interested in getting my mouth vacuumed for the second time.

Instead, I made friends with another group staying in my hostel: Jenny, who was staying in my room, was Canadian; her brother John, along with their friend Tau, who was dark-skinned, gorgeous, and Australian.

I followed them to a pub crawl that night. It was easy to just blend into their group and give my brain a break by listening to their conversations about the summer film program they were attending in Prague. I put up with the normal get-to-know-you questions for a little while, but by the time we got to the second pub, we'd all had enough to drink that we acted like old friends even though we didn't know each other.

Something in me must have been broken, though, because I couldn't even stay interested in what Tau was saying, and the guy was a beautiful specimen of man with a to-die-for accent. John was a bit on the nerdy side, still kind of cute, but there was definitely nothing there either.

I talked to a few guys at each pub we hit, but my eyes were constantly drawn to the door, waiting for someone else to enter.

A very specific someone else.

But that was stupid. He wasn't just going to walk in at random. I knew that, but I couldn't seem to get my head or my heart into the evening.

Between pubs, I must have seen a dozen Internet cafés, each one whispering to me, calling me to go lose myself in messages to friends and the comfort of home (or as close as I could get to it here anyway). I resisted, and made myself do a shot every time my mind wandered to Hunt or Home, both of which were recipes for disaster.

Needless to say, I felt like the walking dead the next day when Jenny plopped herself down at my feet, and pulled the blankets down off my head.

I groaned, and buried my head into my pillow.

"*Fuck.* Too bright."

She clucked. "Hangover. That blows."

I turned my head sideways, just enough so that I could talk and keep from suffocating on my pillow.

"I'm going to blow your brains out if you don't talk a little quieter."

She smiled like I hadn't just taken a stroll into homicidal territory. I had learned one thing the night before . . . Jenny and I were really alike. Scary alike. It was a little like hanging out with my clone. Well . . . a clone that wasn't hung up on some guy she was never going to see again.

She said, "I have a solution."

"Does it involve ritual suicide? I've always thought that would be an interesting way to go."

"*Damn*. You're morbid the morning after. No wonder you say you never have any issues ditching your one-nighters. They're probably *actually* in a ditch somewhere."

"Ha. Ha."

In a much quieter voice, she said, "So, I was thinking we'd get some coffee, maybe add a little something special to yours. You know, a little hair of the dog. Then we're going shopping because we've got plans tonight. Epic plans."

Whoo-hoo. I resisted the urge to roll my eyes. *Epic* plans.

"I'd rather take an epic nap."

"Come on!"

I wanted to bury my head under my pillow and forget the world.

I said, "Go shopping with your friends."

"They're guys. They'll just be obnoxious and impatient the whole time. Besides . . . you'll like this. Trust me. Close your eyes."

Gladly.

"Picture a gorgeous guy. Are you picturing him?"

Despite all attempts to do otherwise, I was picturing a very particular gorgeous guy. The same guy who'd been stuck in my head for two days now.

"Now picture him shirtless, in swim shorts, and dripping wet."

Damn it. Why did my imagination have to be so good? There was no way I was going to get out of my rut if I kept this up.

"Now multiply that times a hundred, add some music and alcohol, and that's what you and I are doing tonight."

"Uh . . . Jenny. I don't know what kind of geography they taught you in Canada, but Hungary is landlocked. I don't see any beach parties in our future."

"Who said anything about a beach, drunky? We're going here."

She literally shoved a flyer into my face. My head ached as I tried to focus on the writing.

I saw the picture first. Some kind of rave with tons of people in bathing suits looking like they were having the time of their lives.

Above that, the title read, "Night of Baths."

When I sat up to take a look at the flyer, Jenny took off rambling. "The guy at the front desk, you know the one with the eyebrow ring?" Oh, I knew him, all right. He'd provided an excellent welcome my first night in Budapest. "He said it's similar to a pub crawl, but instead of bars you go to these thermal bath places that have been around, I don't know, a bazillion years. Everyone wears bathing suits, gets trashed, and stays out all night long."

At the moment, my stomach didn't seem up to another all-nighter.

"I don't know, Jen—"

"What do you mean you don't know? This sounds amazing. *Plus,* it's my last night in Budapest. And I could use a wing woman if I'm going to snag Tau."

Right. I vaguely remembered her mentioning something about liking him the night before. I guessed it was good I couldn't manage to drum up any attraction on my end, then.

"Come on, Kelsey. You'll regret it if you don't. This is like a once-in-a-lifetime party."

Between the regrets I already had and the ones I was scared of having, life was starting to feel like an obstacle course of remorse.

"Okay. I'll go."

She squealed, and I swear my brain screamed in protest.

Quieter, she said, "Sorry. Got excited. You won't regret this Kelsey. We're going to find some hot swimwear, and this will be the highlight of your trip. Just wait."

She was right. I just needed to get rid of this headache, and I'd be able to think a little clearer.

And maybe I would take it easy tonight. I could have fun at this party without alcohol. My liver could probably do with a bit of a break.

I'd help her get Tau and find a guy of my own. Then I'd be back on track, and could move forward.

Jenny, John, Tau, and I bought wristbands that allowed us entry into all of the baths and covered our transportation between the different venues. We shucked our cover-ups, checked our things, and then walked into what I could only assume was an alternate universe.

I'd opted against the sleazy bikini that had first caught my eye, and instead had bought a black-and-white wrap-around number that crisscrossed over my chest, wrapped around my rib cage, and then crisscrossed at the small of my waist once more before tying to my bikini bottoms at each hip. I looked hot, but fashionable; and in the sea of skimpy triangles, I stood out as a challenge, which was exactly my intention.

This venue flashed with neon lights, thumped with re-mixed techno music, and shone with, *dear Jesus,* so much skin. I saw bikinis and Speedos and even an acrobat hanging from the ceiling. And the cherry on top? There were *fire dancers* along the edges of the open pool. As in *people . . .* dancing with *flames.* Serious insanity.

Set against mosaic tiles and marble columns, I felt like I'd time traveled back to the hedonistic festivals I'd studied in theatre history in honor of the Greek god Dionysus; though, I didn't know enough to know if the architecture was Greek or Roman inspired, so I suppose it could have been Bacchus. Either way, it was like Woodstock meets Sea World meets Cirque du Soleil.

AKA fucking crazy pants.

"Is this for real?" Jenny asked.

"Right?" I stood, staring in awe. "Somebody pinch me."

A man with a horrendously hairy chest and a Speedo so tight it was probably cutting off circulation passed by me at that moment, and did just that. I yelped and held a hand to my ass, gawking at his retreating back.

Jenny laughed. "Maybe this place is magic, and whatever we say comes true. Ryan Gosling, please!"

We waited.

The acrobat hanging from the top of the dome above the bath dropped backward, hanging on to her hoop with only her knees, but no celebrities magically appeared.

Jenny snapped her fingers. "Too bad. This is still pretty awesome, though."

Awesome didn't even begin to cover it. This was . . . *incredible.*

"Thanks for making me come."

Jenny smiled. "Like I would have let you miss this!"

The guys seemed to be enjoying it too, though their eyes were glued more to bikinis than the visuals and pyrotechnics.

We walked farther into the room, past a bar and toward the steam-clouded bath. There were men and women of all shapes and sizes. A short guy with blond hair shouted and took a running leap into the water. He landed a few feet away from a chubby guy with a floaty around his waist like a neon green donut. My eyes kept catching on the girl curled around the hoop hanging from the top of the bath's domed ceiling. It reminded me of one of those bird cages, with the circular perch in the middle. I kept waiting for her to sprout wings and fly.

Then there were the abs . . . sweet baby Jesus, it was like there was a factory with a conveyor belt spitting them out because they just kept coming. I didn't even know where to begin. It was a buffet of well . . . buffness, and I was about to be guilty of gluttony.

"Should we get drinks?" Jenny asked.

I shook my head. "I'm okay. Let's check out the water first."

I took my first step into the bath, and I may have let out a strangled moan at the delicious heat. I smiled at Jenny and said, "Bet they don't have things like this in Canada."

"Are you kidding? I would still be *in* Canada if we had shit like this."

I sank in the bath up to my waist and closed my eyes in satisfaction. The water lapped at my chest, and I could feel the tension in my muscles unraveling.

"Can I spend the rest of my life here?" I asked.

"You might get a bit pruney."

"Worth it."

We waded farther into the bath. There were bodies everywhere. People danced and laughed and splashed. With the heat and steam and music and lights—it was a sensual overload.

The guys waded into the water behind us, and I said, "Time to snag you your hot Aussie."

Jenny smiled. "Patience. Trust me, I've been hanging out with him long enough to figure out, he needs a little push. A bit of jealousy should do the trick."

I almost felt a little sorry for Tau. Jenny was gorgeous, all dark to my light. Dark hair, brown eyes, tanned skin. As she scanned the bath, I knew she wouldn't have an issue finding someone to make Tau jealous over.

"And what are you looking to snag tonight?" she asked.

"Just a bit of adventure."

A couple playing chicken toppled into the pool a few feet away, sending a wave of water over both of us.

"I think you've found it!" she shouted, wiping at her eyes.

I did the same, and smiled.

I had found it. *This* was what I'd been looking for. The kind of experiences I couldn't get in Texas. Maybe it was naive, but being here—visiting places and doing things that most people didn't—it made me feel . . . special. It made me feel successful in a way that a college degree and a padded bank account hadn't. Even if I never did anything else of note in my life, if I spent the rest of my days in a loveless marriage or a porcelain home like my mother, at least I had this to remember. At least I had these memories to set me apart from the crowd.

We moved farther into the pool, and Jenny wasted no time before leading us up to two guys. She was kind of the perfect wing woman. Together, we could take the partying world by storm.

"I'm Jenny," she said to the nearest guy. "This is my friend Kelsey. And *you* are gorgeous." He was actually. Tanned skin, killer green eyes, and shaggy hair that was curling in the steam. She added belatedly, "Oh, and that's John and Tau."

Damn, she was good. Her brother and her crush held back a bit from the group, and I could see the way Tau's eyes followed her as she smiled and chatted with her new conquest.

I didn't know whether to talk to Jenny's friends or the cute guy's friend. The friend was attractive too, tall and kind of skinny with long blond hair. But to be honest, I didn't really feel like talking to either. Jenny was easy to hang with because she just talked, and she didn't ask too many questions. She was a party friend, the kind that you click with instantly because you have similar partying styles, but don't have to actually put forth any effort. John and Tau were different. They were both on the quiet side, and I felt like I had to work to talk to them. And the cute guy? Well . . . I didn't have a great excuse for why I didn't want to talk to him. I was trying to convince myself into starting a conversation when he beat me to it.

He said, "Kelsey? That's your name?"

I nodded. "And you are?"

"Lukas." He spoke excellent English, with just a slight trace of an accent. German maybe? He asked, "Are you two sisters?"

Jenny and I looked at each other and smiled. We didn't particularly look alike. She was dark to my light, but our bodies were similar enough.

I smiled at Lukas and said, "We are."

He pushed some of his hair back and gave me a wicked smile. God knows what it was with guys, but there was something about the idea of sisters that drove them nuts.

"Where are you from?" Jenny's guy asked. His accent was thicker than his friend's.

Jenny flipped her hair and answered, "Holland."

I saw Tau roll his eyes and scowl.

Lukas turned to me and said, "Oh?" Followed by a string of noises that I was guessing was Dutch. I gave Jenny a look.

Really? The guy had a German accent, and she picked a country right next door to his? She couldn't have gone for something like, I don't know, Sweden?

I laughed and placed a hand on his shoulder, hoping to flirt my way out of it.

If that didn't work, I could always make a swim for it. My

eyes went to the space between Lukas and Jenny, my escape path, if I needed it. And as if the universe had framed him for me in that space, I saw Hunt.

I blinked once, wondering if I was hallucinating him because of the heat, but he was still there. His head started turning toward me, and I panicked.

I gripped Lukas's other shoulder, and spun him until my back was to Hunt. The water sloshed around us, but there were so many people that he couldn't have seen. Lukas's hands gripped my waist, and I let it happen because the last thing I needed to do was cause a scene.

It was only after my back was turned that I allowed myself to acknowledge how devastatingly gorgeous Hunt looked. I'd felt the muscles beneath his clothing, imagined them this morning, but seeing them in the flesh even for just a second put that all to shame.

And for the first time in a *long* time . . . I was nervous.

Jenny turned and raised an eyebrow at me. "What's up, Kels?" Subtext: Hey, psycho . . . what's your problem?

What *was* my problem? He was just a guy. Guys had never been a challenge for me . . . or not in a long time anyway. But *this* guy . . . he had me on the ropes without even trying. All I knew was that there were a hundred girls in bikinis here, and I was sure I was the only one that had tried to kiss him with vomit-breath.

I resisted the urge to peer over my shoulder and told Jenny, "Nothing. I'm fine. Just someone I'd rather not see." And was dying to see simultaneously. Way to make sense, brain.

Truthfully . . . I didn't *get him*. And when I thought I had, I'd been wrong. It was that uncertainty, that complete lack of control, that made him the scariest damn thing I'd encountered in a long time. And the complete opposite of what I told myself tonight was going to be. I said, "There's five other bath places, right?"

We could just move on. Find another place to party.

"Yes, but . . ." Jenny threw a smile at the guys and said, "We can't leave yet." She moved to stand closer to her catch. I sighed. I didn't want to make her have to start over with operation jealousy.

"They could come with us."

I lifted my chin to look at Lukas, and he tightened his arms around my waist.

Jenny turned and peered past my shoulder. "Who are you running from anyway— Oh!"

"Oh? Oh! What does 'oh' mean?"

A smile crossed her face that made my stomach jump in anticipation.

She turned to the two guys and said, "Could you give us just a second?" She took hold of my shoulders and Lukas's fingernails grazed my skin lightly as she pulled me out of his reach. She moved us over a few feet before asking quietly, "Would the person you don't want to see happen to be a gorgeous piece of man candy with a buzz cut and biceps that some ancient civilization probably worshiped?"

I swallowed. "Please tell me the reason you know that is because you're psychic."

"No, honey. I've just got eyes."

Speaking of eyes, I swear I could feel his on my back, and I thought my spine might curl in on itself from the way it tingled.

"He's watching me?"

"Like you're the last piece of cake."

The water temperature felt like it was rising, and it had already been hot.

Jenny asked, "Just looking for a piece of adventure, my ass. You already have an adventure. Who is he?"

An enigma.

"Just a guy I met the other night," I answered.

"And why the hell would you not want to see him? Did he have herpes or something? Because that's a damn shame. Like paint splattered all over a Van Gogh. Or a naked Ryan Gosling. "

"It wasn't that kind of meeting."

She clucked her tongue. "Also a shame. So, then why are you avoiding him?"

"It doesn't matter."

As intriguing as I found him, I didn't like the way he made me feel. Jumbled and uncertain and naked in a way that had nothing to do with my current lack of clothing. Lukas was the better option. Easier to pinpoint and control.

"Well . . . you're right about that. Because he doesn't seem interested in avoiding you."

That was all the warning I got before hot breath caressed my ear, and a deep voice said, "Nice to see you again, Kelsey."

With my heart on pause, I turned and my mouth went dry. I met his dark eyes through the steam, and my paused heart leapt into action.

6

Standing face to chest with a glorious set of pectorals, I couldn't make my mouth form the appropriate greeting. God bless Bowflex and free weights and whatever other magic gave him that body. Jen was right . . . it was a work of art.

He said, "How are your cheeks this evening?"

Oh, you know, *flaming*.

"Uh . . . good."

Good. My cheeks are *good*.

He stood there, tall and silent and nodding, with that perpetually clenched jaw. The tension between us grew thicker than the steam, and I just couldn't understand why in the world this guy was standing across from me.

He'd seen me at my worst, and then he'd rejected me. Why come back for round two?

He slid closer to me, and I felt the flow of the water around me change. My body instantly responded to his closeness, and his cocky smile told me he could tell. His arm brushed my chest, and the tips of my breasts tightened. I made a strangled sound somewhere between the wheezing of a fat asthmatic and the squeak of a dog's chew toy. In other words, the noise that came out of my mouth was light-years away from being sexy. He chuckled and kept reaching past me to extend his hand to Jenny. With his body invading my space, and my face close enough to him that I could see close-up the stubble on his jaw, he focused on her. "Hello, I'm Hunt. It's nice to meet you."

"I'm Jenny. Likewise."

Even his name sent tingles down my spine.

"Is that short for Hunter?" I'd been wondering.

He pulled back from Jen, but stayed firmly inside my personal bubble. His face tipped down toward mine, and he murmured, "It's not."

"So your parents just named you Hunt?"

"Not exactly."

"God, vague *much*?"

He smiled, and that smile reached into my chest and re-arranged everything in me.

"There you go calling me God again."

Where was a desk when I needed to slam my head against it?

Lukas chose that moment to reappear at my side, and one desk wouldn't have been enough. I needed a whole fucking classroom.

Hunt glanced briefly in his direction, then at Tau and

John standing nearby, before focusing back on me. He said, "I didn't realize you were here with others."

I grinned. "You scared of a little competition?"

He laughed, and the sound unrolled down my spine on a shiver. He looked at me like the idea of him having competition was absurd. And damn it if he wasn't right.

He asked, "What about your other friends? The ones from the other night?"

I shrugged. "We weren't really friends. But this is Jenny." I latched on to her like she was my lifeboat.

He smiled. "Yes. We met. A few seconds ago."

I would welcome Armageddon if it would shut my stupid mouth.

"Right. We're staying in the same hostel." A hand slid across the small of my back, a large male hand that didn't belong to Hunt. Lukas. Damn it. "Because we're *sisters*. And it makes sense for *sisters* to stay in the same place."

Foot . . . meet mouth.

Jenny stood next to me, a peculiar look on her face. And I could imagine it was odd . . . watching me self-destruct. No need to visit Mount Vesuvius, I was my own natural disaster.

Jenny clapped her hands together. "Oookay, I believe it's time for drinks. I *know* I could use one . . . Kelsey?"

Oh God, yes. I could use a vodka IV drip right about now.

But then I looked at Hunt, and remembered where alcohol had gotten me the night we first met. If I hadn't been so drunk, things could have gone very differently. He wouldn't have rejected me, my brain wouldn't currently be a disaster zone, and I would have gotten him out of my system that first night.

But I also needed to relax. He had me wound so tight, that my normal cool, sexy demeanor was nonexistent.

I took a long, slow breath.

"One drink," I told Jenny.

Then I was going to get things back under control. Life was giving me a mulligan, and I was going to take advantage of that faster than a quarterback on prom night. That is, me taking advantage of the quarterback, not the other way around.

I slipped sideways until Lukas's hand fell away from my back, and I stood close enough to Hunt that I could feel his warmth even over the heat of the water. I said, "Come with me?"

"I would have thought you had enough to drink the other night."

I frowned. "It's just one drink. My first of the night. Come, have a little fun."

He hesitated.

"Or I can just catch up with you later." I moved toward Lukas, whose hand was already reaching for me.

I didn't make it more than a few inches before Hunt's hand was at my waist, pulling me back toward him.

"Okay, let's go."

Lukas frowned, but I wasn't about to feel bad. Not when I was getting what I wanted. Just the touch of Hunt's fingers on my waist had my heart sprinting, so I could only imagine what more contact would do. Lukas went to join Jenny instead.

She smiled. "Well, then, to the bar."

I almost laughed. John was up ahead, no doubt trying to ignore the fact that his sister was now juggling the interests of three men, Tau included.

We followed behind them, and I took a steadying breath. I had no idea what Hunt wanted from me, but I knew what I wanted from him.

One night. Enough to erase the crazy in my brain, and get me back on track.

"Your new friend seems a little reluctant to leave you."

My brows furrowed, and I followed his gaze not to Jenny but to Lukas, who kept looking back and forth between Jenny and me.

"He'll get over it. We literally met like two minutes ago."

"I know. I saw you when you came in."

My head whipped toward him so fast, I was in danger of pulling a muscle.

He *what*?

"I really enjoyed that little spin move you did while you were trying to hide."

I couldn't catch a fucking break.

"I wasn't *hiding*. I just . . ."

The words evaporated from my tongue. God, that sexy smirk was going to be the death of me.

"Okay." I rolled my eyes. "So I *was* hiding. It's not every day I make a fool of myself. I wasn't exactly excited about re-hashing that."

"It wasn't that bad."

Those are always the words you want to hear from a guy you're trying to sleep with . . . not *that* bad.

"What are you doing here?" I asked.

His eyebrows lifted, and it drew my attention to his eyes, the color of a thunderstorm.

"It's a room full of women in bikinis. What do you think I'm doing here?"

I tried not to let the sour taste of those words show on my face.

"I meant what are you doing *here*? With me."

We climbed the few steps that led out of the pool, and as gravity pulled the water back down to the earth, my swimsuit clung tight to my skin. I turned to see him standing still on the top step, his eyes cascading down my skin along with the water. He shook his head, and this time he didn't force himself to look away from my body like he had the night we first met. His eyes traveled down my frame, and then up again. The tips of my breasts pebbled, either from the cool air or from his gaze, but his eyes stuck there for a few moments before skipping up to my face. His voice rough and raw, he answered, "What was the question?"

I wanted to smile, but I was so turned on just from the way that he looked at me, that I couldn't seem to remember how to command all my muscles to work.

"I asked what you were doing here with me."

He stepped up out of the bath to tower over me, and he didn't seem to have any issues controlling his facial muscles because his sexy smirk was back. "Oh, you mean you asked a stupid question?"

God, he thought he was so adorable.

And he was. Ugh.

"You still haven't answered it."

"Yes, well." He reached out one finger, and collected a drop of water off my collarbone. "You make it hard to think straight."

And *that* was an answer I would take any day.

Feeling a bit more in control, I turned to follow Jenny, looking back at him over my shoulder as his eyes trailed down my body again. I held back a smile and said, "Come on, soldier. You can finish staring at me at the bar. I promise I'm not going to disappear."

His eyes flicked up to the ceiling, and he mumbled something I couldn't catch under his breath. Whatever it was, I had him on the ropes. Point, to Kelsey.

There were three bars set up around the bath, which was good considering how many people were here. The group had managed to snag a few barstools at the nearest one and were ordering when Hunt and I caught up. I leaned over the bar, simultaneously allowing the bartender a good look at my cleavage while also giving Hunt a clear view of the ass that I had promised him as he sat on his barstool.

"Gin bitter lemon," I ordered for myself, then looked at Hunt. "What do you want?"

"Nothing. I'm good."

I rolled my eyes and said, "Make that two gin bitter lemons."

In comparison to last night, I felt completely in control. Or I did, until I felt two fingers dip under one of the strips of my swimsuit that wrapped around my waist. Then I was tugged backward away from the bar into the space between Hunt's knees. His hands rested on my hips, and my eyes fluttered closed.

This put every other night of my so-far glorious vacation to shame.

The stubble on his chin grazed my shoulder and he said, "Whatever happens tonight . . ."

Whatever. *Whatever*? Please let us be thinking of the same whatever.

"Yes?" I breathed.

"Don't throw up in the pool."

Damn it.

Point, to Hunt.

7

pulled out of Hunt's grasp as a laugh rumbled deep in his chest.

"Just for that, *funny guy* . . . you're buying."

Our drinks arrived, and I raised an eyebrow at him in a challenge. While he stood to pay, I stole his barstool. It was both bizarre and empowering to be in a completely normal setting like a bar, but in a completely abnormal outfit that wasn't much of an outfit at all. But I wasn't complaining. It gave me the chance to get a good look at Hunt and his beautiful back—sculpted in muscles and cloaked in tan skin. My military suspicions were confirmed by the USMC tattoo above his right shoulder blade. It was a lesson in self-control, tracing the letters with my eyes but not my hands.

He turned to face me, drinks in hand, and I didn't even bother pretending like I wasn't ogling him.

He was ogle-able. And he knew it.

A laughing Jen leaned over and clinked her glass with mine, but I couldn't tear my gaze away from Hunt.

Jen whispered in my ear, "Not that you would know it, Miss Distracted, but Operation Tau is going very well."

"Sounds good."

"And I'm guessing you won't be coming home with us tonight?"

"Sounds *great*."

I bit my lip to hide a smile, and Hunt's eyes devoured me even as I sipped the sweet drink, savoring the smooth taste. His gaze flicked to his glass for a second, then back to me.

"So, Hunt," I asked. "Where are you from?"

"Where am I *not* from would be the easier question."

"Military brat?"

He smiled, and it took me right back to that first sighting. It was almost offensive how gorgeous he was. He was like that smart kid in class that ruined the curve for everyone else. Only instead of being good at equations, he was just good at existing. I crossed my legs, and his eyes followed. He said, "Are you calling me a brat?"

"If I were going to call you names, brat would not be my first choice."

His fingers brushed my ankle, and that small touch set my skin on fire.

"What would you call me, then?"

"Well, I've already called you soft." His lovely eyes narrowed. "But I'm not above admitting when I'm wrong."

His fingers traveled from my ankle up the back of my calf. My muscles flexed on instinct, and I really, *really* just wanted to skip the witty banter and get to the part where his mouth was on mine. Or on any part of me, really.

"What brings you to Budapest?" he asked.

I shrugged and hooked my foot around the back of his knee.

"Nothing in particular. It just seemed like an *interesting* place." I pushed lightly, and he stepped away from the bar, closer to me. "What about you?"

His fingertips were close to the sensitive skin at the back of my knee, and he stood close enough now that if I wanted to wrap my legs around him to tug him forward, I could. He answered, "Following a whim."

I wet my lips, and his eyes dropped down to my mouth. I was *so* close to getting him to follow another whim.

I said, "Do you ever get any less cryptic?"

"I thought women liked a mystery."

His voice pitched low, and it must have hit some special frequency because it sent vibrations all the way through me. Yellow and green neon lights flashed, casting a glow across his face.

"Women *love* a mystery. But only if we think we can figure it out." His gaze met mine, the intensity there was at once unnerving and intoxicating. "Are you going to let me figure you out, Hunt?"

He braced a hand on the edge of my stool, and his head dipped down toward my ear. The heat of his breath struck shivers across my skin like lightning. "That's a two-way street, princess."

I was about to tell him that he was dodging the question when Jenny popped up over his shoulder, Tau close by her side.

"We're going back in the bath, you two coming?"

Hunt pulled away, and I fought the urge to wrap my limbs around him to keep him from going too far.

I held up a glass that was still almost full and said, "We're still working on these. You guys go. Have fun."

Jenny gave me a quick salute in lieu of a goodbye, and I had a feeling we wouldn't be seeing each other again tonight.

When she was gone, I took another sip of my drink and met Hunt's gaze. He wasn't holding his glass, and when I looked behind him, it was sitting on the bar completely full.

"You've not touched your drink. I know it looks a little girly, but I swear you'll like it."

He smiled and took a seat on one of the stools that the others had vacated. "I'm okay. Really."

"Oh, come on." I slid off my stool to stand in front of him. Leaning against his knee, I said, "Try mine."

"I'm fine."

"You're so serious. Loosen up a little. Have some fun." I took another sip, then ran my tongue against my bottom lip to catch a stray drop. "Just try it. For me?"

I settled between his knees, and his hands went to my waist.

I imagined what his mouth would taste like, how hot our bodies would burn pressed together. Were his lips as soft as they looked? I could almost feel them, smooth and sure, at odds with the rasp of stubble on his chin. Just imagining it had my body coiling tight. I let out an unsteady breath, and he said, "If you'll answer a question for me."

I tilted my head just an inch, and one of his hands cupped the curve of my neck.

"Deal."

I took another sip of my drink, and then handed it to him. Water dripped off the outside of the glass, and he stared at me for a few seconds. I didn't get his reluctance, and I wondered if it went back to that chivalry he claimed not to have. He acted like he didn't trust himself where alcohol was concerned. And I, for one, was one hundred percent in favor of him getting a little crazy. With me, specifically.

He sighed, and his eyes flicked down to the half-empty glass. He pulled it to his lips, and took a quick sip. I gave him a look, and he took the rest of it in one gulp.

I smiled in victory, and I had the overwhelming urge to taste what was left of it on his lips. I was leaning forward to do just that when he said, "My turn."

I frowned, but a deal was a deal.

He paused, his gaze boring into mine, and his thumb traced my jaw. I could feel the pull of pleasure on my eyelids, and I had to fight to maintain eye contact.

"The other night . . . what did you mean when you said you were tired of being?"

His words crashed over me, and I flinched backward like I'd met a wall of water instead of his curious eyes.

"I don't know what you're talking about."

I turned my face away, but he nudged my jaw back to look at him.

"It's just . . . I look at you, and I see a beautiful woman in the prime of her life, traveling to exotic places, with the world at her fingertips. But I think that's just what you want people to see." I glanced around me, panicked and uncomfortable, as he continued. "And maybe I love a mystery too, because I can't seem to make myself stop thinking about what's underneath all that, what you *don't* let people see."

His other hand came up, one finger grazing my temple like he could unlock some secret gate there. I flicked his hand away, and pulled out of his grasp.

"I told you . . . I don't know what you're talking about. I was wasted. You shouldn't take one person's drunk ramblings as truth."

With my back to him, I leaned against the bar, and picked up his abandoned drink, taking a long pull.

He said, "I don't believe you. I think it was the most honest thing you've said to me. Maybe to yourself, too."

Jesus Christ. Like I needed him trying to play therapist.

"Again with the knight-in-shining armor bullshit. I don't need you to take care of me." I hadn't needed that for a long time. "You don't know anything about me. So whatever you think you're doing, whatever you're trying to *fix* in me, you can fuck off."

I took another big swallow of his drink, but I didn't taste any of the sweetness of it.

"Hey, I'm sorry. Don't be upset."

I could feel him at my back, and my heart was beating up in my throat. How had this derailed so quickly? I'd thought we were heading in the right direction.

"I'm not upset." I finished his drink in another big gulp,

and then tried to wave down the bartender. Before he could see me, though, Hunt took my hand and pressed it flat against the bar. He stood close behind me, and when he breathed in, his bare chest brushed my back.

He said, "Kelsey, I'm sorry. I shouldn't have pushed. But don't drink because you're mad at me."

I angled my head back at him, not bothering to turn around. "Apology accepted. And I'm drinking because I *want* to."

"Just talk to me for a second."

I'd had quite enough talking for the evening.

I raised my other hand to get the bartender's attention, and Hunt spun me around, pressing me back into the bar.

"What the hell is your problem?"

"I just needed to talk to you for a second."

"So you manhandle me like a caveman? Jesus!"

His lips curled into a devastating smile, and I swear if he made some crack about me calling him Jesus, I was going to smack that smile right off his face.

"I just wanted to apologize."

"You already did that."

"I know. But I really am sorry."

"I don't think you are. There's this pattern that keeps cropping up, where you judge me when you have no right to do so. And when you're not judging me, you're prying into my life."

"I'm not judging you. I promise. And the rest? That's just the soldier in me . . . I'm too straightforward. If I want to know something, I just ask. If I want to do something, I do it."

I rolled my eyes. That much was *abundantly* clear.

"Yeah, subtlety is definitely not your strong suit."

His smile widened. "No. It definitely isn't."

"Well, then. If you'll let me go, I think I'm going to go find Jenny and the others. Since I'm not *allowed* to order another drink and—"

I didn't get to finish my rant as his hands cradled my jaw, and he kissed me.

8

froze for a few seconds, in denial that this was actually happening. His lips brushed mine softly once, then twice. I exhaled and his grip on my jaw tightened. Then the softness disappeared as his mouth covered mine. He kissed me carefully, thoroughly, like a man who knew that desire hid with the devil in the details. He angled my head, explored my mouth, and I gave up control to him.

The first taste of him made my toes curl, and when he tugged me forward, bare skin colliding with bare skin, my brain took a much-needed vacation.

He kissed me feverishly, fiercely, like I was a battle he wanted to win, and with all the desperation of a man with nothing to lose.

I gripped the back of his neck and returned his kiss, faster and harder, want quickly burning into need. A low groan spilled from his mouth into mine, and his hand left my face to smooth across the curve of my ribs to the middle of my back. Fire followed his touch, and when his fingers tangled in the ties of my swimsuit, my back arched, pressing us tighter together.

He nipped my bottom lip, and I dug my fingers into his shoulders. His lips coasted down my chin to my neck. The heat of his breath touched my skin first, followed by the tip of his tongue. He pressed me back against the bar, and I was glad for the support at my back because I suddenly felt dizzy.

I pulled in a breath and even though there was no space between us, I tried to move closer. He was hard to my soft; and for a moment it felt as if my brain detached from my body, like I could see the way his hands clasped me tight and his body curled over mine, but I couldn't feel it. The world took on that hazy quality of a dream, and a whimper escaped my lips at the thought that this might not be real.

Then his teeth grazed the sensitive skin over my pulse point, and the world snapped back into focus.

It was *deliciously* real.

He hummed against my neck, the movement of his mouth like a foreign language on my skin—exotic and unpredictable, and sexy as hell.

His kisses burrowed beneath my skin, sparking every nerve ending in my body. And like his kisses really were electric and short-circuited something in me, my legs grew weak, almost numb beneath me.

I took hold of his jaw, just the faintest feeling of scratches against my palm from his facial hair. Pulling his face up to mine, I met his cloudy eyes.

"I think I like your lack of subtlety."

That familiar smirk tugged at his lips seconds before he tugged my mouth back to his. We were touching—from lips to toes—only touching. His hands gripped me tightly, but only in innocuous places. An ache bloomed low in my belly, and the neglected parts of my body were practically singing with need. I wanted him so bad, I was dizzy with it.

Really dizzy.

I began to have trouble matching his pace, unable to move my lips fast enough. I pulled back. My head was heavy, filled with sand, and I had to clutch his shoulders to keep from toppling backward.

"Wow."

His forehead leaned against mine, and he growled. "I should have just done that from the start."

I tried to agree, but he must have kissed away some of my brain cells. I couldn't get the words to leave my mouth, like there was a disconnect between my body and my brain.

His fingers brushed my cheek, but I couldn't feel it. That was odd. How much had I had to drink again?

The dizziness swarmed in my head, thick and buzzing, and the world began to move of it's own volition in my peripheral vision.

"Don't tell me you're speechless, princess."

A giggle poured from my mouth, and he looked as surprised by it as I felt. I let go of his shoulder to cover my mouth, and without that grip, I began tipping sideways.

"Whoa!" His arms wrapped around my waist, and he

pulled me up against him. My head tipped forward, too heavy for my neck to hold up, and I lay my numb cheek against his chest.

"Kelsey?"

I tried to open my eyes and look at him again, but my eyelids were so heavy. I felt like I was on some atrocious carnival ride, one spin or flip away from coming apart at the hinges.

Was his saliva alcoholic? I didn't understand how I could be feeling this way after one and a half drinks. That's all I'd had, right? He'd finished the last of mine, and then I'd had his.

"My cheeks," I mumbled.

His hands settled low on my back, hot and possessive. "What about them, princess?"

I tried to shake my head, but all I managed was to turn my head, my lips grazing the center of his chest. He sucked in a breath, and his grip tightened.

I leaned my forehead against him and whimpered a little. I could feel my insides pushing and pulling, reminiscent of the way I'd felt the other night when I'd been sick. But that didn't make any sense.

He cradled my jaw, and lifted my head back. Our eyes met, and his went from interested to confused in seconds flat.

"Kelsey? What were you saying about your cheeks?"

"Can't feel."

"You can't feel your cheeks?"

I couldn't feel anything.

"Shit."

He tilted my head back farther, searching my eyes. The neon lights overhead flashed, blinding me. Black splashed across my vision, and I pulled away, stumbling. He caught me, holding me so tight against him that there was barely any weight on my feet.

He opened his mouth, but no words came out. He looked at me with dark, glassy eyes and a hanging jaw. He reminded me of a broken doll. I reached out and touched his lips, and his mouth closed. He looked less broken now, but his eyes were still clouded.

"Kelsey, you didn't have anything to drink earlier, did you?"

I opened my mouth to say no, but my tongue felt too big for my mouth. So, I shook my head instead.

"Damn it. My drink."

He lifted me up and sat me on the nearest barstool, and then he turned and called the bartender.

"This drink," Hunt said. "Did you see anyone mess with it? Anyone touch it besides me or her?"

I didn't hear if the bartender replied. My body just felt so heavy.

God, I was exhausted. When did I sleep last?

I didn't even realize I was falling until Hunt's arms closed around my middle, and he righted me. His face appeared before mine, our foreheads pressed together. He said something, but the sound was delayed, a couple seconds behind the movement of his mouth, and I couldn't make sense of it. Hunt said my name, then again a few more times. I laughed because the more he said it, the less familiar it sounded.

"I'm taking you home," he said.

I sighed. That sounded perfect.

I placed another kiss on his sternum, and then lay my head against him. I felt his heavy exhale above me. I wanted to keep kissing him, until there was no breath left in his lungs . . . or mine. But I was so tired. I touched his chest, directly over where his heart should be, and the calloused skin of his fingertips touched my bare waist in a grip that was strong and possessive and maddening.

"I'm sorry," he said, low in my ear. "This is my fault. I should have been watching."

Everything was spinning, while my cheek lifted up and down with his heavy breaths. I was on a carousel, moving in too many directions at once.

I wrapped my arms around his neck, wanting to reassure him. My fingers were numb, and all I got was pinpricks of feeling when I tried to move them.

Then his arms swept beneath my legs, and he held me against his warm chest, and I sighed in relief.

"I've got you, princess. You're safe. If you can hear me, no one's going to take advantage of you. I promise."

I managed to mumble, "Bummer."

He released a heavy breath. "You're something else."

I really hoped he didn't start talking about me being a piece of work again. His arms were so warm, and I'd never felt so comfortable.

We started moving, and Hunt asked me questions in a low, rumbling voice.

My head felt thick and clouded and my body outside my control. It took all my focus to string together words to answer him, but somehow, despite all of that, I was always aware of Hunt's hands and his breath and his heart beating firmly underneath my cheek.

When I opened my eyes again, the world was a kaleidoscope of lights and colors and gray, gray eyes. Just when I thought I knew where I was and what was happening, everything would rearrange into something new and confusing.

Hunt's eyes, though, they were constant. And they were dark and deep and so very unreadable. My head was in his lap, and the world was careening, circling and sprinting around me where I couldn't follow and keep up. Everything tilted, and Hunt's hand laid flat against my stomach to steady me.

I felt sick, but somehow that cleared my head a little, made it easier to think.

"What's happening?" I mumbled.

"We're in a cab. I can't be certain, but . . ." His jaw clenched, and a storm brewed in his gaze. "I'm pretty sure someone slipped something in that drink while it was sitting at the bar."

That's what this was? Suddenly the warmth and the heaviness didn't feel comforting and safe. It felt suffocating. I could feel my heart trying to beat faster in my chest, but the heaviness was there, too.

"Fuck," I groaned.

"I tell you that you've been roofied and that's all you have to say."

"You tell me I've been roofied and expect me to say *more*?"

I couldn't say more. I wouldn't. I didn't even want to think about it.

His expression said he was pissed, but the hand on my waist and the other stroking through my damp hair told a different story.

There was a softness to him after all, and I was glad for it, glad that I wasn't alone for this. Because if he was right . . .

Don't think about it. Nothing happened. You're safe.

I laid a hand over his on my stomach, and tried to just feel and breathe. There was no use in thinking about what *could* have happened. Just as there was no use in thinking about the past.

I must have fallen asleep again because next thing I knew Hunt was pulling me out of the cab and up into his arms. I had that strange out-of-body sensation again. I watched the way he cradled me—careful and strong, almost as though it was happening to someone else. He didn't even break a sweat as he carried me into the lobby of a hotel.

He didn't stop at the desk, so I guessed that this was where he was staying. My stomach clenched.

In the elevator, I blinked up at him, and in my dazed state I saw one thing clearly. It was the way he looked at me, like he already knew me inside out, like he knew something even I didn't—that was what made me desperate to pull him closer and so eager to push him away. I didn't know if he looked at everyone that way or just me.

"You scare me," I said.

His brow furrowed, and his mouth opened, but no words came out. He took a breath and then very slowly said, "You have nothing to be scared of. I won't . . . I wouldn't. I'll help you get to bed, and then I'll leave, get another room."

He thought I didn't trust him . . . that he might do something.

"Not that. I don't think that."

"Then why do I scare you?"

"Because I don't want you to see."

There was a small part of me that knew I should shut my

mouth, that I was saying things I shouldn't, but that part of me felt like it was on the other side of a cement wall. It was too far away and too hard to understand.

"See what?"

He shouldered open a door and I answered simply, "Me."

9

He was silent as he led me across the dark room and low-ered me into a chair. He lay my purse and clothing at my feet. I'd checked those things. He must have picked them up, but I couldn't remember when. He knelt in front of me and perched one hand on the chair beside my thigh.

"Why wouldn't you want me to see you, Kelsey?"

My head was clear enough to order my mouth to stay shut on that one. I was not about to bare my soul to him. I'd lived my whole life as the confident girl, the girl not afraid to be bold or brash or independent. But that was a part I played, just like any other. Thick skin and a mask were necessities of my childhood. But when you grow up wearing a mask, you never really learn the face beneath it. I could guess at the me that hid underneath, though. It was the opposite of my illusion: ugly and afraid and not worth the cost of my manicure. If I lost my mask, if I let it drop, I'd have nothing.

"Kelsey, look at me."

My lids were heavy, and my vision blurry, but I made myself focus on him.

"You are beautiful, that's all I see."

I tried to smile, but I couldn't. Not when I knew how thin a shield that beauty was . . . how weak.

He watched me for a few seconds, and fatigue folded over me like a wave. My head started to droop, and it took all of my strength to keep my neck straight.

He cleared his throat once, twice, three times. Or maybe it was just once, and time or my mind had splintered. He said, "I, um, we should get you out of your wet swimsuit."

I yawned and said, "Okay." I tried to stand, but my legs collapsed beneath me. He caught my arms, and my chest slid against his. The world came quickly back into focus, and my breath caught.

Hunt cleared his throat again, and looked away. My swimsuit consisted of straps of fabric that wrapped around my chest, the small of my waist, and then tied onto my bikini bottoms. I reached for one of the knots tying my suit together at my hip, but my fingers felt useless, like all my bones had disappeared. Even when I managed to grip the fabric, I wasn't strong enough to do anything with it.

My muscles tingled with fatigue, and I felt dizzy.

"I can't."

The strength of gravity seemed to double, and I just couldn't stay upright anymore. Hunt was holding my arms, but the rest of my body began to slump.

"It's okay. I'll help. It's okay."

He lowered me into the chair, but then took a few steps back. He blew out a harsh breath and ran his hands across his head and down his face.

He mumbled, "What the fuck am I doing?"

He flexed his fists and rolled his neck, and I was too tired to do anything but watch the way his body moved, broad shoulders sloping toward muscled arms.

He said okay a few more times to himself, grabbed something from a suitcase, and then returned to me.

He knelt again and said, "Here, slip this on."

I tried to raise my arms to help him slip the dark gray shirt on, but my arms remained stubbornly at my sides. He pulled it over my head, and it smelled like him. I closed my eyes to breathe in the scent. He picked up one of my hands, and I managed to grip his fingers. He smiled reassuringly, and then maneuvered my arm through the sleeve. He did the same with my other arm, and his hand accidentally brushed my chest. I let out a small noise, almost a mewl. His grip tightened around my hand, and he closed his eyes for a few seconds. After a labored pause, he apologized and finished moving my arm into place.

Carefully, he set my hand down by my side, and then walked to the other side of the room. With his back to me, he hooked his hands around his neck, and stood still and silent.

Tension bled from his flexed arms to his rigid back. I

wanted to stand up, cross the room, and trace the lines of his body. I wanted to press myself against his back.

But I couldn't.

"Okay. Next step," he said, focusing on me like I was a problem to solve, a task to be completed.

He crossed the room and reached a hand around my back and another under my knees to lift me. With me in his arms, he bent and dragged back the covers from the bed. He laid me against the cool, clean sheets, and I shivered. He turned on my bedside lamp, and knelt beside me. I inclined my head to the side and met his dark gaze. The dull yellow light cast shadows over the angles of his face, accentuating his strong jaw and straight nose.

I thought he'd given up because he pulled the covers over me. I shivered again, and closed my eyes. Then I felt the brush of his fingertips under the covers against my hip. I pried my eyes open to see his chagrined smile.

"Are you that scared of seeing me naked?"

He finished untangling that first knot with ease.

"I'm not scared, sweetheart."

The ties pulled loose, and he must have thought I was the scared one because he said, "I promise I won't look."

He reached farther under the covers to slide the strip of fabric off my stomach, but the rest wrapped beneath me, around my back to my chest.

"Can you lift yourself up? That might be easier."

I tried to press my hands against the mattress and arch my body, but I was too far gone. The alcohol or the drugs or whatever had hit me hard enough that I felt almost paralyzed by exhaustion.

"I can't." I hated the tremble in my voice and how weak it made me sound, but I felt like my body had turned on me, and I was no longer in control.

Panic unfurled slowly, like the opening of a flower. I made myself keep my eyes open and focused. I knew what I would see if I let them close.

Hunt sat on the edge of the bed beside me.

"Wrap your arms around my neck, and use me to pull yourself up."

Slowly, I managed to snake my arms out of the covers. He made sure the blankets stayed in place before pulling me up and helping me to hook my hands around his neck.

"Just hold on."

He snuck his hands beneath the oversized T-shirt, and I felt him pull the fabric of my swimsuit, but it didn't come undone. It just shifted the rest of my suit.

"Damn it. The other piece is strapped over this one. Hang on."

He slipped a hand under the other strip, and held it out so that he could slip the other underneath it. My arms ached, so I dug my fingers harder into the back of his neck. He sucked in a breath, and his hands at my back faltered.

"Hunt?"

I watched his Adam's apple bob as he swallowed.

"Yeah?"

His fingertips skated across my lower back, dragging the fabric along, too. I skimmed one hand from the back of his neck to his jaw and said, "Tell me your other name. The one most people don't call you."

His eyes searched my face, flicking briefly from my lips up to my eyes.

"You won't remember it tomorrow, sweetheart."

"Doesn't mean I don't want to know, *sweetheart*."

He quirked a smile, but it disappeared almost immediately. He finished working the strap through, and the hand that had been holding up the other strap pressed against my bare skin. His long fingers spread across the entire expanse of my back, and the room seemed to amp up several degrees.

"Jackson. My name is Jackson Hunt."

I smiled, and he returned a small one of his own.

"Well, Jackson Hunt. Stop being a pansy, and just take my clothes off."

He chuckled, low and raspy, and it built into a full, barking laugh.

"You're something else, you know that?"

"Like you said, I won't remember it tomorrow. Let's just get it over with."

He groaned and scraped his fingernails against the stubble along his jaw. He mumbled something under his breath that sounded like, "But I'll remember."

Exhausted and cold and tired of waiting, I eased myself back on the pillow, his hand dragging from my back to my side as I moved. I did my best to shove the covers down. The T-shirt was bunched up around my rib cage.

He jerked, turning his face away. "Jesus, Kelsey."

The cool air embraced me from the waist up, my skin tightening.

"It's not that big of a deal."

"It is, though. I can't take advantage of you like that. Not when you're not sober enough to make decisions with a clear head."

I groaned. "You're not taking advantage of me. Been there. Done that. It felt nothing like this."

His head snapped to mine.

"What did you say?"

I was so tired now that I could feel the tears gathering at the edge of my vision.

That's all it was. Exhaustion.

"Nothing."

"Kelsey—"

"It doesn't matter. Just help me. Please? *Please.*"

I hated the desperation in my voice, but I needed this to be over, and I needed to stop thinking.

After a heavy sigh and a few seconds of staring at the ceiling, he pulled the covers the rest of the way down, and started working on the other knot. When he started unwrapping the swimsuit, his eyes locked on my face.

He leaned down until only a half a dozen inches separated us. His face hovered over mine, and a slow burn stole past the fog in my head. He snuck a hand beneath my back and lifted up my midsection. I swallowed, and he yanked the fabric out from underneath me. He pulled hard enough that the bathing suit slipped off my shoulders and down to my elbows.

I arched my back a little bit more, and my belly grazed his chest. He made a noise low in his throat and closed his eyes. That sound bled through my skin and muscles and lodged itself deep in my bones.

Quickly, he finished unwrapping the fabric, and then pulled the suit free. I heard the wet slap of the fabric as it hit the ground, and though he wasn't touching me, one of his hands was still under the T-shirt, his hand pressing down into the mattress an inch away from my bare skin.

His eyes opened, and the space between us crackled with energy. His eyes dropped to my lips, and his breath fanned across my mouth.

I whimpered, and he growled a four-letter word.

"Jackson."

I closed my eyes and tilted my chin up. My muscles tightened in anticipation. His wrist grazed my ribs, and his lips dipped toward mine.

This felt more like being drugged than anything else.

At the last second, he swerved and pressed a kiss to my cheek instead. He stayed there, his lips and stubble brushing against my skin, and said, "I can't. Not like this. If I'm going to cross this line, I sure as hell want you to remember it."

"It's not crossing a line if I want it."

I held on to him as tightly as I could manage in my current state.

"I want you, too. But you have no idea how many lines I'd be crossing, even if you were sober."

"What does that mean?"

"It means I'm getting you ready for bed, and then I'm saying good night."

"Then get me ready for bed." I took his hand and guided it down to the material at my hips. He hooked two fingers under the fabric, and then started to pull, down my legs and past my feet. When his gaze wasn't on my face, it was directed up toward the ceiling.

He pulled the blankets all the way up to my chin, the smooth sheets sliding against my bare legs. I caught one of his hands at the top of the blankets, keeping it close.

"Don't go."

He ran a hand over the stubble across his jaw.

"I have to. This isn't a good idea."

"I don't want to wake up alone. If I don't remember . . . I'll . . . it will kill me. You don't know . . ."

He was doing it again . . . studying me, and whatever he found made his lips curve into a frown.

"Jackson, please."

"Okay. Just . . . just give me a second."

I relaxed, the panic in my gut loosening. I listened to him moving around the room and then the bathroom, too tired to lift my head to actually watch.

After a few minutes, he flipped off the lamp beside the bed, dousing the room in darkness. I waited for the bed to dip, to feel the electricity that I knew would come from having him close to me.

I waited and waited, but it never came.

"Jackson?"

I heard something creak in the direction of the chair I'd been in earlier, and then his voice came from the same side of the room.

"Are you okay? Do you need something?"

"No." I relaxed back against the mattress. "I just . . . thank you."

"Anytime, princess."

I closed my eyes, and I gave into the weight in my limbs, the pressure behind my eyes.

I'd thought my memories of that night would overwhelm me, that I would see *him*. But against all odds, I felt . . . safe.

With Hunt only a few feet away, I slept.

10

Gentle light poured through window, but it felt more like a full-out assault to me. My limbs were slick with sweat and tangled in my sheets. Just turning my head away from the light felt like an earthquake was rattling through my skull.

"Fu . . ." I didn't even have the energy to finish the curse.

I pulled the pillow over my head, and pressed my pounding forehead into the mattress, then forced my way back into oblivion for a few more hours.

When I woke next, the light was less severe, but my hangover was not. My stomach pitched and rolled like I was adrift at sea, and I barely had time to acknowledge that I was in an unfamiliar hotel and to find the bathroom before I was sick.

There were a few things in this world that I *hated*.

PMS.

Pennies.

Close talkers.

Fran Drescher's voice.

People who say *fus*trating instead of frustrating.

And throwing up. Which I had done twice this week.

With my throat burning, my eyes watering, and my neck sweating, I lay my head feebly against the toilet seat. I rested against the cold porcelain for a few seconds before hurling again.

Life.

Maybe I was doing it wrong.

Again and again my stomach contracted, pushing and pulling until my organs felt like rubber bands. Long after my stomach was empty, I stayed hunched over the toilet with tears streaming down my face, too tired to think or move unless my body forced me to.

It must have been an hour before I felt the chill from the bathroom tile against my bare legs and realized I wore nothing but a man's T-shirt. I thought back to the night before, but the last thing I remembered clearly was arguing with Hunt. Things after that went gray and then black, and even the things before it were fuzzy. I looked back down at my bare skin and around me at the unfamiliar bathroom. Had I gone home with Hunt? I'd certainly been hoping for that. At least, I think I had been. And perhaps the better question . . . if I had, where was he now? I stretched, searching for the telltale soreness of a night spent not sleeping, but my whole body was aching.

There had been another guy, the one before Hunt had showed up, but I couldn't remember his name. Jesus, how much had I had to drink?

I'd worked long and hard in college to have gold-medal worthy tolerance, but for the life of me, I could only remember taking a few sips of alcohol the night before. I'd had hangovers from hell in the past, but none of my nights out had ever been so bad that I blacked out. This made absolutely no sense, especially considering I'd been determined to take it easy last night.

Despite my hollow insides, my stomach began to sink.

What if this wasn't because I'd had too much to drink?

I remembered being frustrated with Hunt and going up to the bar. I closed my eyes, straining to remember. I recalled a snippet or two of conversation, and . . . one drink. I remembered having *one* drink. Maybe two, tops. I gripped the toilet and slowly pulled myself up to my feet. My legs shook like a newborn deer. I was fucking Bambi, hoping the story would take an unusual twist, and I'd be the one facing a shotgun. Put me out of my misery.

Maybe then the pounding in my head would stop.

I dragged myself to the bathroom door and surveyed the hotel room.

"Hello?" I called out. "Anyone here?"

As if my stomach gymnastics in there wouldn't have alerted them to my presence already.

The bed was a mess, sheets and blankets twisted, falling off the mattress. A pillow lay on the floor. But I was alone . . . definitely. And there were no other things but mine in the room. But I couldn't remember how I got here, and that made my headache seem like a soothing massage.

I pressed a hand to my stomach, and for a reason I felt, but couldn't articulate, my heart beat faster and my hands shook.

I had done plenty of stupid things in my life.

I'd slept with people I regretted. I'd done things because everyone else was doing it. I'd made the worst possible choices.

But I owned my mistakes. Because they were mine. They'd been *my* choice.

Except for once. There'd been only once in my life where I'd had no control. That was the moment when I realized that beneath everything beautiful, everything rich . . . there lived an ugly pit that would pull and plunge and smother you if you let it. And once you've been there in that pit, it never quite leaves you. You can try to scrub it off or cover it up, but it lives under your skin, unreachable.

My stomach pitched, and I lurched for the toilet again. I dug my fingers into the porcelain until they hurt. I told myself the tears were just a natural by-product of being sick.

Nothing happened. Not last night. Not back then. Nothing happened. So, stop it. Just stop. You're being dramatic. It was nothing. Nothing.

I wanted to hit something or run or scream. I just needed to *do something.* But the only thing I could get my body to do was to curl up on the cold tile floor.

You're being overdramatic.

God, I'd heard those words so many times, they just happened, like muscle memory. I shivered and pressed my cheek into the tile, hard.

It had taken me so long to stop feeling guilty, to ignore the shame. And now I could feel the ugly emotion curling and winding through my gut like weeds.

I didn't know what happened last night, but whatever it was, it hadn't been my choice. And I had promised that would never happen again. While trying to stay still for my nausea's sake, I slid my hands across and down my body, looking for a clue or hint of what might have happened to me last night. I was scared to even think the word that hung unsaid on the tip of my tongue.

You weren't raped. You've never been raped.

I thought it again. I thought it half a dozen times.

It was a familiar mantra, and it helped about as much now as it had then . . . not at all.

No matter how many times I thought it, no matter that there was nothing torn or painful, I couldn't stop the tears choking at the back of my throat.

If someone was going to drug and rape me, they wouldn't have left me in this nice hotel room. There were no marks or bruises that I could find. I was making a big deal out of nothing.

I always made a big deal out of nothing.

So, I pushed it away. I forced myself off the floor. I willed myself into the shower stall and turned the water as hot as I could stand it.

I kept chanting, *You're fine. Nothing happened. You're fine. You're fine. You're always fine.*

And I *was* fine . . . until I wasn't.

Until the warm water hit my face, and a sob wrenched from my lungs. Until my legs gave out, and my knees slammed into the tile. Until I could no longer pretend that this epic failure was the trip of a lifetime and was going to miraculously show me whatever path my life was supposed to take. That it was going to fix me.

If I couldn't manage to be happy here in this gorgeous, exotic city, how could there be any hope for the rest of my life? I had everything I could want, but it *never* stopped—the ache, the emptiness. Nothing ever satisfied it.

I sat on the shower floor and pulled my knees up to my chest. I leaned my head on my knees and let the water pelt my back.

I hated myself for the weakness, for my inability to just *deal*, but there comes a point when you're so far down in the pit that there is no light at the end of the tunnel, not a pinprick or a soft glow. There is black and more black pressing into you, choking out the world. And asking how you got there and why you can't get out is a pointless exercise because you're too deep to do anything about it.

I knew other people had it worse. I *knew* that. I knew that what happened when I was twelve could have been a lot worse.

I just wished that I knew why I couldn't fucking let it go. Every time I thought I had, life tripped me and shoved my face into the muck of my past, and taught me just how far I was from being over it.

Maybe I should just book a flight back to the States. I could visit Bliss in Philly, build up my resolve, and just go home. What was the use in fighting it?

Whatever I'd thought I was going to do here—the adventure and the living that I'd been looking for—wasn't happening. If anything, I was more confused and more lost than before. I'd been trying to outrun my issues, racing from bar to bar and city to city, but after a while the differences in location didn't matter. Because *I* was the same in every city. Inadequate.

It was stupid, but in my head this trip had become the indicator for the rest of my life. I'd thought it would jumpstart something, that it would give me the momentum to move forward. I had pinned every hope, every doubt on this trip, intending it to fulfill the former and dash the latter. Unfortunately, it was doing the opposite.

Maybe it was time to cut my losses.

The permanent knot in my stomach loosened slightly.

The water battered my back, and I took each tiny blow, willing the water to take some of me with it. Slowly, slowly the tension melted out of my muscles, my lungs lost that aching feeling, and the sting of emotion at the back of my throat receded.

Life was easier when you stopped caring, when you stopped expecting things to get better.

Feeling more in control, I dragged myself off the shower floor. I shut off the water, and reached for a towel.

Then I scrubbed.

At my hair. My face. My skin. I scrubbed myself dry while all my hopes for this trip, for life, twisted down the drain.

I left my hair wet and wavy, and collected my things from where someone had placed them neatly at the foot of the bed. I balled up my wet swimsuit in the T-shirt I'd been wearing and did the walk of shame wearing the wrinkled shift dress I'd worn yesterday before the baths.

It was possibly the shamiest walk of shame in the history of all shaming.

But at least it was short.

I exited the nice boutique hotel to find myself on a familiar block. I was across the street and just a few buildings down from my hostel.

"Jesus . . ."

I jogged across the street, and pushed open the door to the hostel. I reached in my bag for my phone to see what time it was. I didn't actually use the phone to call anyone. It was more of an emergency kind of thing. And it had all my music. I was still fishing around in the bottom of my bag when I entered the dormitory with my bed to see Jenny, John, and Tau packing up their things.

I gave up my search for my phone.

Tau saw me first and nudged Jenny.

"Kelsey! Where did you go last night, you little minx?"

I opened my mouth to tell her where I'd been, that I'd been just across the street, but then pulled my lips closed. I threw on my most convincing smile and said, "Oh, you know me."

There was no point in telling people. Been there. Done that. Fucked things up even worse. Besides . . . there was nothing to tell. Nothing happened. And it's not as if we were really friends anyway. They were little more than cardboard cutouts to me. Superficial people to be with and be seen with. And I was the same to them.

"Oh my God," Jenny said. "I freaking love you. Was it the army guy? I bet he was fantastic. Come out with us and tell me everything."

I moved toward my bed to put down my things. I'd not

found my phone yet, but I was fairly certain it couldn't be much later than noon.

"You're going out now? It's so early."

Jenny shrugged. "We've got to check out in, like, ten minutes, but our train doesn't leave until tonight. So, we figured a little day drinking was in order. You know, to end our Budapest weekend in style. Come with us!"

I worried my bottom lip between my teeth, unsure how to get out of this.

"I don't know if I'm up to day drinking, honestly."

"So come for the company," John said.

I didn't think I was up to the company either.

The hesitance must have shown on my face because Jenny picked up her backpack and handed it to Tau. "You guys go check us out," she said. "I'll be right there."

John waved on his way out, and Tau nodded. Then Jenny turned on me.

"Okay, what's up? I know post-coitus glow, and you don't have it. So where were you really last night?"

I plopped down on the bottom bunk bed that I was currently calling home. The mattress was so thin that I could feel the wooden slats below it.

"Nothing. Just . . ." I sighed. "I've just had a bad week is all. Last night just continued my slump."

"It's probably just mental. Maybe you need a change. New atmosphere. You could start fresh."

That's all I'd been doing. Starting fresh. But I was learning that the stench of the past tended to cling despite changing locations.

"I don't think that will help. I think I'm going to go home."

"Are you serious?"

I threaded my fingers together in my lap and ran my thumb across my palm.

"Yeah." I nodded and said more firmly, "Yeah, I am."

She ducked underneath my bunk and sat down beside me, the bed groaning. "You can't. Not yet. If you go home now, when you're unhappy, that's the only way you'll remember this trip. Go home on a good note at least."

I brushed my thumb across my palm again, scraping lightly with the nail of my thumb.

"You're not wrong."

"Of course I'm not. I get being homesick. And the culture shock can come a bit out of nowhere and bite you in the ass. But you're going to want to look back on this trip fondly. As a good thing . . . right?"

"Right." I nodded. Jenny's advice sounded a lot like what I would have told myself. That is, if I weren't so mixed up and broken down. It was stupid to try to pin all my hopes on this trip. I was expecting too much. Too much pressure.

I still thought going home was the best choice, but I was pretty sure I could handle one last hooray.

"Thanks, Jenny."

She smiled, and lifted one shoulder in a shrug.

"I'm the queen of sabotaging good things, but I'm at least pretty good at recognizing the same tendency in others. One more trip. Do something you'll remember, something impossible to regret. Then take that moment home with you."

I nodded, emotion tickling at the back of my throat.

She slipped off my bunk and headed for the door. "Facebook me and let me know how it goes."

She was almost out the door when I called, "Jenny?"

She balanced a hand on the doorjamb. "Yeah?"

"Would you recommend Prague as a place to remember?"

She smiled.

"Hell, yes, I would. And I happen to know that a train is heading that way in just over eight hours."

Prague it was, then. My last adventure.

11

Even the train station in Budapest was beautiful. It was all archways and glass windows. The glittering night sky was visible through the windows that swept across the arched ceiling. The station was cast in a low yellow light, and the balmy night air crept in through the open archways over the train tracks. I arrived about forty-five minutes early, but didn't see Jenny, John, or Tau anywhere.

The train Jenny had told me about traveled overnight and arrived in Prague just after dawn. I went ahead and purchased a ticket for a couchette in a random compartment, just in case I didn't find them before the train left. There was probably very little chance I would have been able to get in the same train compartment as them anyway.

I took a seat on a quaint wooden bench. I still couldn't find my phone, and I was working on the theory that I'd lost it sometime during the night of oblivion. Unable to listen to music, it was just me and the quiet station, permeated by the humming of the tracks as a train approached.

That hum grew into a roar, and the wind whipped my hair around my face. And for a second . . . for one *tiny* second, I felt good. The worries rolled off my back, and it hit me where I was and what I was doing. I was in a gorgeous European city, where most people didn't speak English. The train station was so grand, it was easy to imagine how magnificent it had been when it was first built. There was a wide, bustling world out there, and *I was a part of it.*

Sure, I had no fucking clue what I was doing with my life or where I fit in this world, but I was a part of it all the same. I'd left footprints across the globe, and though you couldn't see them and they didn't necessarily matter, I knew they were there. And that was enough for now. It had to be enough.

The train pulled to a stop, the wind died down, and with it that *spark* of something more.

The moment was fleeting, but it told me something important. There was hope in this mad world, if I could keep it protected from the darkness.

My train arrived just a few minutes prior to the scheduled time. I picked up my backpack, and did one last sweep of the platform to look for Jenny and the guys.

I didn't see them, but maybe I'd be able to find them once we got to the station in Prague.

I stepped off the platform and up onto the stairs leading into the train. An attendant helped direct me toward my compartment. I slid open the door and shouldered my hulking backpack through the narrow opening. The compartment held six bunks that folded out from the wall bunk-bed style. There were three on each side, each with a pillow and a blanket. I checked my ticket to find that I was on one of the middle bunks. I was not looking forward to climbing into that space. There was only about two feet between the top of my bunk and the bottom of the one above me. Not enough space to sit up unless I wanted to crack my head against the couchette above me.

Now that I knew where I was, I exited my compartment, following the flow of people looking for their own places. I peeked past open doors, checking for a familiar face. I walked nearly the entire length of the train before an announcement came over the speakers. It started in Hungarian, but I didn't need to wait for the translation to know what it meant. We were leaving. And I still hadn't seen Jenny or the guys anywhere.

I was about to turn around and go back to my compartment when I heard a commotion. The train started moving, but the attendant was still at the door, calling out something in Hungarian.

While I stared, a hand took hold of the bar next to the stairs, and a running body pulled itself up onto the train and into the cabin. The person held out a ticket to the conductor, and after they spoke for a few seconds, stepped out into the light.

A small part of me had thought maybe it was Tau or John, and the others would be pulling themselves onto the slowly moving train any second now.

It wasn't.

But the face was a familiar one after all.

The train picked up speed, and I had to brace myself on the wall to keep from falling. He finished tucking his ticket into the pocket of his dark jeans, slung low on his hips, and then his eyes met mine.

Hunt.

I had the strongest urge to run. Or to throw myself into his arms.

He moved forward, reaching a long arm up to the ceiling to help keep his balance.

"You left," he said, his expression troubled.

"I—what?"

"And you left this."

He reached into his pocket again, and pulled out my cell phone.

I stretched for it. "Where did you get that?"

"You left it in your room."

"What?"

My room? The hotel room?

He passed the phone to me and said, "I came over this afternoon to check on you, but you were already gone. I went to your hostel, but you were already gone from there, too. I got lucky and ran into Jenny and Tau at a bar near the hostel. They said you were leaving for Prague tonight."

I was still stuck on that first sentence. "You came over . . ."

He *had* been there last night. He could tell me what happened. He was obviously involved with me ending up in that hotel room. Did he pay for a room for me? How did we go from arguing to him taking care of me? The empty space in my head was infuriating.

His eyebrows tilted, his tanned skin wrinkling across his forehead. "You didn't read my note, did you?" I didn't even have to answer before he was replying, "Damn it. I'm sorry, Kelsey. I thought you would have seen it beside your bed." He came closer, until I could have reached out and traced a finger along the bare strip of skin that showed every time he checked his balance against the wall or ceiling. "I should have stayed. I never meant for you to wake up that way, confused and scared."

"I wasn't scared."

My eyes stayed steady, and my lip didn't wobble. My voice was calm and even.

He paused, his mouth still open in the shape of whatever he'd been planning to say next. "Kelsey . . . you don't have to do that."

"Do what?" I looked away, unnerved by the way he seemed to see right through me.

"I promised you I would stay, so that you wouldn't wake up and not know what had happened. And I was going to stay, I just . . . I'm sorry."

If he'd been there, I wouldn't have freaked out. I wouldn't have had to think about the past at all.

"Why didn't you?"

He cleared his throat and scratched at his neck. "I—uh. I needed a bit of distance. I booked the room across the hall."

I wanted to ask why, to push for more of an explanation, but I didn't want him to know that I cared, and that I had been more than scared. I'd been terrified, split open, and even now I was only barely stitched back together.

The train was at full speed now, and the conductor was sliding open a compartment just a few doors down to check people's tickets. I needed to get back to my seat. *I* was the one who needed distance now. But I had to ask, "Did you just jump on a train to Prague solely to bring me my phone?"

He smoothed a hand over the stubble on his jaw and shrugged.

"Are you crazy? It's just a phone."

"And it's just a train. If I weren't on this one, I'd be on another one. Prague is as good a place as any."

I pushed my phone into a pocket on my backpack and surveyed him. He was a soldier . . . or had been. His hair was still cut short, so either he preferred that style or he'd been in service very recently. But it sounded as if he was wandering just as aimlessly as I was, and I wondered briefly what he was hoping to find here. If he was having better luck than me.

The conductor moved onto the next compartment. I pointed behind me and said, "I better get back to my compartment. You said you saw Jenny?"

"This afternoon, yes. But not since I arrived at the station."

"Oh. Okay. Thanks."

I turned, adjusting the backpack on my shoulders, and heading back the way I'd come. He followed behind me, going to his own compartment presumably, and I wasn't sure whether I should keep up conversation or just maintain the illusion that we'd parted ways.

What exactly did one say to an incredibly hot guy who'd rejected you, hit on you, pried into your personal life, and then possibly took care of you during a drug-induced evening that you can no longer remember?

My resolve to not tell anyone about last night to avoid the pity and the questions and the fallout didn't work so well when there was someone else here who'd experienced it, too. If we talked about it, there would be no pretending that it didn't happen. And as much as I was dying to know, I also knew that there was bliss in oblivion.

I moved through one, two, three train cars in silence. And when I was a few feet away from the door to my compartment, I stopped and faced him.

"What did the note say?"

He pulled up short. His mouth opened and closed. It opened again and he said, "That everything was okay. That nothing bad had happened to you. That you were safe."

"That's it?"

He balanced a hand on the wall next to me.

"Those were the important things."

"And the unimportant things?"

"I told you that you could call me by my first name. You can call me Jackson."

"Does that mean I'm no longer most people?"

He nodded.

"So what am I, then?"

"I'm still figuring that out."

I cleared my throat, feeling like if I turned away from him, the hook he'd sunken under my skin would tear right through. So, I didn't turn. Without looking, I gestured behind me and said, "This is me."

He stepped to the side and held open the door for me. I

passed through, waiting for the pull, the tug to turn around and say one more thing or see him one more time. And it wasn't so much a force as a tingle spreading down my back. When I turned, worried that I waited too long, the door closed, and he was on this side of it.

The tingle spread to my fingertips, and he threw his pack onto the luggage rack that hung from the ceiling.

Quietly, so as not to disturb anyone else in the compartment with us, I said, "Are you following me?"

He smiled unabashedly and said, "Absolutely."

What do you say to something like that? I stood there gaping, my mouth opening and closing like a fish, and he smiled. Even though I couldn't put images or memories to what had happened the night before, my body seemed to remember. I felt both relaxed and exhilarated by his presence.

He touched my shoulder in a gesture that seemed not quite intimate, but familiar. He leaned close to whisper, "Good night, Kelsey."

I struggled to swallow and said, "Good night."

I watched him fold his too long body onto the couchette in the middle, the one directly across from mine.

"Jackson?"

He'd been shifting and turning, trying to get comfortable, and he paused.

"Yeah?"

"Thank you for watching out for me last night."

The look he gave me buried the hook even deeper in my chest, and suddenly I was scared to know what had passed between us last night for an entirely different reason. This beautiful, mysterious man had seen me at my worst twice now, and he was still there across from me.

In every city so far, I'd picked up temporary friends. Some were locals. Some were other travelers. But I never had any issue letting them go. I moved on to a different city, and didn't think twice about them.

But I hoped Hunt would be different. I wanted him to stay.

And at the same time, I was terrified of what that meant, and what it would do to me if he didn't.

12

The couchette was too firm to feel like a bed, and sleeping with my backpack at my feet to keep it safe didn't make for the most comfortable position. Despite that, the low rumbling and gentle swaying motion of the train seduced me into the arms of sleep only a few minutes after I lay down my head. I was still fatigued from whatever had happened to me the night before. I was too exhausted to even stress over Hunt sleeping in the bunk across from me.

Minutes or hours later, I was jostled out of my sleep by the departure of the person on the bunk above me. His bag hit my knee as he climbed down from his bunk. My eyelids felt heavy and swollen, but as I watched him leave, I caught sight of Hunt on his bunk. A dull yellow light shone from above his bed, painting him in highlights and shadows. He lay scratching away at something in a journal. It wasn't the continuous flow of handwriting, so I guessed he was probably drawing.

I watched him as he focused on one corner of his paper. His tongue darted out to wet his lips, and the muscles of his shoulders tensed as he made short, precise strokes on the page. I found myself wishing I could draw too, so that I could capture the power and simplicity of him in that moment.

He glanced up, and his eyes widened when he saw me.

After a few long seconds he whispered, "Hi."

"Hey." My throat was dry, so my reply was barely audible.

"Everything okay?" he asked.

I nodded and rolled onto my side to face him. I tucked my arm beneath my pillow and asked, "You're not going to sleep?"

He closed his sketchbook and tapped his pencil against his lower lip. As if I needed anything else to draw my eyes there.

"Maybe in a little while."

"Were you drawing?"

He nodded. "It's an old habit. It calms my thoughts when I can't sleep."

"Does that happen a lot?"

"Sometimes."

Something rustled in the bunk below me, followed by a breathy moan and noises that were not what you wanted to hear coming from the bed below yours. I met Hunt's gaze, and we both burst into silent laughter.

He placed his pillow over his ear and flipped off his reading light.

"That's my cue," he whispered.

I followed suit and pulled the small pillow over my ear, resting my head on my elbow instead. I stayed staring at the place where Hunt's face had been before the lights went out, wondering if he was looking at me, too.

My eyes were drooping, and sleep had almost claimed me when a light flashed through the train window and gave me my answer.

Our eyes met, and my stomach lurched despite the smooth motion of the train. The darkness took over again a second later, and I was left trying to calm the unsteady beat of my heart enough to fall back asleep.

When I woke the next morning with grimy teeth and oily hair, Hunt was fast asleep.

Thank God.

If I looked half as atrocious as I felt, Big Foot could beat me in a beauty contest. My back ached, either from the stiff bed or from carrying my massive backpack with me through multiple countries. The underwire of my bra had begun to cut into my skin, and the marks itched.

I leaned over the edge of my couchette and saw that everyone was gone but Hunt and me. I pulled my makeup from my bag and did my best to salvage the greasy, smudged mess on my face. I found a piece of gum for my morning breath, and pulled my limp hair into a high ponytail. Feeling a little more alive, I climbed down from my bunk and peeked past the curtain through the window. We were stopped, and people streamed off the train in large numbers.

I went to the other side of the compartment and slid open the door. Judging by the lines of people waiting to get off the train, I was going to guess that we were in Prague.

Damn it. I'd meant to get off the train as quickly as possible so that I could look for Jenny. I pulled my backpack off my bunk, sliding it onto my back. The weight pulled down on my shoulders, and I swore this bag got heavier by the day.

I almost left.

Or I told myself I almost had. I don't think I actually got more than one step toward the door before I turned to a sleeping Hunt.

Almost like he could sense my presence, his eyes snapped open the second I took a step toward him.

He rubbed a hand across his eyes, and then across his shorn hair.

"Hey." His voice was rough with sleep, and that hook beneath my skin pulled taut.

"I think we're here," I said.

He nodded, and with that sleepy look on his face, he looked younger. Softer.

"Damn, I haven't slept that well in a while."

He stretched, and I drank in the flexed muscles of his arms and the strip of hardened skin between his shirt and his jeans.

Before he could catch me staring, I said, "Seriously? I'm going to need a massage just to recover from that sleep."

He shifted his legs over the edge of the couchette, and then hopped down beside me.

"I'm used to sleeping in an uncomfortable bed. Feels like home."

Definitely military. I had a brief flash of memory of a USMC tattoo across someone's back and knew it had to be his.

I said, "Well at least one of us feels good."

He reached forward and curled a hand around the back of my neck. His fingers kneaded softly, and goose bumps prickled across my skin. The gesture was intimate, and the need to know what happened the other night rose up again like bile. And before I could think too much about the answers I didn't want to hear, I said, "What happened the other night?"

He hesitated, and then his hand slipped off my skin.

"Why don't you tell me what you remember, and I'll fill in the blanks."

I leaned my shoulder against his bunk and squinted up at him.

"The last thing I clearly remember is arguing with you. I've got bits and pieces of other things. Conversations. I remember holding a drink, maybe two, but that's it."

"Nothing else?"

He looked both relieved and disappointed.

I swallowed and shook my head.

He sighed and touched my shoulder, lightly this time and only for a few seconds.

"Let's get off the train, and then I'll tell you whatever you need to know."

I nodded. "I need to look for Jenny, too. We were supposed to meet before the train, but I couldn't find her."

"I'll help you look."

I followed behind Hunt, trying to remember for sure where that tattoo had been. Before he descended the stairs down onto the platform, he said, "By the way, that argument we had? You probably don't remember this, but you totally apologized and said you were wrong. Just so you know."

I scoffed, and pushed him to the stairs. "Even without my memory, I know that's bullshit."

He took the stairs quickly, and then held out a hand with a smile.

"It was worth a shot."

He helped me down the stairs and released my hand quickly after my feet were on the platform.

"Better luck next time, soldier."

I flashed back to last night, to before the argument. I remembered the way he looked at me, and I could almost recall the way it had felt when he'd trailed his fingers up my leg. And now he only touched me for *chivalry's* sake. What did that mean? We'd argued, but he still took me home, so the argument couldn't have been that bad. But he was treating me differently. The question was why.

Together we searched the platform, looking for a familiar form. I climbed the stairs leading up into the main part of the station, but even from that vantage point, I didn't see Jenny. We walked from one end of the station to the other, talking as we searched.

Even though he'd promised answers, I didn't ask any questions. Not yet. I kept wavering on whether or not I actually wanted them.

Instead, he asked, "So what are you going to do in Prague?"

I shrugged. "I'm not really sure. Something fun. Something to remember."

"Like what?"

"I don't know. An adventure. I don't want to just do the tourist thing. I want to do something original, you know?"

He nodded. "I get that. "

I checked the stalls in the women's restroom while he waited outside, and I did the same while he checked the men's. After nearly half an hour, we exited the station in a last-ditch effort to see if perhaps they were waiting outside.

They weren't.

"Well, what do we do now?" Hunt asked.

"We?"

"I'm following you, remember?"

That was one of the few things I remembered.

"I don't know. I guess we're on our own."

I could have made more of an effort. I could have found Internet access somewhere and messaged her on Facebook. And maybe I would later. Right now, I was more intrigued with this "we" idea of Hunt's.

"In that case, let's go explore Prague." He hitched his backpack higher on his shoulders and started walking.

I stayed where I was and called, "Should we find a place to stay? I think they have a metro system here and trolleys."

"We'll get to all that. For now, let's just walk."

My jaw dropped. He couldn't possibly serious. I was tired and cranky and my backpack was heavy.

"Why would we do something as stupid as that?"

He smiled. "Because you wanted an adventure."

Then he started walking, and this time he didn't stop

when I called. I stood in disbelief for a few seconds before jogging to catch up with him. My lungs protested from the twenty seconds of almost-running, so I had a feeling they would start an all-out revolution on this "adventurous" walk.

I said, "I can have an adventure without gaining bunions and ruining my pedicure."

He shook his head. "I'm fairly certain it's in the dictionary that it's impossible to have an adventure while worrying about things like pedicures."

Hunt had picked up a map at the train station, and he said there was a neighborhood not too far away that should have plenty of inns and hostels to choose from. We'd go there first.

It wasn't exactly my idea of an adventure. I still would have preferred a taxi or the metro. But I did have to admit, it was refreshing to walk the stone sidewalks and take in the architecture. There were plenty of modern buildings and restaurants, but occasionally we'd turn a corner, and I'd feel like I stepped straight into a fairy tale, complete with stone gargoyles staring down at us from half the buildings we passed.

Hunt and I argued over how to pronounce words we saw on signs. Some of them used almost every consonant in the alphabet with only a few vowels. We argued about what the words meant. I always chose the most unlikely meaning possible, just to see how riled up I could get him.

"There is absolutely no way it means that."

"You don't know. Do you speak Czech?"

"Maybe I'll learn, just to prove how ridiculous you are."

"Good luck with that, soldier."

It was entertaining enough that I didn't pay too much

attention to the slight ache in my feet or the hitch in my lungs or the pinch in my back from the pulling weight of my bag. Or not for a while anyway. After about an hour, my feet were bitching and my back ready to mutiny. I had to concentrate on breathing and talking so that I didn't start panting. Then I looked up at one of the buildings we were passing and stopped in my tracks.

"Jackson! Do you know where you're going?"

He held up the map and said, "Of course I do. We'll be there any minute now."

I let my backpack slip off my shoulders and plopped it on the sidewalk. I was not moving one more step.

I pointed and said, "Why is it, then, that we're passing the Vodka Jell-O Shot place again?"

"I told you, Kelsey. There is no way Minutková Jídla means vodka Jell-O shots. That's clearly a restaurant."

"Yeah, a restaurant that serves Jell-O shots."

"It has to be something to do with a minute or minutes."

"That's because it's instant Jell-O! But the point is . . . we've already been here."

He looked then at the restaurant, and I saw the confirmation on his face.

Fan-fucking-tastic.

"We're lost."

"We're not . . . well . . ." He consulted his map again, twisting it in few different directions and said, "We might be a *little* lost."

"This is your idea of adventure? I thought soldiers were supposed to be good at navigation."

"I have a solution," he said.

My backpack was starting to look like a very tempting chair, but I convinced myself to stay standing. I placed my hands on my hips and said, "Let's hear it."

He crossed to me with the map in his hand, and came close enough that he could probably smell the sweat trickling down my back. I should have been self-conscious, but when I craned my head back to meet his gaze, his smile tore through my thoughts like a tornado, and left them scattered and in pieces. He leaned in, and my heart jumped.

He reached out an arm, and dropped the map in a trash bin just behind me. He stayed there, our chests less than an inch away from touching and said in a low, deep voice, "Problem solved."

13

hat's your solution to getting us lost?"

He shrugged. "If we're not trying to get to any particular place, we can't ever really be lost. We're just exploring."

"But we need to find a place to stay and put our things and—"

"Later. It's still early, Kelsey. We've got all day."

He might be patient, but I wasn't. I was just about to demand that we find a place to stay or get a cab when his hand touched my elbow and skimmed down to my wrist.

"Trust me," he said.

I shivered.

I *did* trust him . . . which made abso-fucking-lutely zero

sense. My memory of the night before was a black hole. I should be wary of him. I sure as hell shouldn't be alone with him now, not without knowing what happened last night. But with his hand circled around my wrist, he could have led me anywhere.

And now I was supposed to go off with him, no plan, no map, no idea where we were heading? It was the opening plot of a horror movie. I might have been in *Hostel,* the reality TV version.

I made myself say, "Tell me what happened first."

His hand slid down from my wrist, and he caught my fingers between his.

"I wouldn't hurt you, Kelsey. And I wouldn't let anyone else either."

"So, someone drugged me. Then what?"

"I don't know that for sure. I just know you were fine. Feisty and ready to take my head off. Then we—"

"We what?"

His eyes dropped to my lips, and he shook his head.

"We were talking, and it was like you were drunk out of nowhere. You were babbling and slurring your words, and you couldn't stand up straight."

"So you took me to a hotel?"

"I didn't want to leave you in a hostel, not when you'd be passed out cold and sharing a room with a dozen people. I took you to my hotel room, then I got another one for me."

"That's it?"

"I suppose I could also talk about you calling me a pansy for not taking your clothes off."

"I did WHAT?"

He chuckled and bent, scooping up my backpack. He threw my bag over his shoulder along with his. Then he tugged on my hand, and started pulling me down the street.

I could have dug in my heels and refused. Or maybe I couldn't have. Not where he was concerned.

"HOLD ON. You can't say something like that and not elaborate."

He smiled. "You can when it's a bribe. I'll tell you later. After I've shown you my kind of adventure."

My mind steered straight into the gutter every time he mentioned an adventure. It was inevitable with a guy who looked like him.

He took a random turn, and pulled me along.

I said, "For the record, I think this no-map thing is a terrible idea."

"Noted."

"Things could go incredibly wrong."

"Or incredibly right."

I dragged my feet a little as we walked, but I was more intrigued than I let on. With him carrying my backpack and our fingers laced together, I was fine with wherever we went.

We walked a few blocks before happening upon a metro stop. He glanced at me over his shoulder, and then pulled me toward the stairs.

"Oh, so now we don't have to walk to have an adventure?"

He shot me a look, and I said, "Fine. I get it. *Trust you.*"

We descended the stairs, and I expected something dark, dank, with that lovely decay-meets-urine smell that seemed to hang around most subway stations. Shockingly, the station was shiny, clean, and modern. Hunt pulled me over to a large map of the metro stops. He dropped both our bags on the ground, stepped in front of me, and said, "Close your eyes."

I tried not to look skeptical.

One thing I'd learned in life: the phrase "Close your eyes" was usually either followed by something very good (i.e., kissing) or very bad (i.e., murder, pranks, or something gross placed in your hand).

I was really hoping this would fall more on the kissing side of the spectrum. His hands squeezed my shoulders in encouragement, and I let my eyelids fall. The anticipation coated my skin, a thin frost that had me shivering. One hand left my shoulder, and I felt him walk around to stand at my back. His breath touched my neck, and the heat melted the frost. I had to concentrate to keep from falling back into him.

"Don't open your eyes," he spoke into my ear.

I couldn't manage to piece together words myself, so I nodded, and his cheek grazed mine.

"Ready?"

That was all the warning I got before he took hold of my shoulders and began to spin me.

"Are you kidding me?"

"Keep your eyes closed!"

He spun me three times, then stilled my body with his hands.

"Point," he said.

"Where?"

"Anywhere."

I threw my hand up and he said, "Open your eyes."

He reached around me and placed his finger on the metro stop closest to where I'd pointed. Malostranská. "That's where we're going," he said.

"Really?"

He picked up our bags and said, "Really."

"What if it's a terrible neighborhood? It could be dangerous."

"I told you I would never let anything bad happen to you."

"Some things in the world are outside even your control."

His shoulders tensed, and his gaze darkened. "I know that. Believe me . . . I know."

A haunted expression stole over his face, filled with ghosts and shadows. It was the kind of look that told me more about him than any words he could ever say. He meant it when he said he would protect me. It was written as plainly across his face as whatever tragedy tore through his memories because of my words.

I couldn't look at that face and *not* trust him.

I laced my fingers with his and said, "I'm in."

When he smiled, it was almost like those ghosts had never been there.

We bought our metro passes, and together figured out which train to take. The metro platform looked like something out of a science fiction novel. Everything I'd seen of Prague before this looked like I'd stepped into the past, but this was the opposite. The walls and ceilings were composed of gold, silver, and green tiles with hundreds of small domes that formed one long tube. A thin, bright line ran the length of the curved ceiling, casting the whole tunnel in an eerie glow.

The train was quiet as it sped into the station, but my hair tossed in the wind it created. The train car we entered was already pretty full, and new riders streamed in front of and behind us. I was still searching for a place to sit or stand or even grab hold when the train started moving. I teetered sideways into my neighbor, then felt Hunt grip my arm and pull me back toward him.

"Grab on, princess."

I clutched at his waist, and used his body to steady myself.

He spoke into my ear. "I meant grab the overhead bar, but that works, too."

I said, "I don't think I can reach it."

In reality, I didn't even want to try. I much preferred holding on to him.

The train was so packed that at any given time I was touching at least three people. On the opposite side of Hunt, a tall guy in his midtwenties with shoulder-length hair smiled down at me every time I brushed against him. The train slowed as it came into the next station, and Hunt's hand gripped my hip to keep me steady. It stayed there even once we started moving, possessive and strong. I could feel the heat from his hand through my jeans like a brand.

As soon as a seat near us came open, he nudged me toward it. I collapsed back onto the bench. I gestured for him to hand me my backpack, but he shook his head.

"I'm fine."

He stood in front of me, directly between me and the long-haired guy, blocking me like a bodyguard. I'd be pissed if it weren't so hot. He lifted both hands above his head to hold on to the bar, and it revealed that same section of skin at his waist that had been driving me crazy for the better part of twelve hours.

My mouth went dry.

Would it be weird if I reached out and touched the toned muscle there? With my face?

If he weren't currently glaring at the long-haired guy, I'd think he was doing this on purpose.

We pulled into the station I'd chosen, and Hunt picked up my hand again as the train slowed to a stop. I followed him out of the station and up to the street, and even once we were out of the crowds of moving people, his hand stayed tight around mine.

Whatever had happened between us last night . . . it had changed him. He was touching me again now, but it was different than the way I could remember him touching me last night. Now he touched me like he knew me, not like some stranger in a bar. He looked at me when he thought I couldn't tell. And he wasn't asking questions, at least not any prying ones.

Something in my stomach began to cave in, and I could feel it falling away.

"Nothing else crazy happened last night, right?"

"You mean besides your pansy comment?"

That actually sounded exactly like something I would say.

"Yes, besides that."

"You might have declared your love for me once or twice. Asked to bear my children."

I rolled my eyes. "Be serious."

"You don't think a declaration of love is serious?"

"I don't think a declaration of love *happened*."

"Are you remembering more?"

"No, I just know myself. I might get touchy-feely when I'm drunk, but it's the other kind of touchy-feely."

He nodded, and no more jokes came, so I guessed that I had hit it on the head. He didn't know my secrets. I'd just hit on him. A lot if I could guess. That's why he was acting differently. And *that* I could deal with.

He tugged on my hand, and together we surfaced out of a stairwell into our spontaneous destination. The neighborhood was quaint and picturesque with narrow, winding, cobblestone streets. Those streets were dotted with trees under a blue, blue sky.

"You're right," Hunt said. "This neighborhood is incredibly dangerous. Downright terrifying. I'd understand if you wanted to go back."

I swatted at him, but he ducked my blow, laughing.

"Come on, princess. Let's see what kind of trouble we can get into."

I wanted to get into all of the trouble with him. Every kind. Multiple times preferably.

We wandered for a while, turning when something looked interesting, taking our time, just admiring the scenery.

(I was totally counting Hunt as part of the scenery.)

"So where to next?" he asked.

"Um, straight, I guess?"

"I meant after Prague. Where are you jetting off to next?"

I sighed, and wiped at a trickle of sweat on my forehead. "Nowhere."

"You're staying here?"

"No. I mean I'm going home. I think."

I pulled my hair over my shoulder, trying to keep it off my heated neck.

"You *think*? Are you homesick?"

If home was my past, sure. Otherwise, not a chance in hell.

"It's complicated," I said. "I don't know what home is anymore."

"I think home is wherever you are happiest."

I wanted the ease and joy of my college friends. At eighteen, they'd been my first real taste of family, and now that family was broken up into tiny pieces and scattered all over the U.S. It wasn't fair that I only got to keep them for four years before they went back to their real families or started new ones with stupid British boyfriends.

"What if home's not a place you can ever go back to?"

We turned from the road we'd been following onto a path that led into a park. The long line of trees and sweeping fields of green relaxed me.

He said, "Then you find a new home, a new place that makes you happy. It's not a once-in-a-lifetime deal, Kelsey. People find home in new places, new dreams, new people all the time. Home should feel effortless, like gravity."

I didn't trust gravity. It seemed to always be pulling me in the wrong direction.

"It's not that simple," I said, then I pulled away and walked a little faster, hoping he'd take that as a clue to change the subject.

"Of course it's not simple. The best things usually aren't."
He caught up beside me and said, "Why go home if it's not
where you want to be?"

"Because I don't know what else to do."

He took hold of my elbow and pulled me to a stop. "You
could keep traveling."

"I've done that. It's not working."

"What do you mean it's not *working*?"

I wasn't about to tell him that it wasn't working because
I was still depressed. This guy had seen more vulnerability
from me in a few days than anyone else had seen in years.

"I just mean . . . I'm not having as much fun as I thought."

"Maybe you've been doing it wrong."

"What's that supposed to mean?"

He let go of my elbow to rub his hand along his jaw.
When he spoke, he did it slowly as though he were choosing
his words carefully.

"You said you wanted an adventure. What's the most adventurous thing you've done?"

I'd done *plenty* of adventurous things. I'd lived completely
in the moment, exactly like I'd planned.

But when I thought back, trying to pick a moment for
him as proof, each day kind of bled into the next. I mean, I'd
met different people, and I'd gone different places, but the
end result had always been the same. We ended up at a bar or
a club. Drinking, dancing, and sex.

I opened my mouth, but I couldn't say any of those things
out loud.

He continued, "Tell me this. Ignoring the fact that you're

in a different place with different people, have you done anything drastically different from what you would do back home?"

I swallowed. And I had to tuck my pride away to admit, "Not really. Not unless you count today."

He smiled.

"The best parts of life are the things we can't plan. And it's a lot harder to find happiness if you're only searching in one place. Sometimes, you just have to throw away the map. Admit that you don't know where you're going and stop pressuring yourself to figure it out. Besides . . . a map is a life someone else already lived. It's more fun to make your own."

I knew, logically, that he was right. As long as I was trying to force myself to be happy, I never would be.

"Don't think too much," he said. "Just decide on something you want to do. The first thing that pops into your head, and do it."

I wanted to kiss him.

There was absolutely nothing I wanted more.

My eyes found his lips, and if ever gravity had been pulling me in one direction, that was it. I pulled up on my tiptoes, balancing a hand on his shoulder. Before I could even get close, he cleared his throat and took a step back.

Just do anything but *that*, apparently.

14

Damn it. Why did I keep doing this to myself? That made twice I'd been rejected by him. Maybe more, considering I couldn't remember half the time we'd spent together.

I could spend time with him without throwing myself at him. I *could* do that. Though, I didn't particularly want to.

I sighed and looked away. Maybe a hundred yards away was a playground. He'd asked me what I wanted. And other than kissing him, *that* was what I wanted.

I wanted a way back to swings and slides and simplicity. A way back to when a butterfly could cheer me up, and a series of puddles could make my day. A way back to a time when happiness wasn't something I had to search for . . . it just was.

So, I took off toward the playground, eyeing the swings and seesaw and merry-go-round. There were these bizarre ceramic creatures that were kind of like a cross between dinosaurs and Gumby. I made a beeline for the merry-go-round. I sprawled across the flat surface and waited for Hunt to arrive. He dropped both of our bags a few feet away and said, "This is what you want to do?"

I shrugged. It was option number two, but it worked.

"Well then, hold on."

I gripped the metal bar closest to me, and he set me spinning. He pulled harder, and I spun faster. It was stupid and childish, but it definitely required no thinking.

"Faster," I yelled.

Hunt gave one more big push, then jumped on the merry-go-round with me. It was moving so fast, he nearly missed, and he had to pull himself the rest of the way on. It was so strange to see him—masculine and reserved—struggling to stay on a merry-go-round. I burst out laughing. Once he managed to lie flat on his back, he laughed too. I lay back beside him, struggling to breathe through my hysterics. But every time I pictured him jumping onto that overgrown child's toy, I descended into giggles again.

This funny thing happens when you graduate college. You hear so much about being an adult that you start to feel like you have to become a different person overnight, that growing up means being not you. And you concentrate so much on living up to the term "adult" that you forget growing up happens by living, not by sheer force of will.

Looking up at the tree branches spinning and spinning

overhead accompanied by the pink and purple palette of the morning sky, I felt younger, or maybe just my age. We lay beside each other laughing at nothing and breathing in everything until the merry-go-round slowed to a stop.

His arm pressed again mine, and when I pulled myself up onto my side, I could feel in my gut that I knew what it was like to kiss this man. That I'd kissed him before. I couldn't remember it. Not in images. But I could feel it. My *body* remembered.

Maybe the spinning had cleared my head a little too much because I said straight out, "You kissed me."

"What?"

"Last night. You kissed me, didn't you?"

He pushed himself up into a sitting position, resting his elbows on his knees. He gripped the back of his neck with one hand and said, "It was before I realized you'd been drugged. After that I didn't . . . I wouldn't."

I knew it.

He grabbed one of the bars and slid off the merry-go-round. Without meeting my eyes, he looked around the playground and said, "What's next?"

I let him change the subject, even though I wanted to push it. Instead, I let him push me on the swings, each touch to my back like a pulse of electricity.

We played on the seesaw, a physical representation of our time together if ever there was one. I gave Hunt my camera, and he took pictures of me sitting atop one of the huge ceramic dinosaurs. Carefully, I held onto the dinosaur's head and stood up on its back.

For the first time, I looked out and saw the view on the non-Hunt side of the playground, and nearly toppled off dinosaur Gumby.

It was a panoramic vista of Prague, and it was *unbelievable.* The city was a sea of orange roofs outlined by a winding river and dotted with cathedral spires. Bridges stretched across the river, beautiful and strong. Here up on this random hill in a deserted playground, we had our own private view of the city. It was beautiful. And I had a feeling we never would have found it if we'd looked through guidebooks or searched on the Internet. We didn't have to share this with other tourists. It belonged to us.

I slid off my dinosaur and made my way closer. A railing lined the edge of the walkway. Plants with small yellow blossoms sprouted everywhere, and other white blossoms like snowflakes dotted the path.

I stared, mesmerized.

"I think you found it," Hunt said.

I spun, smiling, and leaned back against the railing. His steps stuttered, and he paused for a few moments. His eyes swept from me to the landscape at my back, then returned to me. His jaw went slack, and he blinked a few times. My smile widened.

"What did I find?"

It took him a few seconds to answer, but when he did a chill chased down my spine.

"A little piece of home."

He was right. I felt *lighter.* It wasn't quite the effortless happiness of college, but it was certainly the closest thing

I'd felt in a long time. There was just one thing I couldn't let go of.

"Why won't you kiss me? You did it last night. Why not now?"

"I wasn't thinking things through last night."

"And you are now?"

He nodded.

"And what are you thinking?"

"That I want to keep you."

"*Keep* me?"

"Keep seeing you, I mean. I like you. I think we could have fun together. Have *adventures* together."

"A kiss sounds like a pretty great adventure."

"I think it's smarter if we stay friends."

"You promised to fill in the blanks from last night. *This* is a blank."

"Kelsey—"

"It's not that big a deal. It's just a kiss."

He gave me a dark look that made it hard to breathe. My lungs seemed to deflate, swathing around my heart. It was a very good thing there was a railing behind me, or I might have gone toppling backward.

He stalked forward, and I gripped the cold metal of the bar behind me.

"A trade, then." He tipped his head down with a smile. "Give me a week. Travel with me for a week. If I can't find the adventure you were looking for, then we'll go our separate ways."

I'd thought before that gravity pulled me toward Hunt,

but it was more than that. He *was* the gravity. In that moment, he was the push and pull that held my universe together.

"One week for one kiss? That's kind of a steep price."

"That's the deal."

He was so close, my skin felt like it was humming. I could hear the beat of my heart in my ears like the flap of wings, speeding up, trying desperately to stay afloat.

"Okay. I'm in."

His smile wasn't just bright. It was *illuminating*. And for the way warmth spread through my skin, I would have believed that there were two suns in the sky.

Without even a peck, he turned and walked away. He picked up our bags from where we dropped them by the merry-go-round, and looked back at me.

"I said okay," I called, wondering if somehow he'd misunderstood me.

"I'm going to kiss you, princess. But not now, not when you're telling me to. Not when it's just something you want to check off a list. I'll kiss you when it counts."

Hunt took one look at the hostel name—the Madhouse—and raised an eyebrow at me. He may not have been convinced, but when we entered and I saw the Jack Kerouac quote across the wall, I knew it was perfect.

I read aloud. "The only people for me are the mad ones, the ones who are mad to live, mad to talk, mad to be saved, desirous of everything at the same time, the ones who never yawn or say a commonplace thing, but burn, burn, burn like fabulous yellow roman candles exploding like spiders across the stars."

I might have gotten a little caught up in my performance. I was an actor after all. But sometimes someone else just gets the words so right that you feel like they read them off your own heart.

Hunt's eyes stayed fixed on me, and he reached out, but didn't touch me. His hand hovered like I was an artifact, a work of art that would be compromised by the brush of his skin. Still looking at me, he dropped his hand and said, "Two beds, please."

We settled into a coed room with six other beds, and I tried not to think about the fact that his bed was right by mine. That if we both reached out in the middle of the night, our fingers would touch. We locked up our things, even though everyone else in the hostel was already out for the day, and he said, "What now?"

I could have asked to find Jenny. But seeing as we were alone, I saw a better opportunity. I moved to sit beside him on his bunk, close enough that my knee touched his when I turned to face him.

"That's your decision," I said. "You've got me for one week." I leaned back on my hands, and watched his eyes dip down to my body. "So, *Jackson,* what are you going to do with me?"

He touched his fingers to his chin, and his gaze swept over me.

"I've got a few ideas."

"Yeah?"

"I do."

He bent over me, and my elbows shook. Low on my spine, a tingling sensation spread. It reminded me of when you shake a can of soda. You know what will happen as soon as you open it. You can somehow sense all the built-up energy inside, but the idea of opening it is just too tempting.

"I've got a pretty good idea, too," I said.

He hummed, and the scruff on his chin just barely grazed my collarbone. My head fell back, and his breath roamed free across the skin of my neck. His lips brushed across my pulse point in an almost kiss, and all my muscles locked up tight. His mouth moved to hover above my ear, and my arms shook so badly I expected them to give out any second.

He hummed again, and I could feel the vibration against my skin even though we weren't touching.

His mouth brushed the shell of my ear in a second almost kiss, and he said, "Not yet, sweetheart."

My arms gave out, and I flopped back onto his bed with a groan.

His smile was maddening and mischievous.

He gripped the bed frame, and pulled himself up off the bunk, leaving me lying alone on his bed.

What a tease.

"How do you feel about heights?"

15

Y ou're *crazy*," I said.

"You wanted adventure, Kelsey."

"I thought you meant more spontaneous subway rides and playgrounds, not jumping off a bridge!" I heard the scream of the girl I'd just watched disappear over the edge, and I dug my fingers into Hunt's arm.

"I can't."

I'd been on bridges higher than the Zvikov Bridge before, but not ones I was supposed to leap off of. My heart was about to bust out of my chest, and Hunt was grinning like a madman.

I turned to flee, and Hunt pulled me back, his hand settling at the base of my spine. It was almost as if he knew that
that's where I felt him most intensely. When he was near, my
spine became a live wire, sending shockwaves down to every
last nerve ending.

His touch only amplified that.

"You're going to love it."

"Do you have a death wish?" I asked.

"I promise it's going to be fine. We're not going to die. We
can jump together if that will make you feel better."

"Oh, I didn't mean the jumping was going to kill you. I
meant *I* was."

"You can kill me after the jump."

"What if I'm too dead to kill you?" I was a little embarrassed at how hysterical I sounded.

He laced his fingers with mine, and squeezed my hand as
he pulled me forward.

"Trust me."

I did. But that only made me more scared. Trust was a
key that gave him access to places far more breakable than my
body.

It took all of my concentration to keep from crying or
throwing up or both as the instructor began hooking us up
to the same bungee cord. We were harnessed and strapped
and lectured, and the only thing that kept me from having a
complete mental breakdown was the fact that Hunt and I were
chest to chest as they hooked us together. His proximity and
his warm breath fanning across my forehead were enough to
distract me from my impending death.

They had us move closer to the ledge, and I let out an

involuntary squeak of fear when I saw the river winding away from us so far below.

Jackson slipped a hand around my neck and tilted my head up toward his. He placed a sweet kiss on my forehead that made my heart beat faster rather than calming me down. My heart scampered up and hid at the back of my neck, pulsing where Hunt's hand still rested.

All I could think was . . . *that better not count as my kiss.*

He said, "Just try it for me. I'll try something for you later. Whatever you want."

I took a slow, deep breath and nodded.

Once we were all attached, the instructor began adjusting our hands and our bodies to match the appropriate form. My head was tucked into the crook of his shoulder, and his into mine. His skin smelled like the forest around us, but sweeter. We both had one arm wrapped around each other. We laced our fingers and pointed our other hands out toward where we would jump.

"It's like we're dancing," Hunt said, his mumbled words drumming against the sensitive skin of my collarbone.

"Then why didn't you just take me dancing? At least the tango wouldn't kill me."

His chest bounced with laughter below my cheek, and then they were counting down.

"Jackson . . ." I couldn't get out anything but his name.

Then, like he could read my mind, Hunt quoted the Kerouac quote that had been at our hostel. "Mad to live, Kelsey. *This* is living."

He pressed another kiss to my shoulder, and his lips were still there burning against my skin when we went over.

The world paused for one brief second, and my eyes took in the architecture of the land below us. Hunt's arm squeezed around me, and then the peace ended. The wind slammed into me, the ground rushed forward, and my heart got left behind somewhere up above me.

Then I shrieked. A glass-breaking, eardrum-shattering kind of shriek that echoed off the canyon, reverberating back at me from all sides. The cord pulled tight, my insides seemed to resist and pull in the other direction. Despite the tug, we kept falling and falling, and the river rushed up at me, dark and unforgiving. I released Jackson's hand to wrap a second arm around his body. I squeezed as tightly as I could, but it was only half as tight as I wanted. I opened my mouth to cry out, and then suddenly we jerked to a halt and were moving back up again.

I thought maybe the ascension wouldn't be so bad, but then our bodies twisted and flipped, and I might have lost a few other vital organs to the same place my heart disappeared to.

We started dropping again, and Hunt shouted in excitement.

"Oh my God!" I screamed. I couldn't believe I was doing this.

This time I squeezed my arms around him not because I was scared, but because a feeling bubbled up inside me, potent and wild, and I just wanted to hold it all inside.

When we started up again my scream turned into a laughing cackle that would have made Ursula or Maleficent proud.

Hunt was right. It *was* fun.

I screamed some more just because I could, and because

hearing the sound ricochet around the canyon felt like Hunt and I were the only two people in the world. It felt unreal—like I was two parts soul, one part body.

We bounced around a few more times, and I got the courage to let go of Hunt, to stretch my arms down toward the earth below us. I twisted away from him and looked around us and back up to where we'd jumped from.

"You dead?" Hunt asked.

"No." Not by a long shot. In fact, I'd never felt so alive.

I smiled widely, and Hunt smiled back, and I knew my heart was back in place because it thumped so hard it was almost painful.

And then I didn't have to ask if the time was right, and he didn't have to tell me. Our lips pulled together like they'd been replaced by magnets. And all that energy that had sparked inside me began to unspool. I could feel it unwinding around my ribs, pulling from my fingertips, pushing into him.

His hands dove into my hair, and he kissed me like we were still falling, like this is how we were meant to spend our very last moments. His lips pressed hard against mine, and blood pounded in my ears in time with the thrust of his tongue.

I wrapped my arms around his neck, pulling myself as close as possible. But still I wanted closer. I wanted to hook my legs around his waist and feel the skin beneath his clothes. The air pushed against us, soft and sweet, and completely at odds with the frenzy occurring underneath my skin.

Something tugged at our ankles, and we started to rise. I whimpered into his mouth, not ready for the moment to end.

His mouth answered with a faster pace, breath escaping as we shifted and tasted and savored every last second. We didn't pull apart until we had to, until it was time to set foot in the real world again.

Maybe it was the fall or the blood rushing to my head or the reverberations of my universe finally snapping into place, but I had to grip the instructor's arm to keep from falling as he unhooked me.

We didn't talk as we were set free from harnesses and cords. But his gaze was like a touch—tender and aching and possessive.

We walked away that day. We took a bus back to the city. My feet hit the hard cobblestones step after step, but when I climbed into the bed opposite Hunt's that night, I was still falling. My head hit the pillow, but I swore I could feel the rush of wind past my body, could hear it in my ears.

Hunt said something about my inner ear, said it would go away in a day or two, but I wasn't so sure. In the quiet night, I wondered if it was only the beginning of something bigger. One long, exhilarating, terrifying fall. One without the safety of harnesses and cords and a plan. One with no guarantee that I wouldn't hit rock bottom.

I woke up angry the next day.

I wasn't PMSing, and no one had done anything to piss me off (yet). I was just *sour*. And it was only made worse when I hopped on one of the hostel's complimentary computers to check my e-mail.

Bliss had arrived in Philadelphia, and there was a full

novel in my in-box gushing about her apartment and the neighborhood and her *perfect* boyfriend.

I felt like a complete bitch when I closed the message without replying, but anything I would have written then would have caused problems anyway.

And then because I was a masochist, I decided to read the e-mails from Dad. Or his secretary anyway. I skimmed through the dozen or so messages in my in-box, most of which were an account of my whereabouts and my spending habits.

There was no need to worry about Big Brother with a father like mine. I imagined he had assigned his secretary to monitor all of my actions through my bank account.

It was so fucked up.

Not the money part. I was used to that. My only brothers and sisters were bank accounts, and I always came in last.

It was fucked up that he thought he could control everything. He thought himself the great puppeteer, managing and enacting it all.

It was fucked up because I was all too familiar with the fact that he *couldn't* control everything, but he was still pretending like he could.

I wondered what he would do if I told him I'd been drugged. He'd blame me, say it was my fault for being a moral degenerate and spending all my time in places where people got drugged. That much, I knew. But I wondered what he would do after that. Would he care? Would he want me to come home? Or would he sweep it under the rug, smudge it with an eraser, tell me I was being overdramatic again?

While I was sitting at the computer another e-mail came in.

Secretary Cindy, who I had never met and was probably the same age as me, wrote:

> Your father thinks it's time you start making arrangements to come home. Your mother has a charity party coming up the week after next, and he's trying to land a new account with a very family-focused company. He'd like you to be there to make a good impression. Follow the usual dress code, he said. I've attached a document with a couple of options for flights home. Please look it over and let me know which works best for you.

Unbelievable.

That answered my question about him caring. I knew Mom was just a prop to him. That was why he let her drink herself stupid every day. He let her buy whatever she wanted. They ignored it when one or both of them cheated.

Because in my family all that matters is what people see.

They didn't *see* Dad's business partner touch me when I was twelve. There was no mark on my hand from when he made me touch him. The only mark from something like that rests under the skin.

So, of course, *it didn't count.*

When Jackson called my name and stepped into the computer room, I closed the window without replying. Not that the "Fuck off" I'd been planning was much of a reply anyway.

"What's up?" I asked.

"Grab your things. We're heading out."

"Heading out where?"

"Out of the country."

I slid off my stool, but when I tried to move closer, he kept a careful distance between us. Frustration fizzled on my tongue.

"We just got to Prague yesterday."

"And now we're leaving Prague today. You only gave me a week, and there's a lot I want to do."

There was a lot I wanted to do too, but he'd barely looked in my direction for more than two seconds since our kiss.

Not even bothering to muffle my grumbling, I shoved my things into my backpack and left behind the Madhouse hostel. If only I could have left behind my shitty mood, too.

At the train station, I asked, "Will you tell me where we're going now?"

Hunt just smiled. I loved and hated that smile.

"Why are you doing this?"

He said, "Wow, you really don't do well with surprises, do you?"

I rolled my eyes, and crossed my arms over my chest.

"I mean all of this. Why do you care?"

Normally, I never would have asked a question like that, not from guy that I was trying to hook up with. Especially not when the answer could be that he didn't care, not really. He certainly didn't have any qualms about rejecting me.

But I'd spent days with him, and almost everything I knew about him was from observation alone. I mean, it was like pulling teeth just to get him to tell me his first name.

"Because I wanted you to come with me. Do I need another reason?"

"Do you have one?"

He shrugged. "No one likes traveling alone."

And that was the Hunt one-two punch. Pull you in and then plow right over you. Give you the most intense kiss of your life, and then pretend like it never happened and let you fester in your sexual frustration.

I stayed quiet on our way to the station and as we boarded a train to somewhere in Germany. As soon as we were moving, I folded my arms over the top of my backpack, and used them as a pillow.

Just for once, I wanted to know where I stood with him. I wanted to shake him until some actual answers popped out, rather than his charming, sweet noncommittal words.

We changed trains that afternoon in Munich, and even though the train was fairly empty, Hunt sat beside me.

I tried not to react, because any reaction I had was going to be bitchy. Instead, I fished my phone out of my bag and stood to place my backpack in the luggage rack above our heads. I sat back down beside him and slipped one earbud in. I was searching for a song when he said, "You're mad at me."

I glanced at him briefly, then pressed play.

"No, I'm not."

I'd just put in my second earbud when he tugged them both out.

"Yes, you are. I might have spent the last few years in various deserts with mostly men, but I'm not so far removed that I don't know that 'No, I'm not,' means 'I most definitely am.'"

I sighed. "Jackson, I'm not mad. I promise. I'm just tired."

"But you slept on the last train."

"I didn't mean that kind of tired."

"You're tired of me?"

I groaned and ran my hands across my face.

"I'm *frustrated*. I don't know what you want from me."

The look in his eyes reminded me of an ache, the kind you ignore for as long as you can, until you wake up in the middle of the night, short of breath, sweating, and unable to deny it any longer.

He didn't know what he wanted from me either.

"I want several things from you, Kelsey. But at the moment, I just want a friend and to travel."

I didn't even hear the second part of his sentence. I was still hung up on the "several things" he wanted from me, and imagining what they all might be. Maybe I wasn't sure exactly what I wanted from him either.

He wasn't a hookup. He wasn't the kind of guy I could walk away from the morning after. But I also wasn't sure I wanted the kind of thing I couldn't walk away from. Because I was *good* at walking away.

I nodded. "Friends. Got it."

A few hours later, he tugged out my earbuds once more and said, "We're here."

"And where is here?"

"Heidelberg."

I looked at him. "Again, I say, where is here?"

"Still in Germany."

"Okay, then. And what are we doing here?"

He pulled my pack down from the luggage rack for me and said, "There's something I want to show you. Now, enough questions."

I followed him off the train. I waited while he asked someone for directions, and then left the train station with him.

Heidelberg was small and quaint, though not that different from several other cities I'd already seen in Europe. There were cathedrals and narrow roads and a river. It was almost sundown, and the city was quiet and almost deserted. Hunt paused and turned in a circle, searching for something. When he found it, he smiled. I followed his gaze to a castle that sat perched on a hill overlooking the city.

It was both decadent and decaying, emerging out of the dense forest, seemingly untouched by modern society.

"You're taking me to a castle?" I asked.

He smiled. "Come on, princess."

I stared at him, unsure whether I should be frustrated by even more mixed messages or whether I should just be glad to have someone like him trying to make me happy. I could do worse than a friend like Jackson Hunt.

But he could be even better as something more than friends.

I knew how badly things could turn out when one friend was attracted to another. I'd had a front-row seat for the epic disaster that was my friends Bliss and Cade.

But there was a difference with Hunt. I knew he was attracted to me. I might have been drunk that first night, and I might have forgotten most of the evening at the baths, but I could never forget that. And that kiss . . . damn.

He wanted me. But there was something holding him back.

And not knowing pissed me off to no end.

We were on day two of our weeklong trip, which left me five and a half days to figure out what was holding him back and get rid of it.

Sure, it could backfire in any number of ways, most likely

to my detriment. But if I had to get my heart shredded into confetti, he certainly wouldn't be a bad way to go.

I looked back at the castle, and then at Hunt. I placed a hand on his shoulder and raised up on my tiptoes to place a quick kiss on his cheek.

"Thank you, Jackson."

I let my hand coast down his chest as I turned away and began walking toward the castle. I heard his slow exhale behind me, and knew my plan was officially in motion.

We made our way through the city, and arrived at the edge of the town just as the sun started sinking below the horizon. A stairway led up toward the castle, and my feet hurt just looking at it.

"You're kidding, right?"

"Come on," he said. "It won't be that bad."

"Um, you don't get to assume things like that. People *assumed* the *Titanic* was unsinkable, and look how that turned out for them."

"All I'm hearing are excuses, which doesn't sound like someone interested in an adventure to me. In fact, I dare you to race me to the top."

"You *dare* me? Is that supposed to make me suddenly eager to participate?"

"I'm daring you to have an adventure."

"Well, do I get to dare you to do something later?"

He gave me a knowing look, and I was pretty sure he knew exactly what kind of dare I wanted to give him.

"Within reason, yes. And if you win the race, I'll even make it two dares."

I had a feeling that "within reason" was going to bar most

of the dares I would think of. I said, "So, this is how this adventure is going to work? You force me to do something I don't want to do, then I return the favor, and somewhere along the way we both miraculously start to have fun?"

"Sounds about right. It will be an epic montage when they make the movie about our lives."

"My life, you mean. I'm the princess here. You're just my guide."

He rolled his eyes. "Then let me get your bag, your highness."

He took my pack and his and hid them both beneath the leafy branches of a nearby bush. He said, "Wouldn't want anything to weigh us down during our race."

I shook my head and moved toward the stairs. Each individual step had a white painted number on it, starting with a number one on the first step. "How many steps do you think there are?" I asked.

"I guess we'll find out when we get to the top. You ready?"

I nodded.

"On your mark," he said. "Get set. Go!"

We took off running, and the little white numbers blurred into unreadable splotches as I took the steps as quickly as I could. I managed to stay with him through the first twenty steps or so, but then he started pulling away.

My killer stilettos kept my legs in decent shape, but not as good as something like, I don't know, *being in the army.*

By the time I got to step number seventy-five, my calves were burning. By one hundred and two, my lungs had joined the party. By one hundred and thirty, I was ready to cut off my own legs just so I had an excuse to never take stairs again. I paused for a few seconds, panting, and looked up.

Hunt was God knows how many steps ahead of me. Fifty maybe. And he was just over halfway up the stairs.

"Screw this," I whispered. I sat down on one of the steps, wiped a little dirt and grime on my hands and my shins, and then gave an elaborate (and maybe slightly overplayed) cry, followed by a low, painful whine. I clutched at my ankle, and bit my lip, and waited for—

"Kelsey? Are you okay?"

Bingo!

I didn't look up at him, but stayed focused on my ankle. I said "Jackson" just loud enough so that he could hear me, then I sucked in a loud breath.

Thirty seconds later, he slowed to a stop beside me. He knelt on the stair below with hands outstretched and said, "What happened?"

I'd not blinked since I first decided to fake the injury, but I did then and the water that had been building in my eyes ran down my cheek, and I met his gaze.

"I fell," I panted. "My ankle."

He touched my leg, just above where I was gripping my ankle with both hands, and I hissed.

He jolted backward, apologizing.

"It's okay," I said. "It's just tender. God, it hurts so bad."

I wrung out a few more tears for effect.

"Do you want to go back down?" he asked. "I could carry you."

"No, I . . ." I paused for effect. "I'd like to see it. I know

I acted like a bitch at the bottom, but this was really sweet, and . . . never mind."

"No," He said. "I'll carry you up instead."

"I couldn't ask you to do that. It's a long way. I can try to walk."

I was going to try to stand, fake another cry and collapse back down, but I didn't even have to work that hard. Before I could try, he stood and scooped me into his arms. I gave a cry of delight that I quickly masked as pain, and buried my face into his neck so he wouldn't see me smile.

16

The ascent to the castle was slow with Hunt carrying me, but I didn't mind the extra time snuggled up against him. His arms were like bands of steel around me, but his breath against my forehead was warm and soft.

"You still okay?" he asked, and I nodded.

I gave a small whimper just to enjoy the way he pulled me even closer in response. I had both arms wrapped around his neck, and ever so slowly I let one of my hands begin to wander. I used my fingernails to lightly scratch down the column of his neck, and had to hold in a laugh when his step faltered.

He cleared his throat and kept walking.

He walked, and I documented his reactions, like the way

his eyes closed for just a second when my fingertips brushed the hinge of his jaw below his ear, and the hitch of his breath when I dug my fingernails into his shoulder after a particularly "painful" jostle of my ankle.

I could feel his fatigue by the time we hit step 250, and decided to take pity on him. I lifted my head and said, "Jackson."

I wasn't prepared for how close our lips would come when his head turned toward mine. A knot of desire tightened low in my belly, and my thoughts fled.

"Um . . . I . . ."

The word *want* didn't do justice to how badly I hoped he would kiss me again.

His steps slowed to a stop, and my heart went epileptic.

I could have kissed him myself, latched my mouth to his and held him tight. But I wanted him to come to me. I was tired of feeling him pull away. And if I had my way, within five and a half days, I'd have him completely. So I flicked my eyes to his, enjoying the strain I saw in his gaze, and practiced patience. My plan would fall apart faster than Lindsay Lohan post-rehab if I gave in now.

I said, "I can walk now." Then added, "If you'll help me."

He didn't argue, probably because he was glad for the distance. He set me down gingerly, and then wrapped an arm around my waist. I threw my arm over his shoulder, and then slowly we tackled the stairs again. I had to keep reminding myself not to forget that I was supposed to be injured.

When we hit stair number three hundred, we were only about ten to fifteen steps from the top. I sucked in a breath and winced. Hunt stopped and faced me. "What's the matter? Did you twist it again?"

"I don't know. I . . ." He knelt beside me to take a look, and soon as he was down, I took off running up the last of the stairs.

I heard him laugh when I hit step number 310, and I screamed in victory when I hit the last step, number 315.

I turned to find him slowly walking up the steps, shaking his head. His lips were pressed into a thin line, but I could tell he was holding back a smile.

"I won," I sang tauntingly. "I wonder what I should dare you to do."

Hunt approached me slowly, like a predator stalking his prey and my stomach fluttered in response.

I paused to pretend to think about possible dares, and I was too busy gloating to notice him run up the last few steps. I shrieked when he lifted me up and threw me over his shoulder.

"Hunt!" I yelled.

"You're unbelievable," he said.

I laughed. "I'm going to pretend that was a compliment."

"Oh, it was, princess."

"Then, put me down."

"No can do."

I struggled a bit, pretending to be unhappy, but the truth was . . . Hunt had a fabulous ass. And I had a fabulous view.

"What are you going to do to me?" I asked.

"I haven't decided yet. Maybe this place has a dungeon."

I whistled. "Kinky."

He pinched the back of my thigh, and I yelped.

I couldn't see much (other than the aforementioned glorious backside), but the sun must have fully set because the sky in the distance was a vivid purple. I glimpsed a few other tourists wandering the castle grounds out of the corner of my eye. I took a wild guess and said, "Put me down, Jackson. People are starting to stare."

"Let them," he said. "It's a nice view."

Well, at least we were on the same page.

I swatted his back and said, "You're just a sore loser."

"No, I'm just a guy, probably not the first, to fall for one of your schemes."

And now I had five and a half days to get him to fall for another.

I said, "I'll be good. I promise. Unless you want me to be bad, of course."

He laughed, but the sound was strained. Then without warning he flipped me back over and deposited me on my feet. I gave him a sly smile and he said, "You're trouble."

"Me?" I faked innocence.

He shook his head. "Come on, princess. Let's see the castle before I decide to toss you in a fountain."

"Wet T-shirt contest? Only if you jump in the fountain with me."

I'd been mostly joking, but he actually looked tempted. Typical.

He said, "I might have to find you a new nickname. I don't think you're proper enough to be a princess."

"You know the nice ones always have a naughty side. Mine just happens to outweigh the nice by a lot."

He looked at me, and I was beginning to think I wouldn't need those five and a half days to break him down.

"Let's go explore before I . . ." he trailed off and shook his head. "Let's just go."

I resisted the urge to do a celebratory dance for his crumbling resolve, and focused on sightseeing. The castle was gorgeous with grand architecture and even grander ruins. Vines and moss grew over steps and up the stone walls, and it *was* like a fairy tale.

It was now almost completely dark, but the castle was lit up beautifully. Between that and the view of the city down below, there was something stunning everywhere I looked.

But it was Hunt my eyes kept going back to.

We arrived too late to tour the inside of the castle, which apparently housed a gigantic wine barrel that held over fifty thousand gallons of wine.

"We might have to come back to see that," I joked.

"No time. We're on a strict schedule."

And yet we were currently leaning against a wall, quietly surveying the moonlit city down below us.

"So, we can't have maps, but we have a schedule?"

"You only gave me a week. So, yes. We're on a schedule."

"So what if I decide to stay longer than a week?"

"I'd like that."

He didn't look at me as he said it, but stayed focused on the city below us. I tried to read his expression based on his profile, but it wasn't happening.

"And you don't have anywhere to be? No one you have to go home to?"

"I'm yours for the foreseeable future."

As a friend. Greeeaat.

Should I be reading something into this? Did he have a girlfriend back home? Is that why he pushed me away? But then what the hell was he doing here in the first place?

I didn't get any answers before he started pulling me toward the stairs. We didn't race this time. The view was too good to speed up. Black bleeding into purple bleeding into a village that looked plucked from another century. Halfway down my stomach growled loudly. Hunt smiled and draped an arm over my shoulder, like it was the most natural thing in the world. He said, "Let's go get you some food."

This was what friends did apparently.

His arm stayed around me as we arrived back at the base of the hill and wandered back into the city. We found a small café that was empty except for us and one other couple. The owner was also our waiter, and spoke broken English.

"Welcome." He gestured between Hunt and me and said, "Beautiful couple. Have seated."

He put us at a small table in a corner surrounded by artwork and candles. Hunt dropped his arm from around my shoulder and pulled out my chair for me. I smiled in thanks. His hand brushed through my hair and across my shoulder when he walked around to take his seat. I shivered in response.

He said, "Cold?" and I shook my head.

Seriously. This guy fucked with my head like nothing else.

"So what's next on our schedule, soldier?"

"More trains."

Blech.

He laughed at my expression and added, "It will be worth it when we get there."

"There?"

"Italy."

I resisted the urge to squeal. ITALY. Who doesn't dream of going to Italy? And talk about making it easy to seduce Hunt. If I couldn't do it in Italy, someone should take away my vagina because I didn't deserve it.

"I'm guessing by your smile that you approve of the next leg of our trip?"

"I do."

"Good, because we've got fifteen hours of traveling in front of us."

I blinked. "Are you trying to kill me?"

"Of course not, princess. We could fly if you'd rather, but I thought since you already had a Eurail pass, you'd prefer to go by train."

My whiny rant was cut off by the arrival of the owner with our menus, which were in German.

Awesome.

The owner gestured between Hunt and me and said, "Together? New married?"

I started to shake my head, and Hunt said, "Yes. We're on our honeymoon."

I raised my eyebrow at Hunt, and he shrugged.

Mind. Fuck.

The owner clapped his hands, smiling and nodding, and held up a hand. "Wait."

He scurried off, and I faced Jackson. "So . . . husband, huh?"

"Maybe it will get us a free dessert."

I narrowed my eyes. "Are there any other perks that come with being your fake wife?" Because I could totally get on board for some wifely duties.

"My company isn't enough?" he asked. He shot me a charming smile that could have knocked down a row of girls like dominoes.

"I'm not going to feed your ego."

I picked up my menu and started browsing through it for anything that looked familiar. But it had been a long day of traveling and trickery, and all the strange words and letters were just jumbled on the page.

"Speaking of feeding," Hunt said. "Ordering should be an interesting experience."

"What? You mean you don't speak German, just like you don't speak Czech?"

"Well, I'm definitely not trusting your translations. That's for sure."

The owner came back with two glasses of red wine, which he placed on the table between us.

"For you. For marriage."

I smiled. This fake marriage had perks after all.

"*Danke,*" I said to the owner.

He placed his hands over his heart and nodded. I took a quick sip from my glass and smiled my approval. He pointed to my menu, and I panicked.

I pointed at the first thing I saw.

Schwarzsauer, which sounded suspiciously like Schwarzenegger when I said it, but the owner nodded all the same.

"Yes. Yes. Gut."

Then he turned to Hunt, who looked just as lost as I did. He pointed at something and the owner said, "Yes. *Himmel und Erde.* Is you say, 'Heaven and Earth.'"

Great. I got the terminator, and he got heaven and earth.

The owner took our menus and left. I picked up my glass, smelling the dark, fruity scent.

"Are you not going to try it?" I asked.

Hunt eyed the glass for a moment, and then shook his head. "No."

"Do you want a beer? We are in Germany, after all."

"Thanks, but I'm okay."

"All right, spill. You're what twenty-five—"

"Twenty-seven."

That made him five years older than me.

"Okay, so you're twenty-seven, which is—*newsflash*—old enough to drink."

"I've done plenty of drinking before, Kelsey. I just don't do it anymore."

"Bad experience?"

"Bad life."

His hands were stiff and jerky as he unfolded his cloth napkin.

"What happened?" I asked, then regretted it a few seconds later. He'd been charming and funny for most of the day, and a dark cloud rolled over him. He had the same tension in his shoulders as the first few times I saw him. "That was stupid. You don't have to tell me anything."

"No, it's fine. It was what always happens with alcohol. A little became a lot, and my life unraveled around a bottle."

"So you're . . ."

"An alcoholic, yes. I was up to one-year sober this time. Or I was until the other night."

"Was?" I asked. I wracked my brain to try and remember if I'd seen him drink anything. Maybe he'd fallen off the wagon right before I met him.

"I took a drink that night at the baths."

"When?" I searched through fuzzy memories.

He shrugged. "It doesn't matter."

"What do you *mean* it doesn't matter?"

"It just doesn't. It happened. It's over."

A thought stuck in my mind like a thorn. And maybe it was part memory or just because I knew myself, but I said, "It was my fault, wasn't it? Whatever happened . . . you broke your sobriety because of me."

My stomach clenched, and I felt sick. Maybe I drove everyone to drinking. Not just my mother.

"No, princess. It was my choice. Don't take that on you."

He didn't deny it though. He didn't deny it, and my head was spinning. He continued, "It's not my first time off the wagon, and it probably won't be my last" His eyes shot to the wineglass, and he added, "But I'm good for now."

I cleared my throat and pushed my chair back.

"I'll be right back. I'm just going to go to the bathroom."

I tried to make a graceful exit, but the owner ran over as soon as I stood up. He asked me something in German that I didn't understand. I just smiled and said, "Bathroom? Um, toilet?"

Nodding, he pointed me toward a dark hallway in the other corner of the restaurant. I ducked my head and practically ran away.

17

opened two storage closets before I found the unmarked
bathroom, and stole my way inside. I braced my hands on the
porcelain sink and leaned my head against the cool glass of
the mirror. I don't know why it was affecting me so strongly,
but I felt like I'd been punched in the gut.

Jackson was a good guy. A *great* guy. I'd gotten myself
drugged, and he took care of me. I'd oscillated between epic
screw-up and bitch at light speed, and he was *still* here. And
somewhere in between all that, I'd ruined a one-year accom-
plishment.

Now wonder he kept rejecting me.

Not for the first time, I had to wonder *why*. Why did this

great guy give two flying fucks about me? I think he cared more about what happened to me than *I* did.

It didn't matter where I was or how many planes or trains I'd taken to get there, the darkness always caught up to me. Not because of bad luck or karma or anything like that. Disaster followed me because *I* was the disaster. I was a walking, talking hurricane, and my idea of living was taking everyone down with me.

I looked up into the mirror. It was circled by rusting metal, and the low yellow light overhead glowed in the reflection. And there in the center was a girl with pale hair and pink lips. Beauty Queen material. That was what my mother had always said growing up. She wanted me to be the next Marilyn Monroe. She'd tell me that on mornings when she was drunk and retired to bed because of a "headache." But beauty was a poison. A lie. It was a facade, and nothing more.

When I looked in the mirror, all I could see were the things they tried not to see. The bags under my eyes. The smudged mascara and sunken cheeks. The too-thin arms and the lines around my mouth from frowning. But those imperfections had nothing on the ragged soul that resided underneath.

That was the thing I couldn't change. I could paint over it with makeup. Distract myself with parties and guys and traveling. But you can't run from who you are . . . not forever.

And here in this small café in this small German town with possibly the most perfect guy in the world . . . it had finally caught up to me.

A knock sounded on the door.

"Kelsey?"

Jesus. How was I supposed to face him when we both knew he was better off without me? We should just scrap this whole weeklong trip, and go our separate ways. He could continue going wherever he was going. I could go back to Texas and find out if they had rehabs for self-destructive bitches.

"Just a minute."

He didn't listen, because a few seconds later the knob was turning, and the door that I hadn't locked was swinging open.

I rushed to wipe at the mascara under my eyes, and grabbed a paper towel to pretend like I'd been washing my hands.

"Hey," Hunt said.

"Jesus. Impatient much? If you have to go that bad, I'll get out of your way."

I was almost past him when he caught my elbow and turned me toward him.

"Don't," he said. "Don't do that."

"Do what?"

"Pretend that you're okay when you're not."

Funny thing, that. You have to know what's real to stop pretending, and I lost sight of that a long time ago.

"I'm not pre—"

"Kelsey."

Fuck.

His eyes. His goddamn eyes drilled into the very core of me.

"Why do you care?" I was horrified to hear the hitch in my breath.

"Why wouldn't I care, princess?"

"Because I'm horrible. All I do is screw things up. Including you. You should be running as fast as you can in the other direction."

"But then who would carry you when you fake-twist your ankle?"

I choked on a laugh, which turned into a sob, and I covered my face with my hands before he could see me fall apart. "See? Horrible."

He pried my hands away, so I just turned my face down.

"You're not horrible, Kelsey. You are vibrant and beautiful, and you burn. Burn so vividly. Fires can damage, but they're also beautiful and vital and they can purify and give the chance to start fresh. You're not horrible. Not at all."

I wanted to listen to him, wanted to believe the things that he was saying, but my brain could only seem to zero in on the fact that he knew I was destructive, too. I'd spent my whole life wanting to be something more, to be noticed, to burn like Kerouac's roman candles, but I'd never stopped to think about the harm I could do.

"I think I should go home," I said.

His hands on my elbows pulled me in closer, and he said, "I don't know what to do to convince you."

"There's nothing," I said. "There's nothing you can do."

I gave him a sad smile, and the hands on my elbows slipped around to the small of my back, and his lips claimed mine in a scorching kiss.

Except that. You can do that.

I resisted for a second, trying to pull back, but his arms wrapped all the way around my waist, crushing me to his chest, and a few seconds of resistance was all I had in me. I clutched at his back, my fingers scrabbling to hold on to him. His tongue slid between my lips, gliding alongside my own.

This was burning. The heat, the fire between us blazed, and I couldn't be close enough to him. I let one hand trail down to his lower back, and slipped it beneath his shirt to press into his heated skin. At the contact, his kiss turned frenzied, and I felt the cool porcelain of the sink bump against my lower back. I dug my fingernails into his skin, and a rumbling groan poured from his mouth. The arms around my waist slid to my hips, and he lifted me up and onto the sink.

"I should stop," he whispered against my mouth.

I hooked my legs around his waist and pulled him into me. I found that spot at the corner of his jaw just below his ear that I knew affected him and pressed a light kiss there. Then I grazed the sensitive skin with my teeth, and heard his hissing breath above me.

I said, "Don't you dare."

I returned to his lips and used the hand not under his shirt to pull his face closer to mine. My back pressed against the mirror, and the cool contact sent shivers across my warm skin. His hands slid from my bare knees up my thighs to the edge of my shorts. His fingertips dipped beneath the hem, ticking the skin of my inner thighs, and drawing a low moan from my mouth.

I tipped my head back against the mirror, and his lips trailed down my neck. I was so undone by him that my hands and legs were shaking, but that didn't stop me from desperately pulling him closer. I traced the firm muscles of his back with one hand, and his hips pressed harder into mine in response.

I could feel the length of him pressed against the zipper of my shorts, and his mouth was working complete and utter magic on my neck, and I was certain that at any moment I was going to fall apart. I was going to burn so hot and so fast that I would just disintegrate in his arms.

His hips rocked into mine, his arousal pushing right at my core, and I arched into him moaning. He kissed from my neck down to my collarbone, and then nudged my shirt aside to place a hot kiss just above the line of my cleavage.

I reached my other hand down, intending to pull his shirt up and off, when a knock sounded on the door.

It was hesitant, and the voice that followed was the sweet café owner.

He said, "Food, sir. Madam."

Hunt's head dropped into the cradle of space between my neck and shoulder, and he groaned. "Damn it."

Was it terrible that I didn't care about going back out there? Sure, it would look bad, but we were newlyweds. Or they thought we were. I was all for staying in here and finishing what we'd started.

But before I could piece together the right words for this proposal, Hunt had stepped back and turned to face the wall.

I thought of staying there. Maybe I could tempt him back into another kiss. But then he groaned and cursed again, running his hands over his eyes and up to his shorn hair.

He wasn't embarrassed. I was fairly confident he could have shaken something like that off with a smirk or a shrug.

This was different. He was angry at himself. And the sweet glow of desire that had blocked out my earlier insecurities and fears faded, and I felt more ragged, more destroyed than ever.

It was fitting that Hunt had brought me to this particular town with this specific castle when there were so many other castles to choose from. Because this one, though beautiful, had been ravaged by time and left behind, broken and ruined.

I slid down off the sink, my legs still shaky from our kiss, and Hunt turned.

He said, "I'm sorry, Kelsey. I—"

"Don't, Jackson. Just don't." Whatever it was, I didn't want to hear it.

I reached for the door, and he pulled me back to him once more.

He pressed a hard kiss against my temple, sweet, but still tinged with anger. He said once more, "I'm so sorry."

Then led me out of the bathroom.

The owner had fled after his little declaration, thank God. Hunt pulled my seat out for me once more, but there was an intensity between us now that hadn't been there before.

Before there had been attraction and maybe friendship. And those things were there still, but had morphed into something more. The attraction was stronger and tinged with the darkness that only comes when you can't have what you want.

Each step, each breath took on a voice, and I could hear it whisper *why*. It wasn't enough to think of this gap between us as a line or a wall. I needed more than a metaphor. I needed to know what exactly stood between us.

We spent the rest of the evening pretending that the darkness wasn't there, pretending we hadn't just shared the most intense kiss of my life. We forced ourselves to talk and laugh over anything that could be even remotely deemed funny, like the fact that the food I'd ordered was some strange soup that looked like a mixture of oil and blood and smelled like whatever dead thing the blood had come from. I used one of my dares to make him switch food with me because if I had to touch that stuff, I was going to be sick all over the table.

By comparison, his meal was mashed potatoes with onions and some kind of blackened, oozing sausage. I would definitely be avoiding the sausage, but the mashed potatoes looked promising. That is until I took a bite and found lumps of something sweet that might have been apples mixed into the potatoes.

Heaven and Earth, my ass.

We kept up our facade through the entire meal. Hunt took my hand as we stood to leave, and we both thanked the owner, who had been smiling like a maniac since Hunt and I stepped out of the bathroom together.

He came forward and grasped our linked hands in his.

He said something in German that I didn't understand, but I got the feeling it was a blessing, not that we deserved it.

Our hands stayed linked as we made our way through the darkened city to the train station where we'd first arrived.

"We're leaving now?" I asked.

Hunt nodded. "I thought you'd rather travel through the night. But we can find a place to stay if you want."

He didn't look at me as he offered. Clearly, the idea of being anywhere near a bed with me right now was out of the question.

"No, the train is fine. We have a schedule to keep after all."

I'd like to think I kept most of the sourness out of my tone, but the slow sink of his shoulders said otherwise.

18

might have said to hell with Hunt's issues and demanded we find a place to stay if I'd had any idea what I was in store for that night. I thought we'd be on another overnight train like the one we'd taken from Budapest to Prague. Instead, he'd lined up a series of seven trains. SEVEN. For a total of roughly fifteen hours.

It was a recipe for disaster (me being the disaster, of course).

The first train was just twelve minutes and took us to another station in Germany. From there we had just over ten minutes to jump on board another train to Basel, Switzerland. That one was about two and a half hours and filled with restless attempts to sleep on my backpack or the window or whatever surface looked appealing to my bleary, bloodshot eyes. Because I sure as hell wasn't talking to Hunt, not without biting his head off.

We arrived in Basel just before midnight with six minutes to transfer to our next train. Hunt had to pick up my bag and pull me along at a run to keep us from missing our train.

I collapsed into the first two open seats I could find and said, "Remind me to never go on *The Amazing Race*. This is not as fun as you would think."

We took that train, transferred to another in Olten, and arrived in Bern, Switzerland, roughly an hour later. We weren't in any one spot long enough to even think about sleeping, which left me plenty of time to seethe in my frustration.

"Just keep thinking of Italy," he said. "It will be worth it when we get to Italy."

"Is there a shower, the world's softest bed, and a professional masseuse waiting for us in Italy? Because that's the only way I can see this being worth it."

Exhausted, we arrived in Bern and I said, "Where to, captain?"

He pulled out the printed schedule that the ticket seller in Heidelberg had given him and flipped through the pages of timetables and information.

When he found the page he was looking for he said, "Oh."

"Oh? What does oh mean?"

"We have a little more time for this transfer is all."

"How much is a little more time?"

He scratched absentmindedly at his jaw, still staring at the paper instead of meeting my eyes.

"How much more time, Jackson?"

He offered a sheepish smile and said, "Five hours?"

"My brain is too foggy with sleep to pick which way to kill you, but give me five minutes and I'll figure it out."

"Kelsey—"

"Sharks," I said. "I would like to give you a few paper cuts and feed you to sharks."

"I don't think there are sharks in Switzerland."

"Then I'll find an aquarium!"

"I'm sorry. I should have paid more attention when she gave me the itinerary. I was just concentrated on getting there. But it's going to be okay. We'll kill some time. Maybe go get some food."

"It's one in the morning, Hunt."

We did manage to find a McDonald's that was open, though. So, I had to eat my words.

I said, "McDonalds in Switzerland is not exactly my idea of an adventure."

He didn't have to know how much I was worshiping these fries at the moment, though. After our last food adventure with apple mashed potatoes and blood soup, McDonald's fries were more valuable than gold. When we'd approached the restaurant and gotten our first whiff of fried goodness, I was two minutes away from falling on my knees and proposing to the pimply counter attendant just to get some freaking fries.

I made myself eat slowly, but every time Hunt looked away I did a Hoover vacuum impression and inhaled the stuff.

With my stomach achingly full, we made our way back to the train platform. It was summer, so it wasn't exactly cold, but the night wind blew in from the openings on the tracks, and I shivered. We found a bench on the platform our train would leave from roughly four hours later, and started making camp. Hunt pulled a jacket from his backpack, and handed it to me. I turned it around backward, and used it like a blanket.

"Come here." Hunt took a seat and pulled me closer to him, his hands reaching underneath the coat to touch my shoulders.

"What are you doing?"

"Just relax. You're tense and tired."

And bitchy. That was the word he didn't and probably wouldn't say.

"You wanted a professional masseuse in Italy. Well, this is Switzerland, and I'm no professional, but I bet I can get the job done."

His thumbs pressed into muscles that ran from my shoulders to my neck, and I swear my whole body went numb for a few seconds. Words fled my mouth, and all I managed was an unintelligible noise of approval.

Screw having a professional masseuse. It was so much better when he touched me.

"Is that okay?"

Okay was beyond my vocabulary at the moment. My eyes nearly rolled back in my head and I said, "Huh?"

"Harder?"

I groaned. He was so not helping my sexually starved brain.

"It's perfect."

His hands traveled the landscape of my back from the

path of my spine to valley of my waist. I melted in his arms until I felt like I was no longer solid, as insubstantial as water cupped between his hands.

Those hands skated across the sides of my rib cage, and my body jerked in an involuntary shiver.

"You okay?"

Yeah, there was no way I was managing words right now. I was just as turned on now as I was by that kiss in the bathroom. Maybe more now that I'd brought up that particular memory. So, I nodded.

I pulled my legs up to my chest and rested my cheek against my knees. Then I gave myself up to the glorious manipulation of his hands, and I let myself imagine what might happen if I turned around and straddled his lap and kissed him senseless like I wanted to. I imagined it so much that I fell from wishes into a dream.

When I woke, I wasn't leaned forward against my knees, but back against Hunt's chest, settled between his legs. We were turned sideways on the bench, and he was propped up against his backpack, and I was propped up against him. My knees were still bunched up because the bench was too short, and the armrest at the end of the bench kept me from stretching out my legs. But it wasn't the mildly uncomfortable position that woke me.

It was the gentle stroke of Jackson's fingers along my ribs from just below my bra to my waist and back again. It was soothing and maddening, and I was hyperaware of everywhere that our bodies touched. The rise and fall of his chest beneath me was like the rise and fall of ocean waves, and my feelings for him were just as tumultuous. I'd given up trying to decide what was the right thing to do in this situation or what I thought was best. The truth was . . . I didn't want to think. And when we were touching like this, I didn't have to. I could just feel.

While his hand was stroking down to my waist, I shifted and turned onto my side. I laid my head against his upper body, pulled one arm up to my chest, and casually tucked the other around his waist. When I'd turned, his hand had shifted from my side to my stomach, dragging my shirt up on accident.

I held my breath, hoping that he would stay exactly where he was, that he wouldn't pull his hand away. The second stretched on until I was wound so tight from anticipation that I thought I might explode. Then his tentative touch turned sure and his hand pressed closer to my stomach, half his hand touching bare skin.

We both knew the other was awake, but we lay still as if we weren't. It was like a game to see how close we could get to the line without crossing it. The hand that I had so casually wrapped around his waist slipped underneath the back of his shirt, pressing into the same skin that I had dragged my fingernails across a few hours ago. I didn't push further, not yet. And neither did he. But I lay there, my heart beating wildly, staring out at the empty train tracks and absorbing the warmth from where our bodies aligned. Still cradled between his legs, my hip was even with the juncture of his thighs but not quite touching. After a few minutes of stillness, I slowly edged my way closer to him. Our bodies pressed more intimately together, and my head rested higher on his chest so that my lips were nearly at his neck.

His head moved, his cheek pressed against my forehead. I could feel him looking down at me, but I couldn't meet his gaze. If we didn't look at each other, neither of us had to think. I didn't have to think of how I could screw this up, and neither of us had to think about whatever it was that made him keep pushing me away. We didn't have to do anything more than touch. His touch was all I needed to erase the rest of the world.

I could still feel his eyes on me, and I willed him to turn away. After a few more long moments, I felt him exhale, and I seemed to sink further into him. He turned his face more so that the edge of his lips touched my forehead, and the hand on my waist began the same slow stroking motion that he'd started on my side, but this time his hand slipped completely beneath my shirt.

That was where it started. Those soft touches. Each one pulled us a little closer. Each one gradually smudged that imaginary line between us.

And soon, the pull between us wouldn't just erase that line. It would obliterate it.

19

When our train came, we didn't talk about what was happening between us. I slipped Hunt's coat all the way on, we gathered our things and boarded. On the train, I sat next to him, he lifted the armrest, and we wordlessly fell back into each other's arms.

We did the same on the next train that took us from Brig, Switzerland, to Milan, Italy. I assumed that was our final stop, but when we boarded one last train to Firenze, in Florence, I was glad for one more chance to touch him. Because I wasn't sure this weird peace would last once we emerged back into the real world.

But despite my intentions to savor our closeness, fatigue

caught up to me and I was asleep within ten minutes of the train taking off. I didn't stir again until we were pulling into the station a little over an hour and a half later.

Hunt's fingers were combing through my hair and he said, "We're here."

I yawned and pushed myself up off his chest. His eyelids were heavy, and I knew he probably hadn't slept at all. His face was normally all angles and hard edges, but sleepy, he looked younger, less intimidating.

He yawned, and I laughed because he was just so damn cute.

"I thought we'd start by just walking around the city. Maybe go see the statue of David. Eat some gelato."

I caught his yawn and said, "Sounds good, but . . ."

I trailed off, unwilling to admit how exhausted I was. Thankfully he did it for me.

"But sleep first?"

"Oh, please God, yes."

He laughed and agreed.

We stumbled from the train station, little better than zombies. A hostel was out of the question. It was almost impossible to sleep during the day at those because you shared a room with so many people, so we stopped at the first decent hotel we found a few blocks south of the station. I didn't even have the energy to read the name. It was too long. It started with a B and ended with hotel, and that was all that mattered.

I leaned my head into Hunt's back as he spoke to the concierge, and then handed over my credit card.

I didn't think about much at all until we arrived at our room, and found a giant king bed in the middle of it.

"I'm sorry. I didn't think to ask for two beds," Hunt said. "I'll go back down."

"No, don't. That bed looks amazing, and I'm going to collapse if I don't get into it right now."

"Are you sure?" he asked.

I didn't bother answering. Instead, I kicked off my shoes and collapsed onto the bed still fully clothed.

"Oh God, I have never been happier than I am in this moment."

I heard Hunt's faint laughter, and then I was out.

I woke later as Hunt pulled back the covers and maneuvered me beneath them. A certain familiarity crept through my bones, like this had happened before. I peeled my eyes open, and found Hunt. He must have showered because his face was still slightly damp, and he was wearing nothing but a pair of pajama pants that hung low on his hips. His abs could have rivaled all of Tuscany for the most gorgeous rolling hills I had ever seen.

He pulled the covers up to my neck, and then stepped away from the bed. He settled onto the burgundy sofa situated across the room on the opposite wall.

I said, "What are you doing?"

"Ssh. Just go back to sleep."

"No, I'm not letting you sleep on the couch, not after the night we've had. If you're too afraid to sleep in the same bed as me, we'll go downstairs and get a different room."

I pushed back the covers and started crawling out of bed. He was off the couch and in front of me before my feet even settled on the floor.

"Don't, Kelsey. Just go back to sleep."

I set my lips in a firm line and scooted over, leaving space for him to climb in.

"You're not going to let this go?" he asked.

I shook my head.

"The couch is actually pretty comfortable. And it's not a good idea to—"

Tired of the same old argument, I grabbed his hand and tugged hard. He toppled on the bed next to me, and I said, "No more excuses."

My patience had been brushed away by every smoothing stroke of his hand across my waist last night. It disappeared like sand in the wind bit by bit until all that was left was the longing underneath.

Still gripping his hand, I laid back and turned on my side, facing away from him. I tugged on his hand until he lay behind me, and then I let his hand drop onto my stomach.

I wasn't going back to how we were before. I was sick of the will he—won't he. I just wanted to be close to him. The consequences be damned.

His body was stiff behind me at first, and he was holding his arm so that it made as little contact with me as possible. I snuggled back into him, and he froze.

"Jackson . . ."

I let his name hang in the air, and after a few moments he relaxed. His arm curled around my waist, and the movement of his chest grew to match my own as we fell into sleep.

I woke again in the afternoon, and sunlight was pouring through the window, stronger than a jack and coke, hold the coke. I rolled over to get away from the light, and abruptly met the wall that was Hunt. He lay on his back, completely dead to the world. I'd only ever seen him sleep on that first train ride to Prague, and then it had only been a few seconds before he woke up.

In sleep, I got to study him in a way I hadn't been able to so far. He had a small scar that ran through his right eyebrow, and another on his chin. His nose wasn't quite as straight as I thought it was, but had a slight bump at the bridge. I wondered if he'd broken it before.

His chest I'd seen several times, but that didn't make it any less mesmerizing now. It too had several scars, one toward his shoulder that was small and thin, and I guessed was from a surgery. Another on his side was more jagged, and spanned the length of several ribs.

When I'd soaked in as much of him as I could without turning him over or removing those pajama pants that framed his hips so deliciously, I decided to try to catch another hour or so of sleep. Gently, I laid a hand across his abdomen. When he didn't wake, I laid my head across his chest.

I'd barely released a satisfied sigh when I was flipped over onto my back, and my shoulders were pinned to the mattress. I cried out in shock, and then in pain at the force Hunt exerted on my shoulders. He was strong and all of his weight was bearing down on me, bending my shoulders back in a way they definitely weren't meant to. His eyes were wild and dark and unseeing. His breath came in heavy, shaky pants, each one punctuated by a little more pressure on my shoulders.

"Hunt," I said, but he didn't react. I bent my arms at the

elbow, and managed to grasp at his forearms. "Jackson. It's Kelsey. Wake up." I whimpered, desperate to make the pain stop. Louder, I said, "*Jackson,* please *wake up.* You're hurting me."

I don't know if it was time or my words or something else that snapped him out of it, but he released me, and a look of horror dropped down over his previously blank expression.

Even though it was over, his breathing was still harsh and uneven, and it was several long seconds before he said anything.

"Oh God. I'm so sorry, princess. I'm sorry."

His expression crumbled, ruins hidden in his eyes, and he started crawling backward to get off of me.

My hands shot out, and I gripped his arms.

"Don't. Don't do that." I repeated the words he said to me in that café bathroom.

"Kelsey . . ."

I tugged on his arms, but they were immovable stone columns. I said, "Come back to me." I tugged again, and this time the stone gave way. His hip hit the bed beside mine, but his chest draped across mine. He dropped his face into the hollow between my neck and shoulder, and his hands went to my shoulders, his touch now soft and soothing.

"I'm sorry," he said again.

"Ssh." I wrapped my arms around his shoulders and held on to him as tightly as I could. I didn't know what plagued him, but I could guess, and all my guesses put my problems to shame.

"I never wanted to hurt you," he whispered.

This was why he'd pushed me away. He'd thought I couldn't handle this or wouldn't want to. But the truth was . . . I'd grown up in the kind of world where people hurt you on purpose. To prove a point or to play a game. I'd take Jackson's kind of hurt any day.

"Hey," I said, pulling his face up until his eyes met mine. "You haven't hurt me. I'm fine."

He shook his head. "You don't know, Kelsey. There's this thing . . ."

"We've all got things like that, Jackson. I don't care."

I grasped his jaw and pulled his lips closer to mine.

Millimeters away from my mouth, he jerked back. "You *should* care. You don't know anything about me."

"Then tell me."

He rolled over onto his back next to me and ran his hand across his face. I shifted onto my side, and laid my head on his chest.

He said, "Kelsey . . ."

I closed my eyes, settling into him. "You're going to have to pry me off because I'm not going anywhere. And I can be pretty damn stubborn."

He paused, and then breathed in an impression of a laugh. After a few seconds, breathing became breathing again and the laughter disappeared, but his arms settled around me. And that was enough.

We stayed locked together in bed for the rest of the day. Sometimes sleeping. Sometimes not. But no matter how we shifted or in what positions we lay, we never stopped touching for more than a few seconds.

And each time I was shocked by the ache I felt in those moments. It uncoiled quickly, piercing and pulling and opening a hole in my chest that echoed like an empty cavern until his skin met mine again. Each time I would sigh in relief, and hold him tightly, probably too tightly for a few seconds. But he never said anything. Neither of us did. Not about his dream or the way I was clinging to him. Not about the darkness that was so clearly lurking in both of us, filling up the spaces between the skin and muscle and bone.

We didn't say a word, and I was reminded of those first few seconds when we'd leapt off the bridge in Prague. There had been so much noise and fear and adrenaline, but most of all there had been a permeating, inevitable, and calming silence as we fell and fell and fell.

When we finally climbed out of bed, we spent the evening walking around Florence. We did get that gelato. And we saw the replica statue of David outside the museum, which was close enough to seeing the real thing for us.

We had dinner on the garden terrace on the roof of our hotel, and we slept in each other's arms again that night.

But still . . . all we ever did was touch.

And feel.

20

was fairly certain that Hunt had meant to leave and jet off to another place the next day, but he hadn't counted on spending the whole first day in bed. I'd thought once that Hunt was like gravity, but the real gravity was between us. Neither Hunt nor I had anticipated how much that pull would take over.

It was irrational, but I kept feeling like we'd lose whatever this was if we left our little hotel in Florence. Sometimes, I felt like we'd lose it if we even left the bed. It was an awful thing to be terrified of waking up, of standing, of going outside.

It was stupid, and when I wasn't petrified, I was berating myself for it.

I was not this girl. I was not the girl who let her whole world revolve around a man. But then again, I'd never really let my world revolve around anything else but me. Now that I had stepped out of the center, and put someone else there, it was hard to go back.

So, he didn't admit it, but I think he changed his plan. Instead of heading to another city, we stayed in Florence. Sometimes we ventured outside the city, like the day we took a bike tour of Tuscany. We spent an entire day, exhausted and sweaty, exploring hill towns that weren't the typical tourist destinations. In most of the towns, we were the only tourists to be found. Hardly anyone spoke English, but they were so excited to have us.

In one village, we toured an art studio where the artist worked with alabaster, crafting everything from statues to lamps to chess sets. I bought a pale alabaster heart pendant, and looped it onto the necklace I was already wearing.

Outside one walled city, we found the most stunning ruins of a Roman theater. We couldn't get very close, but we found a great view of it from the wall of the city, and I told Hunt everything I knew about Roman theaters. I told him the Roman names for all the parts of the structure like *scaena frons* and the *cavea* and *vomitorium*. I'm sure he didn't care, let alone remember what I said a few minutes later, but he listened and smiled.

We biked along the winding roads, sometimes going hours without seeing a car. We stopped and had a picnic lunch in the grass. I stared up at the sky, finding shapes in the clouds while Hunt drew in his sketchbook. Me, I think.

When we saw a town in the distance, we went there, having no idea what it was called or where we were heading. I had the most delicious homemade pasta in someone's actual home. We'd been looking for a restaurant, and were instead invited inside by Giovanni and his wife.

And even though the day was amazing, and we could have stayed in any of those towns or kept exploring forever, we couldn't bring ourselves to move on. We rented our bikes for a second day and rode off in a different direction, meeting new people and exploring new places, but both days we were back in Florence by nightfall. Back in our sanctuary of silence where we didn't have to question or label or analyze anything between us.

It was perfect.

Except for the fact that I was wound so tight from being close to him, from touching him that at times it became difficult to sleep at all.

He fell asleep faster and faster each night, and I stayed up longer and longer, my body aching from neglect. On the fifth night of our weeklong adventure, I couldn't take it anymore. While he slept, strong and silent next to me, I let a hand trail down my stomach, and into the pajama shorts I'd worn to sleep that night. I was already slick and aching, and just the first touch had me pointing my toes and closing my eyes.

I sucked in a breath and bit down on my lip to stay silent, but my body was buzzing with pent-up energy. It was the same buzz I felt coming off stage, high from the lights and the applause and the attention. Only this all came from *him*. From being near him and being unable to have him.

I circled my fingers, my back arching with pleasure.

I was so caught up and focused on my own touch that I didn't realize Hunt was awake until he gripped my wrist, pulling my hand up and pressing it against the pillow above my head.

My eyes snapped open, and my jaw dropped. I didn't know what to say. But I knew I was turned on even more by the sight of him leaning over me, and the feel of him pinning my wrist. I whimpered, and his eyes were so dark, they shone black.

Without saying a word, he touched the flat of my stomach, and then replaced my hand with his. The calloused pad of his middle finger pressed against me, and a galaxy sprung up behind my closed eyes as I bucked up into him. He pressed again, circling this time, and I didn't have to be quiet now. I cried out and with my free hand, I gripped the wrist of the hand that shackled mine above my head.

He leaned over me, his head finding the hollow where my neck sloped into my shoulder. He inhaled deeply, the tip of his nose trailing a line up my neck. His finger swirled around my most sensitive part again, and I was so close already.

My fingernails dug into his wrist, and something like a growl tore from his mouth. He pressed his finger down, hard, and that was all it took to send me over the edge. I came apart with a low cry. Nearly a week of built-up of frustration lit and burned in my blood, and the rush of pleasure started in my head, as bright and deafening as a fireworks show. It shot down my spine to my center, and then flooded out to every part of me.

I arched up into him because the only thing that was missing was his mouth on my mouth, his skin on my skin. But before I could even drag his head up to mine, he rolled away from me and off the bed. He stalked into the bathroom without a word. As I lay in bed, my bones gone soft, I heard the shower switch on.

We woke up on the sixth day of our adventure, and neither of us mentioned what occurred the night before. Hunt's eyelids were heavy as though he didn't sleep, and I didn't know what to say to make him stop feeling guilty. I didn't know why he should. And every time I let myself brainstorm, my heart seized up the same way it did whenever I had to get out of bed and leave our sanctuary behind.

We only had two days left in Hunt's week.

Two days.

And even though our deadline was arbitrary, I didn't think we'd make it past that deadline without talking about something. And I was afraid that something would bring this all to an end.

With my now-routine morning regret, I rolled out of Jackson's arms. He stopped me with a touch to my elbow. I turned and was struck by how surreal it was to see sheets draped over his bare chest. Our few nights together felt like years, and yet I knew so little about him. It wasn't unusual for me to share a bed with someone I didn't know, but it was unusual for me to be bothered by it. Maybe it was because in addition to not knowing his mind, I'd not learned his body either. His hand tickled at my elbow again, and he said, "Sorry about the nightmares."

He'd had several last night after the thing we apparently weren't talking about. Instead of curling into me after they were over, he took to pacing the room or sketching at the window.

"It's okay."

I shifted to leave again, only to feel his hand wrap around mine. He played with my fingers for a few seconds, as if that was the only reason he stopped me. Then he asked, "Tell me about your life back in the states."

Not a subject I particularly wanted to hash out this early in the morning, but he obviously wanted to talk. Maybe talking about this would help him talk about the rest.

"Like what? It's nothing that interesting."

"Tell me about your favorite Christmas growing up."

"You're kidding, right?"

"I'm serious. I'm trying to get the full picture of Kelsey Summers."

It wasn't a pretty picture, but if he wanted it . . .

"Fine," I said. "My favorite Christmas has got to be by default the one *before* the first one I can remember."

He looked down, squeezing my fingers between his own. "That's really sad."

"Yeah, well, my family is sad."

"What made it so bad?"

I propelled myself back against the pillows, letting go of his hand.

"Can we talk about something else?"

He wanted to push. I could hear it in the silence, in his careful breaths, in the creak of the bed as he leaned forward for just a few seconds before rolling away.

"You go shower. I'll figure out what we're doing today."

God, we were both so bad at this. There was no way it could work, not that I really even knew what "working" would entail.

Released from his questioning, I fled for the bathroom.

I took my time, enjoying the way the hot water loosened my sore muscles, but ever conscious of the other body just outside the bathroom with only a wall between us.

I decided we'd been still long enough. Neither of us was good with words. We were action people, which was why last night had worked. We didn't talk. Maybe it was time for a little push. So when I got out of the shower, I ignored the pile of clothes in the bathroom and exited the room in my towel.

"I told you everything is fine."

I said, "I forgot my—"

Then stopped because Hunt's back was to me and he was on the phone.

He whipped around, and I lowered my voice, "I, um, I forgot something. Sorry."

In a quiet voice, he said into the phone, "I have to go now. No. No. Thank you, but I have to go."

He lowered the phone, but I could still hear the faint sound of someone talking on the other end before he hung up.

I picked up a pair of socks, the first thing I saw in my backpack, and said, "Who was that?"

"What?" He didn't look at me. "Oh. Just the concierge, wondering if we'd decided when we were checking out yet."

I stood there, a puddle collecting on the floor below me, in nothing but a towel holding a pair of pointless socks, and still he didn't even glance my way.

I couldn't tell whether I was more distressed by his lack of reaction or the tense set of his shoulders. A conversation with the concierge shouldn't do that. And if he was only asking if we were staying, shouldn't that have been a simpler, shorter call?

Maybe he was just tense about us, and the phone call had nothing to do with it.

I stayed staring for a few more seconds before fleeing to the bathroom. I had almost closed the door when I heard him ask, "What do you think about taking a train to the coast? Maybe the Italian Riviera?"

I poked my head back out of the bathroom, and he was sitting stiffly on the bed, his hands clenched into fists at his side.

It looked like we'd be saying goodbye to our Florence refuge after all. Perhaps our secrets were getting too big for this small room.

I said, "Okay. Sounds good."

The words echoed off the tile walls around me, and I felt that hole in my chest opening up, and the fear creeping in.

The small village of Riomaggiore was set into a cliff side on the Italian Riviera, and I knew from the moment that I stepped off the train that I was going to love this place. The air smelled fresh and salty, and the wind curled up from the ocean, tossing my hair. At the edge of the train platform was a wall, and beyond that a turquoise blue sea.

I rushed to the edge, desperate to soak in the view. Craggy black rocks were decorated with white sea foam, and stood out against the vibrant blue waters. Waves crashed against the rock, and I swear I could feel the spray all the way up on the platform.

I squealed and threw my arms around Hunt's neck.

"This is good?" he asked.

"Very good."

This was worth leaving Florence.

Hunt had told me on the train where we were going. There were five villages collectively called Cinque Terre that sat along the coastline. They were part of some kind of protected wilderness area or park, so there was almost nothing modern about the villages, just the train in and out. We would spend today and tomorrow, our last two days, exploring and hiking from village to village.

If all five villages were as beautiful as this train platform, I was sold.

We left the station and headed to the city to find lunch and a place to stay. There was no lack of either. We stopped at a small restaurant, and I had the most delicious pesto in the history of the universe. I didn't even particularly like pesto, but Cinque Terre made me a believer.

The waiter at the restaurant recommended a family down the road that rented out an apartment attached to their home. On the way, I marveled at the village. The homes were stacked up like building blocks and painted in vibrant colors. There were orange and yellow and pink buildings with blue and green and red shutters. Everywhere I looked was something worthy of capturing in a picture—from a fading turquoise door, whose stories you could almost detect through the splintering wood and peeling paint, to a small boy, skin tanned from the sun, with bare feet toughened by rough roads and the sweet cradle of a soft stray cat in his arms.

Hunt's hand touched the small of my back, and I leaned into him instinctively. "This is wonderful," I said. "I just . . . I've never seen anything like it."

"So have I done it?" he asked.

"Done what?"

"Given you an adventure?"

I stopped, and looked at him. His face was tense, and I got the feeling he was asking about something more than if I was just having fun.

The sea and sky joined in a dark blue horizon over his shoulder, and I wanted to stop time. A picture could never be enough to capture this moment, and I was afraid if I didn't imprint it upon my brain I would forget the breeze rustling the laundry hanging out of the shuddered windows, the shine of the sun off the water, and the deep gray of Hunt's eyes. It would be a crime to forget those things. I wanted to stop time because that one-second pause wasn't big enough to feel the things my body wanted to feel and think the things my mind wanted to think. So, I told him honestly, "Adventure doesn't seem like a big enough word for what this has been."

His smile put the sun to shame.

He draped his arm across my shoulder, and we went to see about a room.

Each of the villages was connected by both a train and a path. After settling into our cozy, albeit simple, private apartment, we set out to explore. We chose the path because there was no way that Hunt would let us get away with the train. Not that I would have even wanted to.

We followed the trail map from Riomaggiore to the beginning of the path that would lead us to Manarola. The path was named Via dell'Amore, the lover's path. Carved out of the side of a cliff with a flat stone trail, the path made for a pretty easy trek between the first and second village. It wrapped around the cliff, giving us a beautiful view of Riomaggiore as we left, and the ocean as we moved forward.

The path led us to a stone alcove with window openings that allowed us to peer out at the water and rocks below. As we moved farther through the tunnel, I started to notice locks hung from the railing and ropes on the ceiling and every available surface. There were locks of every size and shape. Some were shiny and new, while others were rusted and aged, but there had to be thousands of them in all.

Following the locks led us to a chair that had been sculpted out of stone. The seat was big enough for two and the back had been carved to look like two people kissing. The chair was placed in a stone archway with railings behind it to keep the chair and people from tumbling into the ocean below. Not that you could see the railings anymore. They were covered in locks, overflowing. There were locks hooked onto other locks, framing the lover's seat with the help of an ocean backdrop. The chair and much of the tunnel around us were covered in graffiti, but it didn't matter. You could feel how special this place was. The horizon lined up almost perfectly with the lips of the lovers, as if the sea and sky and life converged to make this perfect representation of what it means to be with another person. The permanence of it.

I didn't know how many couples had placed locks around this chair, nor did I know how many of them were still together. But it didn't matter. When you love someone, really love someone, it's a lasting mark on your soul. There's a lock on your heart that you'll carry with you always. You may lose the key or give it away, but the lock stays with you all the same.

A man approached us, and asked if we'd like to buy a lock. He had a box with all different kinds, and I started to say no, but Hunt said, "Why not?"

He handed the man some cash, and picked a lock out of his assortment. The lock he chose was plain, but sturdy.

"Where should we put it?" he asked.

I looked at the chair, but the way my heartbeat lurched made me look for another place, a place with less *pressure*. I took a few steps farther down the tunnel toward where it opened back up to the regular path. At the mouth of the tunnel, I could see locks hanging down near the ceiling.

I pointed and said, "There."

Up close I could see that netting had been placed around one of the boulders on the side of the cliff, and locks had been clipped to that net. This was perfect. We were still leaving our mark, but without it meaning more than I was willing to say.

"I'll lift you up," Hunt said.

I took the lock from him, and he bent, wrapping his arms around my knees. He pulled me up, and I balanced myself with his shoulders. When he was standing upright, I put one hand up on the boulder and picked up a piece of the netting. I opened the lock, slipped it around a bit of the rope, and clicked it closed.

I smiled.

"All done."

Hunt loosened his arms around my knees, and I slid down his body. And just like the lock, it felt like we had clicked into place.

21

Heat crackled across my skin. Hunt's gray eyes bore into mine. And my gaze was drawn to his lips. Those lips. I had spent days thinking about those lips, maybe even days looking at them. I'd agonized over Hunt's excuses and what might be keeping us apart, about what he wasn't telling me. But here with the ocean at my back and the memory of that lock against the skin of my palm, I couldn't think of a single reason. Or maybe I just didn't want to.

I tipped my chin up, and he tipped his down. The world shrunk to include only the space between our lips, space that only our breath crossed.

My heart was about to beat out of my chest, and I swear

I could hear his beating, too. I knew he wanted this just as much as I did. And I was tired of letting some imaginary line dictate my actions. So, I leaned in, and for the barest of seconds my bottom lip grazed his. And that small world, expanded, exploded, and we were at the fiery hot center of it.

I pressed my lips harder against his, curling my hands around the back of his neck. And for just a second, he pulled me in closer. My chest smashed against his. My feet left the ground, dangling centimeters above the stone path. My head was spinning with want.

Then just as suddenly, he released me. My feet hit the ground. My head stopped spinning. But I felt dizzier than ever.

He said, "Kelsey, I can't."

"You can't? It seems to me like you just won't."

"You don't understand."

I stepped out of his arms, and backed away to the other side of the path.

"You're right. I don't understand. I don't understand what about this is *not* okay." People were starting to stare, but I didn't care. "I don't understand how we can spend every waking moment together, how you can *touch* me, how we can sleep in the same bed, sleep in each other's arms, but this? *This* is somehow not okay? No, I don't understand that. I don't understand how you can kiss me the way you kissed me and feel the way I *know* you feel, and keep pushing me away. But I'm done trying to figure it out."

I spun and ran through the tunnel, passing the lover's seat that moments ago had seemed so poignant and perfect a representation of what I wanted and where I thought Jackson and I were heading. Maybe they didn't choose locks because love is permanent. Maybe they chose locks because emotions bind us into place. They weigh us down. They pull your heart into a thousand different directions until the only option left is for it to break.

That chair was stone, stuck forever in that chaste kiss. It was hard, cold, and lifeless. A lot like Hunt could be at times.

So, I ran, my sandals slapping against the stone path. The tunnel was dark with rectangles of light pouring in through the window gaps. I got far enough away that I couldn't feel Hunt's gaze on my back or the gravity that pulled us together. Then, I slowed. My breath rasped like the sound of fabric tearing, threads ripping apart.

And then because the universe has impeccable timing (and because it hates me), a droplet of rain splashed against my forehead. Followed by a second and a third. Then the sky opened, and dumped an ocean on my head.

I yelled, "Fuck! Of course." I looked up at the sky, raindrops pummeling my face and yelled, "Thank you. Thank you so much."

The hard path jarred my ankles as I ran, but I kept running, more concerned with finding shelter. I could have turned back and headed for the tunnel, but then I'd have to face Hunt again.

No, thank you. Not after I literally ran away from him. Not after he pushed me away at every turn.

The stones turned slick under the downpour of rain, and my foot slid. I tried to catch my balance, but there was nothing to hold on to. I teetered backward and prepared myself for impact.

But my back didn't hit rock, well, not the rock path anyway. A familiar pair of arms circled me. I saw Hunt's soaked tennis shoes first, but I would have known it was him regardless. Even soaking wet and pelted with rain, I felt a shock of warmth at his touch.

"Are you okay?" he asked.

I jerked out of his arms. "I'm fine."

I continued down the path, walking as fast as I could on the uneven, slippery stones.

"Kelsey, just wait."

I yelled back. "I'm tired of waiting, Jackson. I think I'm done."

I followed the path down into the village, and the streets were grimy with mud. I could feel tiny drops flicking up and landing on my calves and thighs.

I reached the home where we were staying, and ran up the rickety stairs that led to the apartment upstairs we'd rented. I threw open the door, and slammed it closed behind me.

I knew it was childish, and I couldn't keep him out there in the rain, but it felt good all the same.

I tore off my sandals, splattering mud and water on the floor and my clothes. Then, maybe because I was crazy or because I was a mile past giving a shit, I tugged my soaking shirt over my head. It hit the ground with a slap at the same time that the apartment door blew open.

I heard it slam back against the wall once, then again, knocked by the wind. I turned and found Hunt frozen in the doorway.

His eyes went to the bare skin of my stomach, slick with rainwater and pebbled with goose bumps.

Spitefully, I said, "You're welcome to stay outside. You know, if this is another thing you *can't handle*."

He stayed locked in the doorway, his hands gripping the jamb.

I unbuttoned my shorts and slid them over my hips, letting them fall to the ground.

I said, "Actually, I *dare* you to come inside. I still have one dare left from Heidelberg. So, I dare you to come inside and kiss me."

His body leaned into the room, but his grip stayed tight on the entryway, and his feet firmly planted on the porch. His face screwed up like he was in pain, but he dropped his head and looked away.

I scoffed. "That's what I thought."

I spun and walked toward the shower in the corner of the room. It wasn't even a room by itself, just a raised tile platform circled by a shower curtain. I turned the knob, and heard the pipes whistle at the same time the door slammed closed.

I'd thought maybe he'd left, but then I heard his gruff voice behind me say, "Fuck it," and his hands seized my waist and pulled me back against his chest.

His wet clothing met my bare skin, and I shivered from the cold. His mouth found my neck, and those shivers became tremors. He nipped the juncture of my neck and shoulder, and I stumbled forward into the spray of the shower.

I gasped when the water hit me, and he squeezed my waist, pulling my hips back against his. One of his hands trailed upward and cupped my breast through my wet bra, and my head dropped back against his shoulder with a moan.

He spun me around, and my back hit the tile wall just below the showerhead. Water spewed down onto both of his, but he didn't seem to notice as he dragged my mouth to his.

God, we needed to argue more often.

He kissed me hard, his tongue prying my lips open. He cupped my jaw, and angled my head to kiss me deeper. I grew dizzy with desire as his mouth plundered mine. I grasped his forearms, my fingernails biting into his skin.

I was still frustrated and angry, and so was he. That made the connection between us all the more explosive.

I reached greedy hands for the bottom of his shirt, desperate for skin on skin. I ripped the shirt over his head. Water ran down his face and chest in tiny rivers, and I wanted to taste each one. I couldn't resist touching him. I started at his chest, pressing both my hands flat against pecs, and he groaned in response. I slid my hands down to his abs, dragging my fingernails lightly over his skin. He growled, his fingers digging into my skin. I dipped my head, and licked at a trail of water at the center of his chest.

He gripped my jaw and pulled my face up to his. "You're irresistible."

I would have taken it as a compliment if he didn't seem so pissed about it.

Okay, maybe I took it as a compliment either way.

"That's funny," I said. "Then what the hell took you so long?"

I curled my fingers over his shoulders, and his hands slid down my body. His thumbs pressed into my hipbones hard, his fingers splaying over the curve of my ass. And the only answer I got to my question was him tugging my hips forward to meet his. His strength undid me, sending every nerve ending up in flames.

His arousal pressed against my stomach through his jeans, and I sucked in a breath. He took advantage of my open mouth, his tongue winding and flicking against mine.

His hands explored my body, bold and strong like his kiss. My heart felt like a bird loosed from a cage, like it couldn't stay perched in one spot in my chest.

He slid a hand up my back, unsnapping the clasp of my bra with ease. He broke our kiss just long enough to pull the fabric from between us, before crushing me against him again. I heard the wet slap of my bra hit the tile floor.

When my bare chest met his, a growl sounded low in his throat. His mouth pressed and pulled and coaxed mine into movement, and time seemed both too fast and too slow at once.

When my lungs burned for air, I pulled back, panting.

I said, "You're the most confusing person I've ever met, and sometimes I hate you."

Not the most romantic thing to say, but it was honest.

He pinned me back against the wall again, and this time gripped my wrists, locking them in place above me, too.

He growled, "This counts," before nipping my bottom lip.

I didn't know what he was saying, but I nodded because his leg pushed between mine, anchored at the juncture between my thighs, and every shift or movement caused something to rend and then mend inside me.

"Say it."

I arched my body into his, pulling at his shoulders.

"Say what?"

"Say that this is real. Tell me it *counts*."

He pressed his forehead against mine, and that thing that tore inside of me was so loud that it had to be real. Something hung in the space between my heart and lungs, detached from where it had been.

"This is real." I shivered, suddenly cold under the spray of water.

He released my wrists and turned off the shower, pulling me out into the bedroom. Water streamed down our bodies, forming a puddle on the floor, but he didn't even give it a second glance. He wrapped an arm around my waist and the other around my thighs, lifting me up above him. His head was in line with my stomach. He paused to taste the wet skin just below my breasts, and I closed my eyes. I clenched his shoulders, every muscle in my body pulling tight as his tongue darted out to flick over the sensitive skin of my ribs.

I said, "Jackson."

I didn't know what I was going to say next. It could have been more angry words or confusion or a romantic declaration. But I forgot it completely when he lifted his head higher, and took the pebbled tip of my breast into his mouth. I cried out.

Slowly, he loosened his grip, letting me slide down his body the way I had out on the path. But now, our wet skin melded together. My softness pressed against his hard muscle, and all I could think of were four-letter words.

When our faces aligned, he said, "This is what I should have done out there. This is what I've wanted to do a thousand times over."

He claimed my mouth in another kiss.

I opened to him immediately, his tongue tangling with mine. He tasted like warm summer days and hurricanes, like everything I wanted and everything I didn't know I needed. He caught my bottom lip between his, sucking and nibbling, and I was reminded of the first time I saw him. That terrible kiss in the ruin bar brought Hunt into my life. I never thought I would be grateful for the worst kiss of my life, especially not while enjoying the best.

He kept one arm banded around my ribs to hold me up, and the other dragged down my back to my ass. He cupped me, grinding me against his hips, and I wrapped my legs around his waist for better friction. But then I wished I hadn't because my legs met his wet jeans, which I wanted off. Like ten minutes ago.

My fingers found the waistband of his jeans. I was pressed too tightly against him to manage the buttons, and I whined into his kiss.

I tugged on his jeans, and felt him begin moving toward the bed.

He dropped me on my back without warning, and I bounced against the mattress.

Shocked, I yelled, "You—"

I swallowed whatever insult had been coming when he flicked open the button of his jeans and slid them down over his naked hips.

When I managed to pick up my jaw, I followed his lead, slipping my underwear over my hips. I kicked them off, leaving us both bare before the other's gaze. We were getting the sheets wet, but who the hell cared? For several long seconds, we both just stared at each other, drinking in the sight that for so long we'd denied ourselves.

Hunt smiled darkly and said, "My imagination didn't do you justice."

"Imagine me naked a lot, did you?"

"Only every other second."

I smiled and the last of my frustration fled to be replaced by anticipation.

I sat up so that my face was level with his abdomen.

He ran a gentle hand through my hair. I turned into his touch and kissed his wrist. Then I leaned forward and licked a stray water droplet from his bare hip.

His hand tightened in my hair, and he exhaled sharply.

I circled my hand around him, and he choked out a groan. He stayed still for a few seconds, his eyes directed toward the ceiling.

"Why didn't you?" I asked. "If you thought about me so much, if you wanted me . . . why push me away?"

He pulled my hand away from his body, kissing the back of my knuckles instead.

"I couldn't do this lightly. Not with you. I needed it to mean as much to you as it meant to me."

He leaned down and kissed me sweetly on the lips. So sweet it burned, like sugar around the rim of a Molotov cocktail.

Gripping my hips, he slid me back farther on the bed, until just my feet were dangling off the edge. I sat up on my elbows and watched him as his eyes surveyed me from head to toe.

He picked up my right foot, and placed a tender kiss on the inside of my ankle. That kiss started a fire deep in my bones that ran through the rest of me like a lit fuse. As he kissed my calf and the inside of my knee, my bones melted down to liquid. His hands started at my heels and ran up the backs of my legs, tickling the sensitive skin. I squirmed, pulling my knees together, and he placed a hand low on my abdomen stilling me.

"Patience, princess."

I had no patience left. Especially not if he was going to do the same thing he did every other time and pull back when he came to his senses.

I said, "You're not going to change your mind, are you, Jackson? Because I can't keep doing this."

He said, "I hope you can keep doing this. Because I don't plan on letting you out of this room until my seven days are up."

22

His mouth trailed up the inside of my thigh, and I was breathing so heavy that I was on the verge of hyperventilating. One of his hands still pressed into my stomach, and the other pushed my knees apart. His teeth grazed my skin, and my hips bowed up.

He was going to kill me.

I could actually die like this.

"Please," I said.

"Please what, princess?"

His breath fanned across my inner thigh, and just that was enough to send shockwaves of pleasure through me. The hand on my stomach slid down to the juncture between my thighs, and I completely lost it.

I turned my head to the side, and swallowed a moan.

His fingers drew me to the edge, working me until all I could do was whimper and breathe, whimper and breathe.

"Tell me what you want," he said.

My body clenched around his fingers, and all I could say was "You." His thumb pressed hard against my most sensitive spot just like it had the night before, and I said, again, "Oh God, you."

All I knew was that he was too far away, and I didn't need any more foreplay. Our whole damn relationship had been foreplay. I wanted him now.

I reached a hand down toward him, and he laced his fingers with mine. I tugged, and he stood from where he'd been kneeling. I pulled again, and he put his knee on the bed between my thighs.

He hovered above me, his body lean and muscled, and his eyes predatory. He looked like he wanted to devour me, and I was all too willing to be his victim.

I released his hand to touch his waist, and then I pulled his body down on top of mine. I threw my head back and moaned at the contact.

His mouth went to my shoulder, tracing along the line of my muscle to my collarbone. His thigh pressed up and against my center, and I held my breath. He lifted his head to look at me. When our eyes met, he pressed against me again, and the breath I'd been holding tore from my lungs.

He bent to taste my lips, gentle and focused. I clutched at

his back, marveling at the way his muscles flexed and moved as kissed me.

"Please," I said again. "Please Jackson."

His eyes softened, and he pressed his forehead against mine. His eyes closed, and he took a slow, deep breath. Then he leaned down and placed a kiss on my sternum, between the swell of my breasts.

"Give me a second."

He slid off of me, and I felt like I was drowning every second that it took for him to grab a condom and come back to me.

I rose up on my elbows, and he crawled above me. He kissed me sweetly, slowly, and the frenzy of our previous moments disappeared. There was a level of intimacy in just kissing him that I'd never experienced, and it left me excited and terrified of what came next.

Sex had never been a big deal to me. But everything about Jackson was a big deal. I was afraid I wouldn't be good enough, afraid that I wouldn't know how to have the kind of sex that meant something. What if when it was over, he regretted crossing that line?

His hand smoothed over my cheek and he said, "Don't. Don't do that."

I didn't know if he knew the exact line of my thoughts or just that I was worried, but it soothed me all the same.

He kissed me, and then slowly eased me back on the bed. He lay beside me, and I turned on my side to face him. I laid my head on his arm, and he pulled me into his chest, just holding me for a moment. We'd held each other like this before, but this time was different. My heart was thundering, and my skin sang. His hand traced down the line of my spine, and I arched into him. He continued over my hip and down my leg, his fingers curling behind my knee. A zing of electricity shot from my knee up to my core as he pulled my leg over his hip.

Our mouths met and he said, "God, I love the way you taste."

He leaned into me, situating his leg between mine, and aligning our hips. He pushed inside me, and for a moment my whole body seemed to forget how to work. My blood forgot to pump, my lungs forgot to breathe, and my hips forgot to move.

His hands tightened on me, and he released a low groan into my neck.

He growled, "I love the way you feel."

Laying on my side like this with our legs twined together, he reached deep inside me. I'd never had sex like this, wrapped up in another person until it was impossible to find the divide between us. His hips withdrew and then pushed again, and the friction had me arching my back.

My hips stayed aligned with his, but I bent backward until my head and half my back rested on the bed. Jackson leaned with me, curling around my body. His mouth burned a hot path from my collarbone down into the valley between my breasts. He kept a hand at the small of my back and used it to pull me in every time he surged forward.

He rained kisses down on my chest, and I clutched the back of his head, needing to feel him, to hold him against me.

He trailed up again, flicking his tongue over my collarbone and scraping his teeth against the column of my throat. My skin broke out in goose bumps, and I shuddered in his arms. He placed a kiss on the underside of my jaw, and I dipped my head down to meet his.

His tongue plunged into my mouth, mimicking the deep movement of the rest of his body, and I clung to him as he wrung pleasure from my body with each slow thrust.

"Kelsey," he whispered.

I had to pry my eyes open, and even then each time his skin slid against mine I had to fight to hold up my eyelids. He pressed his forehead into mine, and rather than falling into his dark eyes, they seemed to pour something into me. Confidence, maybe. Or affection. Whatever it was, I stopped worrying about how this would play out. I stopped thinking of the ways I was inadequate. I stopped everything that didn't have to do with this moment.

He said, "God, do you have any idea what you do to me? Any idea how long I've wanted you?"

I didn't have any ideas about anything, except that I was so close.

I hooked my hand around his hip, my fingers splaying from his lower back to the curve of the rest of his body. I pressed my fingers into his skin, my fingernails spurring him on.

"Harder," I begged.

His hips pushed forward, and I felt it all the way to my toes.

He slid the arm out from underneath my head and lifted himself up. He kept one knee between mine, and our hips fitted together. He used the leg I'd had around his hip to guide me onto my back. Then clutching my leg to his chest, he gave me exactly what I asked for.

His hips rolled into mine first, as I adjusted to the new position, then rocked forward harder. On his second thrust, I reached up and pressed my hand flat against the headboard.

His pace shifted from slow and steady to fast and hard and the bed creaked beneath us. I sucked in a breath, holding it as I drew closer and closer, and then I was falling all over again. Falling from that bridge. My heart in my throat. Falling for him. My heart in my hands. Falling apart. Falling together.

Falling into place.

It felt like hours before my heartbeat slowed, and I was strong enough to open my eyes.

When I did, my head was both clouded and clear. I couldn't have remembered fractions or the state capitols or maybe even my name. Those things had been locked behind a wall of bliss. But Jackson's face above mine? That was clear, as was the way just the sight of him made my heartbeat pick up again.

He lowered my leg to the outside of his hips, so that he was cradled between my thighs.

He leaned down and teased my tired lips with his own.

He said, "I could watch that a hundred more times. A thousand."

I scrunched my nose up, certain that I'd probably made some hideous face in the throes of the moment. He smoothed the lines on my forehead with his thumb and said, " I want to memorize the way your eyes clench shut and you bite down on your lip, so that I can sketch your expression from memory. I want to know the exact angle of the way your neck curves, and how many times your heart beats a minute. I want to know everything."

I swallowed, my heart speeding up when it should have been slowing down. There were things about myself that even *I* didn't want to know, let alone share them with him.

Changing the subject, I asked, "So you don't regret crossing that line?"

His mouth trailed across my jaw, and he hummed under his breath.

"I can still think of a few other lines I'd like to cross before the night is through."

He rolled, pulling me on top of him, our bodies still intimately connected. The friction teased my sensitive skin, and I had to steady myself with my hands on his chest.

He traced the curve of my body from my breast to my waist to my hip and said with a wicked grin, "You're adventurous, right?"

Now, this was the kind of adventure I was always on board for.

Hours stretched into days, and we only left the apartment in Riomaggiore when we had to. We got whatever food and supplies we needed, but we never lasted very long before our tastes turned away from food.

Our seventh day came and went, and neither of us made any move to leave or end our time together. And I began to understand the Via dell'Amore a little more, that chair and all those locks. I realized it wasn't the lock that mattered so much as the fact that it required a key.

Jackson had found every little sensitive nook that made my toes curl and my eyes roll back in my head. He knew what made me hold my breath and what made me cry out his name. He unlocked my body, and in doing so unlocked doors that held nothing but stale air and bad memories.

If I believed the stories I learned growing up, God made the world in six days and on the seventh day he rested. I wondered if, like me, the eighth day was when he watched it all begin to unravel.

23

woke, my breaths pushing from my lungs like broken glass. Jackson wasn't in bed beside me, and I curled into a ball, glad for his absence.

Pieces of my dream were slipping away, and I couldn't decide whether I wanted to try to hold on to them to examine or to push them away so I wouldn't have to.

I'd been twelve again, but in that way that dreams don't make sense, I was also twenty-two. Mom and Dad were arguing in the kitchen, and Mr. Ames, Dad's business partner, had come upstairs. He said he was looking for a bathroom, but there were two on the bottom floor. He touched my shoulder. He told me I was soft. And like those animated flip books I played with as a kid, the sheets of my dream began to fan, and it wasn't Mr. Ames's hand against me, but the boy I'd lost my virginity to just a year and a half later.

He trailed his fingers to my neck, and then down to my chest. The pages flipped. More hands, a different one on every page. Some looked familiar. Some didn't. But with each page, the hands swept across my body. The pages flipped and the locations began to change along with the hands—the back of a pickup truck, my freshman dorm, my apartment, a few hostels.

The scene shifted, and it was me and Mr. Ames in all those places, and I screamed and cried long after the dream had shifted on to a new person, a new place. And each hand carved away a part of me, sanded and chiseled until I was hollowed out, a wisp of a girl.

I pulled away, crying, and stumbled from a hostel bed to my parents' living room couch. This time I was just me, present day, but my parents looked down at me like I was still only four feet tall.

Dad was talking, saying I was blowing things out of proportion. He morphed into Mr. Ames for just as second as he said, "Quit playing the victim."

Mom asked me questions, asked me how Mr. Ames touched me and where. When I showed them, when I put my hand to my chest . . . I knew what was coming next. I knew the words like they were carved into my skin, like the pulse of my heart beat them out in Morse code.

I waited for them, cringed for them, begged for them because I needed to hear that *it didn't count.*

But instead, my world was filled with Hunt, with his all-seeing eyes, with his blistering touch, with his consuming kiss and the words, "Tell me this counts."

His hands, large and callused lay atop my chest where the heart beneath had been sanded down to a tiny thing. In my dream, he held my crumbling body, and he told me that it was okay. His touch was soft and perfect and exactly what I wanted, but I didn't stop crumbling in his arms, no matter how gentle he was.

That was when the lies I'd built so high that they scraped the sky shattered. Every brick I'd laid between me and that day when I was twelve crumbled as if they were made of something less than sand.

Because *it mattered*.

Who touches you, whether it's your skin or your soul, *matters*.

I sat, huddled alone in bed in that Italian apartment, shaking from a dream that I knew was nothing more than synapses firing in my brain, collecting recent thoughts and putting them together regardless of sense or order. I knew that's all it was, but things didn't always have to make sense to be true.

And I could feel every hand that ever touched me, the ones that I'd welcomed along with the one that I didn't, as if they were bearing down on me, pushing me below the current until I had no choice but to breathe in that shattered glass of truth.

It all counted.

Hunt walked through the door of our poisoned oasis, held up a bag, and said, "I've got breakfast."

It took everything in me not to cry. Because he was perfect. So *goddamn* perfect. And I was a mess.

"Thanks," I shrugged, the corners of my lips jumping briefly in a similar motion. "I'm not hungry, though."

He laid the bag, probably containing some kind of pastry on the bedside table, and toed off his shoes.

Lifting one knee up onto the bed, he smirked, before crawling toward me. "I can think of a few ways to work up your appetite."

He pushed my tangled hair to the other side of my neck, and lowered his mouth to my shoulder. I closed my eyes thinking he might be just the thing to clear away the cobwebs from all those newly opened doors.

Instead, his kiss was like a puncture wound, and I couldn't decide which part hurt worse—the beginning or the end, the knife going in or pulling out. His sweet kiss only made me think of all the other kisses I'd given away without a thought. It only made me think of how much I didn't deserve him. Or rather . . . he didn't deserve to get stuck with someone like me.

I moved away from him in the guise of facing him instead.

"How long have you been up?"

He settled back against the headboard. "A while."

"Couldn't sleep?"

I wished *I* had never gone to sleep.

"Something like that."

"More nightmares?"

He took hold of my waist, and pulled me back between his thighs. My back rested against his chest, and he tucked his chin over my shoulder.

"Enough about that. Any thoughts on how you'd like to spend the day, princess?"

The scruff on his jaw grazed my neck, and I shivered.

His hand smoothed up my thigh, and panicked, I said, "Let's go out."

He paused for a few seconds, and then wrapped his arms around me in a loose embrace.

"And do what?"

"I thought you were the one with all the plans."

"Yes, well." He pulled me close. "I'm easily distracted."

God, first I can't get him to make a move, and now he's full of them.

"What about swimming? There was that swimming hole that the lady at the restaurant mentioned."

"As if I could say no to you in a bathing suit."

I donned the same swimsuit I'd worn that night in Budapest. His eyes went dark when he saw me, and he grasped one of the ties hanging off my hip, tugging me forward.

Against my better judgment, I melted into him. His touch was an addiction, and addictions don't become any less desirable when they're joined with pain. He kissed me, and his lips were an introduction to light after a life of darkness. The brightness hurt, but not nearly as bad as the thought of a life wasted in the black.

I made myself step away before I fell into pieces at his feet. I peeled his hands off my hips and said, "Later."

Later, when I could get a grip. I just needed to shove all these emotions and memories into a box and pack them away into the back of my mind. Then things could go back to normal.

I saw his eyes drop to my lips, and I knew what he was considering, so I moved toward the door, putting several feet between us.

I said, "Absence makes the hard grow fonder."

I turned the doorknob, and he embraced me from behind.

"I don't think I could be any more fond of you."

We followed the lover's path once more toward Manarola. When we passed our lock at the mouth of the tunnel, he pulled me tight against his side and kissed my temple.

The easy path led us into the village within ten to fifteen minutes. Manarola sat perched on a rocky outcrop of land right on the coastline. It was even more colorful than Riomaggiore, and seemed to be more reliant on the sea than the first village. There were boats everywhere we turned, even if we weren't down by the water.

We had some of the best gelato of our trip so far at 5 Terre Gelateria e Creperia. Another couple there directed us toward a swimming hole down by the rocks. The village streets declined steeply as we approached the harbor, and the swimming hole that the couple had mentioned was a natural pool encircled by rocks. Judging by the dark blue color in the center, I'd say it went fairly deep, too. We could climb down onto the rocks ourselves or there were some ladders that led down to the ocean. But it was a warm summer day and the water was already crowded with tourists. I saw a pasty, middle-aged, white man in his forties strip down right there on the rocks to change from his clothes into his swimsuit.

Hunt pressed his face into my hair, laughing.

We knew there were more places to swim in the other villages, so we decided to pass on that particular swimming hole and keep exploring.

The path that led from Manarola to Corniglia, the third

village, couldn't have been more different from the lover's path. It was more of a true hike, winding upward away from the coast to the rocky hills. Eventually, the rocks gave way to green fields of lemon and olive trees, and grape vines and wildflowers. The smell of sea salt combined with the perfume of the flowers, and when Hunt caught me sniffing repeatedly at the air, he laughed.

I laughed too and shoved him. "What? It smells good."

He dropped a kiss on my shoulder and said, "You smell good."

Each time he said something like that, an ache formed in my chest. Not in my heart. Or my lungs. But in hollow places, in the gaps. Like a phantom limb, it ached in the places where I had lost a piece of myself along the way.

As we neared the village, we could see it set up above the rocks. As it turned out, there was a long flight of stairs at the end of the path that led up to the village. And based on our recent experience with the epic stairs in Heidelberg, I knew enough to know that getting up to the village was going to be a bitch.

I looked at Hunt.

"Don't even think about pretending to sprain your ankle again. I'm on to you."

I smiled. "I would never use the same con twice, sweetheart."

Desperate to avoid the stairs, I started looking for another option to get up to the village. Maybe a train or a funicular. Instead, I stumbled upon some hand-drawn signs on a rock that said, "Guvano Beach" with an arrow. The word *secret* was scrawled above Guvano, and I was sold.

"Jackson!" I yelled. He followed, and together we took off in the direction of the arrow.

But it quickly became clear that an arrow was not going to suffice, and we had no clue where to head next. We walked down to a nearby house and an old woman stood hunched and sweeping on the porch.

Hunt tried to talk to her, but she didn't speak English. I said, "Guvano."

Her expression changed, her mouth making a small "o" and she nodded. She gestured for us to go around behind the houses and then mimed pushing a button.

We stood there unsure, and she gestured us away with her broom.

"Um . . . okay."

Hunt took hold of my hand and together we walked behind a few houses down an ever-steepening slope until we found an old abandoned train tunnel. Another scrawled note said Guvano with an arrow through the tunnel. We found the button that the woman must have been referencing, and it said lights in both Italian and English above the button. Hunt pressed it, but nothing happened. He pressed again, still nothing.

"Let me try."

Pitch-black.

We found a breaker box, and flipped every switch. Nothing.

"Are we doing this?" I asked, eyeing the dark path of doom ahead of us.

I mean, I wanted a beach, the more private the better. And since it seemed we had to travel to hell and back to get to this one, I was willing to bet it was pretty private.

Hunt shrugged his backpack off one shoulder, and pulled it around in front of him. "Hold on." He rifled through his bag and came back with a cell phone.

"You have a cell phone with you? How did I not know you have a cell phone?"

He shrugged.

"I don't really use it. For emergencies only, you know."

I pulled mine out of my backpack and followed his lead. "Mine too."

We passed through the entryway. The cell phone lights were feeble in the vast darkness of the tunnel, and it did little more than light up our arms and give us a vague, shadowy view of our feet.

I grasped Jackson's elbow, and we shuffled slowly through the tunnel as it sloped downward. It was dank, and I could feel the grime settling on my feet as we walked, but I kept telling myself it would be worth it once we got to the beach.

We walked for a few minutes, and I kept expecting to see a light at the end, but there was nothing. The darkness stretched on forever and ever as we walked down and down, our footsteps echoing through the empty chamber around us.

When we were about ten minutes into the tunnel, a low rumbling began below my feet and then migrated to the walls. I heard the whisper of tiny pebbles falling and scattering to the ground. I looked at Hunt in horror, but it was too dark for me to see his face.

I clutched his waist and said, "Jackson. Train!"

The second word was drowned out by the roar of a train passing by. Not through. By. Still squeezing Hunt with all my might, I realized it was in the tunnel next to us. I breathed a sigh of relief that was swallowed by the noise of the train, and Jackson brushed a kiss across my forehead. I was too numb to react.

After that, we walked a little faster and within minutes we saw the light at the end of the tunnel.

We jogged the last one hundred yards or so, just ready to be back in the daylight. Here in this decrepit tunnel, I desperately missed the sweet air that I'd been enjoying earlier on our hike.

I tried not to think about how closely this resembled my earlier thoughts in the room. Thoughts about light and darkness. I was doing everything I could to *not* think about this morning and that stupid dream.

We emerged out into the sunlight, and it pierced our eyes at first. I squeezed my lids shut, and waited to adjust to the light. When I looked again, I saw a man waiting at the end of the tunnel, and we had to pay him five euro for the use of the passage.

Hunt was skeptical, but I rolled my eyes and pulled the money from my pack. I was reaching to hand him a few coins when a man about Jackson's age walked past completely nude, a lit cigarette dangling from his mouth.

My jaw went slack, and I dropped a euro. It went skipping down the rocks in the direction the naked man had gone.

I laughed hesitantly, and fished out another coin for the tunnel troll.

Hunt said, "Are you sure you want—"

"We're already here, aren't we?"

I gripped his hand and pulled him away from the tunnel down toward Guvano Beach. It wasn't a sand beach like I had pictured; instead, it was rocky like the rest of the villages, a small pebble slope that reclined into the water. There were less than ten other people on the beach, half of them completely naked.

We walked past a nude man and woman sun-bathing on a nearby rock and Jackson said, "Before you ask, no."

I pouted. "Aw . . . come on. Don't tell me you're self-conscious. *Believe me,* you have nothing to worry about."

"I was talking about you, actually. But no, I'm not doing it either."

"Me? Are you telling me what to do?"

I stepped away from him and pulled my sundress over my head. His eyes raked across my swimsuit-clad body. And he reached a hand out to the small of my waist. His thumb grazed the underside of my breast and he said, "I'm not sharing you with complete strangers."

I slipped off my sandals too and said, "Look around, Jackson. They could care less. Besides . . . this is an *adventure*."

My argument fell flat because he never took his narrowed eyes off of me.

I stepped out of his reach, and my hands went to the tie at my waist that kept the straps wrapping around my body in place.

His eyebrows pulled down into a warning glare. "Kelsey."

"Jackson." I smiled back.

This was good. This was what I needed, to live in the now and let go of the past. If I could cement myself in the present, all the craziness that had been drudged up could be washed away.

Slowly, I untied the knot at my hip. When I finished, the

strap unfolded, uncovering more of my stomach. I let it hang down behind me while I reached for the knot on my other hip. When this one was untied, I would be able to unwind the suit completely, baring much more than my stomach to the air and sunlight.

"Kelsey, you're not funny."

I pressed a hand to my heart, pretending to be wounded. Then I smiled, and pulled down the fabric over my chest just a little, just enough to tease him.

He gave me a heat-filled look. Whether that heat came from anger or something else, I wasn't sure. Nor did I care.

"What?" I shrugged. "Nobody likes tan lines."

I untied the second knot, and started unwrapping the fabric, but before I could reveal much more than my stomach, Hunt charged.

He threw me over his shoulders, stopping me from unwinding into nudity.

"Jackson Hunt! You can't just do this every time I do something you don't like."

"It's worked pretty well so far."

He started wading into the water with me on his shoulder. Two could play at this game.

I reached down for the waistband of his swim trunks, and tried to push them down over his hips. One of us was going to be naked one way or another.

I didn't get his trunks down but an inch before he tugged me over his shoulder and tossed me into the water.

The salty water went up my nose, and I rose out of the water coughing, and Hunt burst out laughing.

"Oh, you're going to be sorry, Hunt."

I pushed the soaking mane of hair back from my face and glared at him. I backed away, knowing I'd need space for my next maneuver. When the water was up to my ribs, and I was far enough away from him that I felt sure he couldn't get to me quickly, I grabbed my bathing suit top and tugged it over my head without unwrapping it the rest of the way.

The cool air hit me first, and I managed a small smile before Hunt reached me, and shoved me under the water, which seemed a little colder on this second dunk.

Thankfully, I kept my head above water.

"Jackson," I tried to stand, but his hands shoved my shoulders back down at the same time that a wave crested against my back.

The bathing suit slipped out of my hand, and when I tried to reach down and grab it back, I came back with only water.

"Uh-oh," I said.

"What does that mean? Are you okay? Did you get stung or cut yourself?"

I held off answering for a moment, hoping his fear for my safety would soften his reaction to the fact that I now had no way of covering myself up.

"This is your fault," I prefaced.

"Kelsey, just tell me what happened," he yelled.

"I might have lost my bathing suit."

His lips pulled into a thin, angry line.

I smiled." Adventure?"

He shook his head, and exhaled through his nose.

I swam backward a ways, and he followed. Then I lay back

and let my body float up, my chest rising above the water. "Adventure," I teased again. I waited for him to say something, but I seemed to have distracted him from his anger.

His eyes were glued to my chest, and I smiled in victory.

"You could join me, you know."

He was still almost fully clothed since he hadn't bothered to take off his shirt or shoes before dragging me into the water.

He looked tempted, so I added, "We could swim out a little farther." I pointed to an outcropping of rocks on the side of a cliff that was far enough away from the beach for us not to attract too much attention. "You could put your clothes there until we're ready to go back."

It was remarkably easy to get him to agree with me while I wasn't wearing a top.

Once we reached the rocks, I slipped off my bathing suit bottoms and the now ruined sandals that I'd been wearing when he tossed me in. He followed suit, shedding his shirt, shorts, and shoes.

Then we were naked and somewhat alone in a blue green ocean.

Treading water, we moved closer to each other, until our knees bumped.

"It's later," he said. "You *did* tell me later."

I swallowed. I could do this. It was a matter of will power. Of control. I *wanted* this.

He touched a strand of my wet hair, and I wrapped my arms around his neck. My wet breasts smashed into his chest, and he said, "All right, maybe I'm a little okay with nude beaches."

Shivers chased across my skin. I pressed my cheek to his, concentrating on breathing. His tongue tasted the salt on my shoulder, and I dug my fingernails into his back, not because of desire, but because of fear.

I wanted his touch to heal the hurt. I wanted to lose myself in his kiss, so that I could forget. But he didn't heal or eclipse, he illuminated. Every *single* second I spent with him was *perfect,* which somehow only seemed to excavate more pain.

I pulled his head away from my shoulder, needing a break. His eyes locked onto mine, deep and warm. I wasn't sure exactly what I saw in his gaze, but it felt too big to fathom, like explaining the unexplainable. Like seeing the light of a star and knowing that light is billions of years old. Like the way time slows near a black hole.

And as we stared, unnamed truths passing between us, Hunt's kicking feet weren't enough to keep us afloat. The water moved from my chest to my shoulders, from my shoulders to my neck.

And I thought drowning was the perfect word for the way he made me feel. Drowning after a life of drought.

He laughed and said something about deep water not really being the ideal place for the kind of exploring he wanted to do. I might have laughed. Sound was muted, like we'd slipped below the water, and I was still trapped there beneath the surface.

We slipped our clothes back on, and Hunt tried to make me take his shirt.

"I'll just have to take it off when we get up there. I'm not wearing your soaking wet shirt when I could put my sundress back on."

Reluctantly, he agreed.

He didn't put his shirt back on. And when we were close enough to shore that our feet could touch, I climbed onto Hunt's back, and he carried me out of the water, my bare chest hidden against his back.

He found a small, rocky alcove and he tried to block me from view as I changed, even though no one on the beach was even paying attention to us. Then together we headed back for the tunnel.

I stopped him and unzipped one of the pockets on his bag.

"Let me get your phone."

"Kelsey, wait—"

I'd already grabbed the phone and swiped my finger across the screen.

He had seventeen voice mail messages.

My brows furrowed, and I looked up at him. "I thought you said this phone was just for emergencies. Why haven't you listened to your voice mails?"

"Because they're not emergencies. I'm sure of it."

I asked, "Who are they from?"

"Nobody important. We should hurry through the tunnel. We've got to head back to Riomaggiore for the night."

I should have pushed. I should have dug my feet in and refused to move until he told me the truth. That's what I should have done.

I didn't.

I let him take the phone, and I followed him into that pitch-black tunnel without saying a word.

He kept my hand clasped loosely in his, and I began to consider what I really knew about him. Which was not a hell of a lot. And the more I thought about that, the more I was certain that he was hiding something from me, something that would break apart our already fragile relationship.

Still, I didn't ask. Not even in the tunnel where he couldn't see my face, and I couldn't see those eyes.

Because there was a part of me, small but not silent, that saw this as an escape. It was the same broken part of me that preferred the dark to the light. If I didn't know his secret, he never had to know mine.

24

We didn't sleep together that night. Not because either of us made an excuse, but just because. When our backs hit the mattress, both of us were so in our own worlds that the thought of closing the distance between us never occurred. At least not for me.

The room was pitch-black. The village was so untouched by society that they didn't even have street lamps. The occasional house would have a light out front, but not ours.

The darkness was filled with silence covered in stillness, and when I listened for Jackson's steady breathing, I couldn't hear it.

I wondered what kept him awake. Could he tell I'd been

off? Could he feel the way I recoiled when he kissed me? Or was it his own secrets that kept his brain moving, unable to rest.

I'd thought I was exploring the world, but maybe I'd been running. Maybe I'd been running for a very long time, and perhaps he was, too. And whatever he was running from—a girlfriend, family, a mistake—it wasn't giving him up easily.

The silence grew a heartbeat, and I listened to the rhythm to pass the time, until *finally* Hunt's slow breaths joined the symphony, and I could relax. I slipped off the bed, not to go anywhere, but just because I needed to be on my feet.

I shuffled slowly, my hands outstretched until I found the wall, then I sunk into it, pressed my cheek against it and tried to breathe.

You're overreacting.

The thought came automatically, like a song on repeat, and it nearly swept my feet out from under me.

Those words had been thrown at me too much, and I'd taken them up like armor, and I'd used them to close off all the ugly emotions inside of me. I guess I'd had to sacrifice some of the good ones, too. Because now that those were back, all the ugly ones were, too.

The effort of pretending all day today had worn on me like sandpaper, and my skin felt raw. There was a truth that I needed to face. It screamed from the back of my mind, and I didn't think I could survive listening to it.

I needed something to drown it out.

I didn't think as I fled that tiny apartment. I pulled on a pair of shorts and some sandals. I told myself that my nightgown top could pass for a blouse, and I descended the rickety stairs slowly, ignoring the impulse in my blood that told me to run. Far and fast.

Riomaggiore wasn't exactly the picture of nightlife, but I found a bar by looking for lights and listening for people,

It was filled with mostly tourists, and I took an empty seat at the front. I told the bartender to bring me anything, anything at all.

He started telling me about a special lemon liqueur called limoncello that was homemade from the lemons his family grew. I tuned him out and reached for the small glass he held, and tipped it back in one go.

I'd expected it to be sour, but it was bittersweet. It tasted like lemon drops with just a hint of Pledge, but I didn't care.

"Sip!" The bartender mimed sipping, like maybe I was misunderstanding his broken English. I understood it perfectly.

I held up a finger and said, "Another. Wait, no. Bring me the bottle."

His brows furrowed, and I said louder, "The whole bottle. All of it."

I laid a few of my largest bills on the counter, probably twice as much as the bottle was worth, but I didn't care. I took the neck of the bottle when he handed it over, and I tipped it straight back.

It burned, but not enough.

Alcohol was supposed to sterilize, right? Because I needed that. I needed to burn out the infection and numb my wounds.

A guy came up to talk to me, and I was so at a loss for what to do that I felt the tears collecting like rain at the back of my throat. In the end, I sent him away, even as I thought about following him.

I'd come here with every intention of losing myself the way I used to. I just wanted it to stop hurting, and it hadn't hurt so badly when I'd spent every night in a bar with a different guy. It had been a different kind of pain then. Hollow, almost. The pain of absence. Like missing someone you haven't seen in a long time. That, at least, was the kind of ache you could learn to live with.

This current pain was sharp. Unexpected. And I couldn't control it. Sometimes it happened when Jackson would touch me, but often it didn't even take that. Just a thought or a feeling or a memory could conjure it. And each time I felt like my lungs had been punctured and I was drowning without any water.

I took another swig from the bottle, and it was too damn sweet for a moment this sour.

The only thing I could think of was that this was the price of trying to be whole again. I'd turned myself off all those years ago, so that I wouldn't have to feel the things I'd lost. And unbeknownst to me, I was losing more of myself every single day. The universe wouldn't let me move on without feeling those things.

But maybe I could get stuck again. Maybe I could find my way back to that stagnant life where nothing ever changed, and things were never very bright, but they weren't too dark either.

I could find my way back there. *I could.* And it would be better when I did.

"Kelsey?"

No. No, please, no.

I took a bigger gulp, hoping it would transport me out of this moment. I was like a child wishing for Narnia in a coat closet, but I wasn't so naive to believe I would get what I wished for.

"Kelsey, what are you doing here?"

God, I didn't know how to answer. I didn't know whether to be cold and push him away or to fall into his arms. Either option would hurt, and that's what I was trying to avoid.

So, I stayed silent and took another drink.

"Hey," he snatched the bottle from my hand. "Look at me. You don't need that."

I pressed my cheek against the cracked, worn wood of the bar, and watered it with the steady leak at the corner of my eye.

I squeezed my eyes shut and mumbled, "Just leave me alone. Please. Leave me alone."

"Princess, what's the matter? What happened?"

"Nothing happened. I'm fine. Can't a girl get a drink?"

I reached for the limoncello, but he stepped between the bottle and me.

"Not like this. Not in the middle of the night, still wearing what you wore to bed." His fingers plucked at the lacy strap of my top, and he continued, "Not when you're clearly upset. I don't know what happened, but this isn't the answer. I've been there. I thought it was the solution, but it only amplified the problem. Come talk to me."

"I am the problem! Don't you get that? This is who I am. This is the only way I can survive."

"That's not true. You have so much more than this.

Whatever you're running from, it's just a thing, a memory. It can't dictate your life."

I pushed my hands up into my hair and squeezed, trying not to cry.

"It already did. And now it's not just one memory . . . it's a thousand. And I can't run. This isn't me running. This is me giving in."

I raised my hand and called the bartender. He started moving my way, but then Jackson pointed a finger at him and said, "No. Don't give her anything else."

Damn it. Now I was going to have to search for another bar because Hunt was sure as hell more intimidating than I could ever hope to be.

"I understand what you're doing, Jackson. And it's sweet, and I'm thankful, but it's not going to work. Let me save us both the time and the trouble."

We had only known each other a matter of weeks, and already the darkness had crept in. If we couldn't beat it at the beginning when everything was fresh and the emotions were the most intense, there was no hope for a future here.

He moved in close, gripping my jaw and drawing my eyes up to his. "I told you the night we met that I didn't care what you think you needed, and now is no exception. I'm not letting you do this."

He took hold of my elbow and started pulling me out of the bar.

I tugged my arm loose, and stumbled back a few feet.

"You can't just drag me along or throw me over your shoulder to get what you want, Jackson. Not this time. You'll only make it worse."

"Make what worse? Explain to me what's happening. What's changed?"

"Nothing." I pulled at the corner of my lips like puppet strings. "That's the point. I've been acting like I've changed. Like I'm the kind of person who can run away for an adventure with you or waste days in your bed. Like I'm the kind of person who can fall in love. I'm not. That part of me disappeared a long time ago."

I brushed past him and out into the night, wondering if there would even *be* another bar in a village like this.

"Is this because of what happened when you were younger?"

I froze, stiff as a stone. I could feel the tiny pebbles that had snuck between the bottom of my foot and my sandal. I could hear the scratching noise in my lungs from trying to inhale and hold my breath at the same time. I could sense Hunt at my back by following the waves of my panic like sonar. I turned. "How do you know about that?"

"You said something . . . the night you were drugged. No details, just that . . . you knew what it felt like to be taken advantage of. I didn't want to push you to talk about it if you weren't ready, but I've been picking up clues, and if that's why this is happening, you have to know it wasn't your fault. Whatever was done to you . . . it was outside your control."

"That's not why I can't do this. It's a part of it, yes. It's what came afterward, the part that *was* in my control."

That's what was killing me.

"Just tell me what you're thinking. Talk it through. Maybe that will help."

That was the last thing I wanted to do. The more I opened up, the more it hurt. That's how all of this shit started.

I turned and started walking, the slope of the village down toward the water making it impossible to do so slowly.

"I'm not letting you walk away from this," Jackson said behind me. "I've watched you let go and open up. I've watched your smile change from forced to brilliant. I won't watch you back peddle just because it's hard."

I turned, furious.

"Screw you. You don't get to belittle what I'm feeling and tell me I should suck it up. That's all I've ever done is ignore what hurts, and look at where it's fucking gotten me."

His hands cradled my jaw, his fingertips pressing just hard enough that it cut through the haze of alcohol.

"I'm not belittling how you feel. I would *never* do that. I'm just asking you to let me in. Let me feel it with you."

I tried to pull my face away, but he held strong. "You don't really want that."

"Try me."

Rage bubbled up in me. I couldn't tell what from or if it was for him or myself. All I knew was that I was overflowing with it. I pushed him away, his fingertips scrabbling at my cheeks.

"You want to hear it? Fine. It's a simple story really, about a pretty girl who was pretty stupid. She let a man touch her because she was scared to say no, and then she told her parents because she was scared to say nothing. Then they were scared to do anything that might ruin their pretty little lives, so they told the girl that it was nothing. That just being *touched* wasn't enough to fight for. Too scared to prove them wrong, she kept going like it *was* nothing, and she let more people touch her, never knowing that she was handing out pieces of herself. Or, hell, maybe she knew deep down, and she just hated herself so much that she was glad to be rid of them. And life wasn't pretty, but it also wasn't scary until she met a man with two names who touched her without taking and made her miss the pieces she had lost. And now things aren't just scary, they're fucking terrifying, and I can't do it. I can't live like this, knowing all that I've ruined and that it can't be fixed."

He caught my hands as they pulled through my hair, and pulled my body against his, and I felt all the holes in me. My sobs echoed through them like caverns, and I never would have thought *empty* could be made of such weight.

I couldn't breathe around it.

25

A tightness was forming in my neck, like it was clamped in a slowly tightening vise.

Crushing.

Constricting.

If I didn't get outside, I'd never be able to breathe. If I didn't get outside, it felt like I was going to turn inside out, that my body would just give way and my insides would pour out. Wait . . . I was outside. It was dark and the air was cool, but I still couldn't breathe. Why couldn't I breathe?

I had to hold on to Hunt to keep from stumbling backward and falling. Panic pooled in my body, lapping around my chin, threatening to pull me under any second now.

"Sit down."

Hunt's face appeared in front of me, blurry then clear, blurry then clear.

"Kelsey, just sit down."

Now that I thought about it, my legs *were* shaking. I didn't think I could walk long enough to find a place, so I just reached for the gravel road.

Instead, Hunt scooped me up and placed me on a bench. I looked around. We were in a boat. A boat of blue that someone had tied up outside their pastel green house. The details helped somehow, so I searched for more. Dark green shutters. Three floors. A mangy dog sleeping on the porch. A child's toys forgotten in a corner.

Hunt was there beside me, asking me questions. His mouth was moving forever before I was able to understand him.

"You're having a panic attack. Breathe. Just breathe. Close your eyes."

I did what he said, and all I could say was, "Sorry."

I was many things, but mostly I was sorry.

"Oh, princess. Don't be. You never have to be sorry with me."

I noticed my chest jumping before I noticed I was crying.

"You're okay." His voice was deep and calm, and he pulled me into him. It didn't make sense, but with my face buried in his shoulder, it was somehow easier to breathe.

"I don't know where to start. I'm not that good with words. I'm a visual person. I know what I see, and I know that you are not missing any pieces. Not any, sweetheart." My lungs ached, and my head spun. I held him tightly just waiting for it all to stop. "You're bruised and battered from dealing with things you should not have had to face, but you are not less because of that. You're more." His hands smoothed through my hair, gentle and soothing. "Your parents were wrong. What happened to you was *wrong*. And they should have fought for you. You were brave enough to tell them, and they failed you, and I'm *sorry*. And I'm sorry that you had to learn how to medicate your own pain, and it's not your fault that you had to do that. Someone should have been there to help you in another way. They weren't, and that's awful, but it's also over. And this time I'm here, and I'm telling you there are other ways."

I pulled back, wiping at my wet cheeks and said, "I thought that's what *you* would be. I thought being with you was helping—but, oh God, it hurts worse." I curled over onto my knees, as if making myself the smallest target possible would keep the pain from finding me. "Being with you made me realize what I'd been missing."

"Shouldn't that make you happy? That being with me feels good?"

"It does make me happy. When it doesn't make me sad. I don't know how to balance the two."

His hand slid up my back, and then he pulled me up, prying me open. His hand curved around my cheek, and his thumb brushed over my bottom lip. "Not how you tried tonight. That doesn't balance anything. It throws away the scale. I did the same thing once on leave. I went back to that life, tried to drink away what I saw in the sand. It made it easier to face when I was drunk, but twice as hard to see when I was sober."

"God, I'm terrible. Making this huge deal when you've seen so much worse."

"Stop." He pulled my face close. "Don't do that. Your parents may have made light of what happened to you, but there was nothing light about it. I signed up for the military. Mine was a choice."

"So how did you deal with it?"

He smiled. "Trial and error." His eyes dropped to my lips. "And I make sure there's always another option that I want more. Just stay with me. We'll beat it together, okay? Say you'll stay with me."

I swallowed, hoping that was enough. "Okay."

"Okay?"

"If you'll tell me one thing."

"Anything."

"The voice mails," I began, and he tensed immediately. "There's not . . . someone back home waiting for you is there? A girl?"

"Oh God. No, Kelsey. There's no one but you. I swear."

I nodded. "Okay." Anything else I could deal with.

He pulled me into his lap. And this time, at least, it didn't hurt.

We spent another few days in Cinque Terre, airing out our issues on hiking trails and ocean-side cliffs. There was no magic fix. I had trouble sleeping, and so did he. We reverted back to the way we'd been in Florence, finding sanctuary in simple touches only.

Jackson decided we needed a change of scenery to shake things up, so we went to Rome.

How crazy was that? Need something different, so hop on over to the home of arguably the most powerful ancient civilization. No big. For the first time, we acted like tourists, and I didn't even care.

It was easy to pretend in the daylight. We were both good at that.

We took a walking tour of the city, saw the Colosseum and the Roman Forum and the Theater of Marcellus. Rome was a city I'd studied extensively in my theatre-history class, so I became a walking *Wikipedia* page as I told him about how the Colosseum had worked and the other crazy things the Romans did for entertainment.

"Mock sea battles," I said. "They would actually fill up an entire arena with water, and watch two ships full of people battle until one sunk."

"Sounds awesome."

"Hell yes, it does. Except for, you know, the hundreds upon thousands of people who probably died."

"Right, of course," he said, laughing. "You know, you seem to really love this stuff."

"Rome? I don't think there's anyone in the world who doesn't love this stuff at least a little. Thank Russell Crowe."

"No, I mean, the history. You could be a teacher."

I raised an eyebrow. "Me? Um, I would probably cuss out a student on the first day."

I thought about that day in Budapest with my young artist. It had been exciting, helping him, but I'd also wanted to punch that bully in the solar plexus.

"No, you wouldn't. You would be great. And all your students would actually listen because you're gorgeous."

"Yes, that's what qualifies me for being a teacher. Having boobs."

He shrugged. "That would have been enough for me when I was in high school."

I shook my head and changed the subject. "I know you told me you don't have anything waiting for you back home. Does that mean you're still in the military?"

"Not anymore, no."

I touched his shoulder where I knew he had a thin scar, wondering if that had something to do with it.

"And you don't have anything to get back to?"

"I told you, Kelsey." He pressed his forehead against mine. "I'm all yours."

That night, he set out to prove it. Slowly, like we were starting all over from scratch.

He kissed me until there was no trace of pain in his touch, until I couldn't remember any other lips but his.

He found every little sensitive nook that made my toes curl and my eyes roll back in my head. He knew what made me hold my breath and what made me cry out his name.

He particularly enjoyed that discovery.

He explored my body like he was the very first one, and in many ways, it felt that way for me, too.

He held me close, his fingers wrapped up in my hair and our bodies connected. His breath tickled across my lips, and I thought . . . this is what it means to trust someone.

I didn't realize I was crying until he kissed away the tears.

I didn't realize a lot of things when I was caught up in him.

From Rome we headed to Naples, where I had three goals: pizza, Pompeii, and more pizza. And maybe to surreptitiously take pictures of Italian men in suits that I thought could be part of the Mafia. But that was an unofficial goal.

We boarded a regional train from Rome and found an empty compartment in the last car. There were three seats facing each other on each side of the compartment. Hunt took a seat by the window, and I sat in the middle and snuggled up against him.

"So, I was thinking we might go to Capri after Naples. It's not too far."

"Are there more nude beaches?" I asked.

He pinched my side, and I squealed, contorting my body away from him. He pulled me back to him laughing, and the train slowly pulled out of the station.

I said, "Fine. Then I'll have to go shopping for another swimsuit."

He shrugged. "I'm okay with that. As long as you model the options for me."

I said, "I think I can handle that," and launched myself into his lap, giggling.

He slid away from the window a little, so my knees could fit on either side of him. His eyes flicked to the compartment door, checking that the curtain was drawn.

"Now, this is by far the best way to travel."

I found that spot on his jaw that drove him crazy and concentrated my energy there. His hands gripped my hips, pulling me down against him.

"Kelsey."

I ground my hips against him, and his head dropped back against the seat with a groan. God, I would never get tired of doing this to him.

"Kelsey, how are you feeling?"

"Really?" I pressed my chest against his. "Do you actually have to ask that?"

He pulled my hands from his shoulders and pushed them down by my thighs. "I didn't mean that. I meant about the things we discussed in Cinque Terre. These days in Rome have been fun, but I need you to be honest with me and tell me where you're at."

"At the moment, I'm in your lap."

"I'm serious. There are some things I want to talk about, but I don't want to push you too fast."

That didn't sound even remotely like a way I wanted to pass this train ride.

I pulled his face forward and said, "Kiss now, talk later."

"Kelsey—"

"I don't know, Jackson. I don't know how I feel yet. I'm so used to pretending, to shoving it all away and pasting on a smile that sometimes I don't even realize I'm doing it. I'm trying, but I don't know."

His eyes searched mine for a few seconds, and I saw something flicker there that looked like pain, and I didn't want him to pity me any more than he already did.

So, I leaned down to kiss him again. He hesitated, and I pulled his bottom lip between my teeth. His hips lifted up into me, and his mouth seized mine.

"Irresistible," he breathed.

"So you keep telling me."

His hands ventured up from my hips to tease the skin just below the hem of my shirt. Then he stopped teasing and slid one hand up my spine to the clasp of my bra. My whole body seemed to bloom at his touch, like my heart expanded and my ribs had to unfold like petals to make room.

He broke our kiss and said again, "Kelsey."

"Jackson." I rocked against him again, and his body locked up, his grip so hard on me that it was almost painful. Almost. Really it just made me want him more.

"I didn't think I would feel this way."

"What way?" I asked.

"Like life is worth living again."

I pulled back so that I could look into his eyes, and that feeling, that attachment I'd felt to him was no longer a hook, but an anchor buried deep in my rib cage.

"I didn't believe you when you told me I would find another place to call home." I kissed him tenderly, trying to pour all my gratitude and affection and all the other unnamed things that I felt into my kiss. "This feels like home."

26

We subsisted on pizza, gelato, and coffee for two full days in Naples before taking a train out to the ancient city of Pompeii. I was so fascinated by the history there, and the way their lives were so perfectly preserved by the volcanic eruption that stopped this place in time. We wandered the ruins, looking at the frescoes and columns and homes that had been left behind.

There were stray dogs everywhere, and a small mutt with gorgeous blue eyes that I named Chachi followed us for almost the entire day. The ruins held not one, but two theaters. Yet, all that paled in comparison to seeing the plaster casts of the bodies. When the town had been buried, the people were buried along with it. And when the ancient city was rediscovered, the people had returned to dust, but the shapes of their bodies in their last moments were preserved in the volcanic rock. There were people with their hands over their mouths or trying to shelter another person. Some had barely even had time to protect themselves before they died.

And now they were frozen in time, stuck forever as an example of the tragedy that took place here.

I could identify with that. Despite being able to move and breathe and talk, I'd felt stuck for a long time, leaving a past I wanted to forget and headed toward a future I didn't want. Until Hunt.

He made me feel like I didn't have to keep heading in the same direction. I'd thought I needed this trip to give me a story, one that I could take with me through the rest of my miserable life for comfort or consolation. But he made me think I could have a bigger story, one that didn't end when this trip was over.

Maybe being a teacher wasn't such a bad idea after all. My father would scoff at the idea, and think I could do so much better. But history was filled with stories, some good and some bad, and I loved the way those stories made history about more than just dates and names and places. History was filled with people just like me, who just so happened to make a choice that impacted the way the time unfolded. I was so eager to leave my own mark on the world, but maybe I was meant to study the mark of others.

"What are you thinking about?" Hunt asked.

"History."

"Yours or the ancient kind?"

"Both."

He laid a hand across my shoulder and asked, "And what have you come up with?"

"Just that history matters. Mine, and yours, and the world's. The past is frozen. Written in stone. But the future isn't."

As we explored more history over the next few days, I thought a lot about the future. Jackson and I went scuba diving to look at another ancient city just off the coast of Naples that had sunk into the sea hundreds of years ago.

I watched him swimming past coral and fish and Roman statues that had been claimed by the sea, and knew that I wanted him to be a part of my life. But I didn't know how to tell him that.

Sure, we'd said things that implied what we meant to each other, hints at how we felt. But actually talking about the future and how the two of us fit together in it? That was uncharted territory.

Even at just a few weeks, this relationship felt more serious than any of the others I'd had in my life. I'd never felt this way. I was used to the kind of relationship where the guy was more interested than I was. I spent my time worrying about when the guy would say he loved me, and how that would ruin the delicate balance of our relationship. I'd never been on the other side, wanting to say those words, but terrified that I was just feeling caught up in the moment. Terrified that I was wrong or that he wouldn't say them back.

But I could feel our trip drawing to a close.

And I needed to know that I would see him again.

We took a boat to the island of Capri the next day. If ever there was a perfect place to broach the topic of a future between us, it was Capri. The crystal waters, high cliffs, and green landscape made the island look like paradise.

Indeed, it was so much of a paradise that it took us nearly an hour to find a place to stay.

Every place we found was already fully booked. Tired of lugging our packs around, we stopped at a small coffee place with an Internet café attached. Jackson searched for a place to stay while I caught up on my e-mail.

I sent a Facebook message to Bliss telling her about my adventures, but I left out any mention of Hunt. It wasn't that I didn't want her to know about him. With the way I felt, I wanted the whole world to know we were together. But . . . I didn't want to say anything until I knew for sure that this would last.

With a degree of unease, I opened my e-mail just to check and make sure there wasn't anything super important that I'd been neglecting.

As expected, I had over twenty unread messages from my father's secretary. I didn't have the patience to read them all. Except for the last one.

That one was from my father. Or at least my father's e-mail.

I hesitated. Then opened the message.

Kelsey,

Your mother and I are very disappointed that you've neglected to answer our e-mails during the last few weeks. We expected you home for the charity event, and you caused your mother and me both great embarrassments with your absence.

You might also think of your mother. It's not good for her to worry about you.

If you're going to waste your life and spend all my money, you could at least have the decency to let us know you're okay. If I don't hear from you, I'm hiring a private investigator, and he will bring you home.

Sincerely,

Richard N. Summers

That was my dad. Good ole Richard N. Summers. Gotta love being treated like an employee by your own father. I almost hit reply. I had so many things I wanted to say to him, "I'm alive, douche-bag" being just the first.

But I believed him when he said he'd hire a private investigator. We'd gotten in the habit of paying in cash because they hadn't really taken cards in Cinque Terre. I don't think I'd used my card since Florence. He'd have a hell of a time finding us. His patience had run out, and if I told him where I was now, the odds were he'd have someone here tomorrow to drag me home.

Or I could keep going, and maybe it would take him another week or two to find me. I'd stopped using my card to pay for things after that last e-mail in Prague. I only withdrew cash from an ATM when we were leaving a city and moving on. So, other than the occasional ATM transaction, he wouldn't have much to go on.

Tomorrow, I told myself. I'd take care of it tomorrow. I didn't want him dragging me home, but I was also tired of running. If I had learned anything on this trip, it was that running from something didn't mean it stopped chasing you. And I was tired of living life with all my problems nipping at my heels.

Today, I would talk to Hunt and find out where this was going. And then depending on how that went, I'd e-mail my father tomorrow. Either to tell him I was coming home . . . or to tell him something, anything that would let me hang on to this paradise a little longer.

"You ready?" Hunt asked over my shoulder. "What are you reading?"

I closed the window and logged off the computer.

"Just an e-mail from my father. Still trying to control me even with an entire ocean between us."

He frowned, and I linked my arm with his. "It's fine. I'm done letting him interfere with my life."

It took several long moments for his eyes to clear, but then he smiled at me.

I asked, "Did you find a place for us to stay?"

"I did. It's kind of a trek from here, so we should get whatever we need for our stay now so we don't have to come back to the city center unless we want to. But the good news is it's not far from a harbor where you and I have a reservation for a boat tour around the island."

"Sounds perfect."

We gathered our things, did a bit of shopping (including a new swimsuit for me), and found a taxi to take us to the bed-and-breakfast where we were staying.

I closed myself in the bathroom to change into my bathing suit, a simple black bikini top to go with the old black bottoms that I hadn't lost in Cinque Terre.

I looked in the mirror, trying to gather my courage. Instead, I marveled at the way I had changed in the last few weeks.

In that bathroom in Heidelberg, I'd looked in the mirror and been disgusted with myself. I had looked sad and small and pathetic and ragged. Now . . . I looked happy. I mean, sure, I was tired from all the traveling and lugging my backpack around. My brow was lined with sweat from the non-air-conditioned taxi that had brought us here. And I was wearing just a dash of mascara, and nothing more. I had definitely looked prettier. But happier? Never.

That was all the pep talk I needed.

I pulled on another sundress, opened the bathroom door, and located Jackson sitting on the bed. I took a running leap, and threw myself at him.

His reflexes were too fast for me to surprise him, so instead he caught me, and rolled me underneath him.

I laughed, and he looked at me with such tenderness in his eyes. He propped himself up on one elbow, and ran his fingers through my hair splayed across a pillow.

"Someone is happy," he said.

I nodded, and pulled him down for a kiss. I wrapped my legs around his waist, and he lowered himself down on top of me.

I hummed into his kiss and said, "It appears someone else is happy, too."

27

We were five minutes late for our boat reservation.

Totally worth it.

We rented a boat and hired a man named Gianni to captain it for us. Gianni was a plump, older man with a near-permanent frown and white eyebrows so bushy they looked more like a patch of whiskers. But even his grouchy, broken English couldn't ruin this moment.

Gianni set off in silence, leaving Hunt and me toward the back of the boat just to enjoy the ride.

We rode straight out of the harbor first, the small inlet filled with boats disappearing quickly behind us. Then when we were far enough out that we could only see a few boats like ours out on the water, he turned and began circling the island.

I leaned back against the seat cushions and placed my feet in Hunt's lap with a quick smile. His returned smile was devastatingly handsome. He glanced at an oblivious Gianni, and lifted up my foot, placing a sensuous kiss on the inside of my ankle the same way he'd done the night we first slept together. A shiver snaked down my spine, coiling low in my belly.

After a while, we settled into a comfortable silence. The boat's motor was too loud to allow for much conversation anyway. So, I leaned back against the cushions to watch the land rise and fall around us, and Hunt pulled out his notebook, scratching away at another sketch.

Once we'd seen a good portion of the island at a distance, Gianni brought us close to the land again, this time a section devoid of a harbor and seaside buildings. He began to slow. The water below us was a vivid turquoise, but as we came into shallower water, we could see straight through to the fish and coral that lined the ocean bottom.

There were numerous other boats ahead of us gathered around one outcropping of rock. Gianni slowed to a stop and lowered a tiny rowboat into the water off the edge of our larger boat.

Gesturing toward an opening in the rock, he said, "Grotta Azzurra."

I took a wild guess, and assumed that Azzurra was related to the word *azure*.

"Blue?" I asked.

"*Sì*, Blue Grotto."

He motioned for Hunt and me to climb down the ladder on the side of the boat, and into the canoe/small boat/thing-amajig. Jackson went first, and I followed, and then Gianni came down last. It was a seriously *small* boat. I was a little worried about how it was going to handle the three of us. But I wasn't going to argue with Gianni's very serious eyebrows.

He pointed toward the mouth of the cave again, and said, "Grotto."

I moved closer to Hunt to make a little room, and he pulled me into the V of his legs.

Gianni rowed us toward the grotto, where we waited in line as other small boats like ours entered and exited the cave. We had to duck our heads just to fit under the overhanging rock, but as soon as we got inside, I knew how it got its name.

The waters inside the dark cave glowed a florescent blue. At first, I thought it was just a reflection from the light coming from the mouth of the cave, but the light seemed to be shining up from underneath the water. I dipped a hand under the surface, and it too glowed blue.

"Wow." My voice echoed around the cave, bouncing back at us from craggy walls.

Then our surly guide began to sing, and my jaw dropped in shock.

His voice was low and rich as he sang a song in Italian, slow and mesmerizing. The sound echoed around us, filling the chamber, and making my breath catch in my throat.

Jackson's arm tightened around my waist and he rested his lips against my shoulder.

Too quickly, Gianni was maneuvering the boat around and we were heading back for the bright light of the opening. I wanted to slow time down, to freeze us in this moment for just a few seconds longer.

I turned my head and met Jackson's eyes. They looked almost blue in the cave, and my heart beat at a frenzied pace. Before I could change my mind, I said, "I'm falling for you."

His eyes searched mine, and I felt like I was falling still, waiting for him to answer. My ears rang like I was plunging toward the earth, and my eyes watered like the wind was flying directly into my face. And I waited. And waited. His expression, unreadable.

He opened his mouth, and my heart leapt in my chest.

Then Gianni said, "Duck."

Hunt's large hand cradled my head, and he pulled us both down as the boat glided underneath the rock. My heart was splintering, cracking and peeling every second he stayed silent.

But I shouldn't have worried.

The very second we were past the overhang, he pulled me up and pressed his lips to mine in the perfect, scorching kiss.

He didn't say anything. Just melted me with his mouth and pierced me with his eyes, and I supposed I would have to settle for that. He was an action-over-words kind of man, and I liked him that way.

After that, Gianni led us to a private inlet. He tied the boat to an outcrop of rock, gestured for us to jump out, and then pulled his hat down over his face for a nap.

Jackson and I took advantage of the privacy, and with the help of a not-too pointy rock face, we managed to achieve what hadn't been possible out in the deep water at Cinque Terre.

When we returned to our room that night, our skin was several shades darker, my hair smelled of salt, and we'd managed to get salt and sand in a few inconvenient places.

We both needed a good shower.

"You go first. It's going to take me forever to get everything out of my hair."

"I could help."

As appealing as that sounded, I knew where it would lead, and I was honestly too tired to even think about sex standing up, let alone perform it.

"Thanks, Casanova, but let's just get clean first. You can get me dirty again later."

"Looking forward to it already."

I laughed, and turned to throw my things at the foot of the bed. They hit the floor, and then an arm swooped around my waist, spinning and dipping me backward.

He kissed me slowly, the scruff on his chin tickling my skin. I was constantly amazed at how every kiss with him felt different, felt new. I hoped it would always feel that way.

He stood me up and gave me one more quick kiss.

He said, "I've not been this happy in a long time. Ever. Maybe."

"Me too."

He whistled as he retreated to the shower, and a smile burst open on my mouth, impossible to contain. I closed my eyes, and stretched out my arms like I'd just finished the only race that mattered.

God, he was perfect.

Well, except for the mess factor, but I could live with that. He'd dumped his things by the door, and I began moving them to the desk.

I could see his phone in the open outside pocket of his backpack, and in a small moment of curiosity and desperation, I picked it up.

I unlocked it. Not to search it, not really. Just to see.

My stomach sank.

Twenty-nine voice-mail messages.

Twenty-nine.

My finger hovered over the screen, and I wanted to listen. Just a quick check, just to make sure they were really nothing to worry about. I touched my finger to the screen, but then immediately pulled it back.

I wasn't going to be that way. Jackson had been so good about respecting my privacy as we got closer. He hadn't pushed even though it had been obvious from the very beginning that that went against his nature. He'd done so much for me, more than I could put into words.

I wouldn't betray him like that. I couldn't.

I returned the phone as I caught sight of his sketchbook. Somehow the impulse to know what he drew in there was even stronger than the one that wanted to listen to the phone calls.

I told myself I was just going to pick it up, but when I did, a few loose sheets of paper drifted to the floor. I scrabbled to pick them up. I picked up a few sheets, sliding them back into the book. When I turned the last one over, I froze.

For a few seconds, I thought it was the drawing that I'd gotten from that little boy in Budapest. It was the same fountain. I recognized the man at the top, proud and bare like he'd risen up right out of the sea. The same thoughtful women sat below him, their shoulders hunched, their bodies smoothly sculpted.

The drawing was different, though. Darker. Whereas the boy had drawn the world as he saw it, trying to capture the reality of the curves and the physicality of nature, this drawing seemed . . . sad. The shadows melted into each other, throwing the statues into sharp relief. This drawing gave words to the stone women, frozen forever in time, unable to do anything but exist. The boy had only begun to sketch me into the picture, so that I was almost a ghost, little more than a smile, blonde curls, and a flowing dress.

I was a ghost in this drawing, too. Not because I wasn't fully realized, but because I *was*. I sat on that bench, both stiff and somehow wilted at the same time, and I watched the world around me with longing buried beneath detachment, covered over with a paper-thin smile that was little more than a smudge on the page.

I looked to the bathroom, where Jackson was currently just on the other side of a door. Maybe I hadn't imagined him that day. There'd been a glimpse, just the briefest sight of a head that might have been his, but I'd written it off as wishful thinking.

But if he had this, if he drew this, he had to have been there.

I stopped worrying about getting the chair wet, and I stopped worrying about privacy as I took a seat to scan through the rest.

I'd thought I might find comfort in his sketches. He'd seen right through me with his sketch of Budapest. He'd seen that I was hurting when I was only just coming to terms with it. I wanted to see what he saw now. He was so confident that I could beat the darkness in me. Maybe he saw something I didn't.

I flipped open the sketchbook, full of hope and fear, wishing that somewhere in those pictures I would find my next foothold, a hand to pull me up.

Instead, they sent me tumbling over the edge.

28

"Your turn, sweetheart."

I couldn't look at him. I was barely holding it together, and I knew if I looked at him, I was going to fall to pieces. I just wanted to rewind time, take back a few more precious seconds of happiness. I would have cherished them more if I'd known they were coming to an end. But that's life, I guess. We're always a half a second late and one word short of what we really need.

"Kelsey? You okay?"

Jackson walked toward me. He reached out, skin to skin, and I moved so fast that my chair toppled over.

"Don't touch me. Don't you dare."

His expression crumpled like a discarded ball of paper, and it looked so authentic, so real that my heart jerked.

I threw my gaze up to the ceiling so that I wouldn't have to see, so that I wouldn't get fooled again.

"I don't understand," he said. "Did I do something?"

There weren't words for the horror I felt, so I grabbed the sketchbook off the seat of the stool next to me, and slapped the picture of the fountain in Budapest onto the bar.

"That was the day after we met."

I covered it with a second picture of me sleeping on the train from Budapest to Prague. My face was soft, angelic even, but still sad.

"A few days later."

"I—" He opened his mouth, maybe to make an excuse, but I cut him off with another sketch.

"And that's me in front of the monastery in Kiev. Now, I'm not great with time and dates, but that's roughly a month ago. *A month.*"

"Kelsey, I can—"

I slammed down another page, and I felt the force echo up through my elbow to my chest.

"And here's Bucharest. I'm not in this first one, but, oh, look, there I am." I laid a second and a third. "And I sure as hell don't remember seeing you at that club in Belgrade, but I guess you *were.* You captured the light perfectly on that one, by the way."

I went to lay down more sketches, angry and fighting with tears, but my hands shook. Like leaves, the papers drifted to the ground. Places I'd seen. Cities I'd visited. The last month of my life sketched out in black and white.

"Kelsey—"

"Just explain something to me, Hunt. Is it a game? Or are you a stalker? Are all those missed calls your parole officer? I called you a serial killer that first night or, well, the first night for me. I'd been kidding, but maybe I'd known something was off even then."

"I swear it wasn't like that, Kelsey. I know it looks bad, but it was never my intention to—"

"To what? Follow me across a continent? Worm your way into my life? Into my bed? God, but you were fucking patient, weren't you? If you'd slept with me that first night, I would have left and been on my way. But no . . . that wasn't enough."

He gripped my shoulders, and for the first time, fear coiled around my anger because I had no idea what he was capable of. Even now, I had no idea what he wanted from me.

"It's not a game. I meant every moment, and I can explain all of this if you'll just give me a chance."

A vibration buzzed on the desk, and I snatched Hunt's phone from where I'd set it down.

I held it up to him. "Or I could find out the truth for myself?"

He threw out a hand as I pressed answer, but I ducked, pulling back a few feet. I stood near the door of the bar and pressed the phone to my ear.

I saw Hunt's expression first—devastated and defeated. Then I heard a familiar voice through speaker.

"It's about damn time, Hunt. Tell me what the hell my daughter is doing or you're fired."

The phone slipped from my hand, and time seemed to

move into slow motion as it dropped. My heart fell at the same speed, long enough that it could have passed through galaxies before it hit the floor. The phone at least made a satisfying crack when it landed, but the crash of my heart was nothing more than a dull, hollow thud.

"Not just a stalker. A *paid* stalker."

I guess it wasn't me he wanted something from after all.

It's a quiet thing when your heart breaks. I thought it would be loud, louder even than the air rushing around us when we'd dove off that bridge. I thought it would drown everything else out.

But it happened like a whisper. A small, clean split. It broke in a second, and the pain was little more than a pinprick.

It's the echo that kills you. Like the echo inside the Grotta Azzurra, that tiny little sound kept bouncing around the cavern of my ribs, getting louder and louder. It multiplied until I heard a hundred hearts breaking, a thousand, more. All of them mine.

"Kelsey, just listen."

How could I listen? I couldn't hear anything over this pain.

Outside. Outside maybe the sound would have somewhere to go.

I grabbed my bag. It didn't have everything in it, but it had the most important things. It had what I needed to run.

I blew past him, and I didn't even look at his body, at the towel slung around his hips. I couldn't let myself. My mind was decades ahead of the rest of me. My body still remem-

bered the shape of his and that damn gravity still pulled and
pulled and pulled.

So I pulled back, and broke out into a run.

I thought I would make it farther, that maybe I could
make it down to the main road, and for once there might be
a taxi nearby without having to wait or call.

He overtook me before I'd even worked up a sweat. He'd
pulled on a pair of gym shorts and two unlaced tennis shoes.
He panted like he was running from the devil himself.

"Don't come near me."

"I never meant to hurt you, Kelsey. I love—"

"Don't say it. Don't you fucking say it."

"I didn't mean for this to happen."

I didn't know whether to cry or scream or collapse, and
my body shook with the force of everything pent up inside me.

I scoffed. "Yeah, I can see how you just did this all by accident. You accidentally followed me all over Europe, and accidentally got paid for it. Shit like that happens all the time."

"I was going to tell you."

"*I don't care.* It wouldn't have mattered. I *told you* about my
parents. I told you about everything."

"I know. *I know.* And I haven't talked to your father in
weeks. You saw the voice mails. I've not told him anything important."

I was moving to dart around him, but I stopped cold.

"When was the last time?"

He hesitated.

"Damn it, Hunt. When was the last time you played spy
for my father?"

"Prague."

Oh, God. I was going to be sick.

Prague was everything, the beginning of it all. We'd met before then, but I couldn't even remember half of that now. Prague was where he'd spun my cares away on that merry-go-round. Prague was where he convinced me that I could find another place that felt like home, or another person even. Prague was when I'd started *falling*.

Goddamn it.

He continued, "You used your card at the hotel in Florence, and he called then on the room phone."

I knew something had been strange about that phone call with the concierge. He'd lied to me.

"But Kelsey, I swear I didn't say anything. And I made sure we left the same day."

That was why we'd left and gone to Cinque Terre.

Even when I thought I was free, I wasn't. I was a bird with clipped wings.

When I thought I was having the adventure of a lifetime, I was a dog on a leash taking a stroll through the park.

And when I thought I was in love, it was a lie.

I'd wanted a story, and this was it.

And, boy, wouldn't it make a great one when I was old and unhappy and bitter.

It unfolded just like the rest of my life so far. A smile to my face, and a knife in my back. A hug in public, and a thinly veiled disdain at home. A pretty face and a rotten soul.

I was a fool to think my reflection had changed.

"I checked in when we got to Prague, while you were in the bathroom looking for Jenny. I still knew so little about you, and the night with the roofie had scared me. I didn't know what I was dealing with. But that was the last time. Once you and I started getting to know each other, I ignored his emails and his calls."

"Did you tell him I'd been roofied? Did he even blink a fucking eye?"

"I didn't tell him. I thought . . . I thought that would come better from you."

"Too bad. You missed your shot to see just how much my family can *suck*."

"I know you're angry, and you have every right to be. But please . . . just listen. Just let me explain."

"It doesn't matter what your explanation is. Don't you get that, Jackson?"

"No one's called me Jackson since before I joined the military. No one but you."

"That's supposed to make me feel better?"

"Jackson was the old me. The kid from a fucked-up family where money was more important than love and society more important than the individual."

"If you're trying to bond with me, it's too damn late."

"By age seventeen, I was having a glass of whiskey for breakfast. I had to be completely smashed just to get out of bed. I drank myself out of college. I hurt myself and my friends and everyone who cared about me. Even when I was trying not to, I hurt people. I guess I'm still doing that."

I felt the tears gathering in my throat, and I tried to will them down.

Quiet and cold, I said, "I guess you are."

"I joined the military mostly to piss off my father, not unlike your reasons for going on this trip."

I hated that he thought he knew me. And hated even more that he did.

"At first, I was miserable there, too. I got in trouble. I pissed people off. I pissed myself off. But then I got transferred to a new unit, and . . . they got me. Don't get me wrong, they called me out on my bullshit and beat me into place, but they understood and they helped. They were like family. My first real taste of what it was supposed to be like. I got sober. Slowly, and with a lot of missteps and failures. But I got there. And life started to look up. I started to believe that things could be better. That I could be better. You would have thought I was in paradise rather than Afghanistan for the way I felt. I couldn't have been happier. Then one day we were following intelligence and checking out an old meetinghouse that was supposed to have been abandoned. Only it wasn't. The thing blew with my unit inside. I was near a window, and managed to jump and avoid the brunt of the blast. But I separated my shoulder when I landed and had half a dozen bones broken by debris. In a flash, I lost everything I'd gained. I was medically discharged, and I spent the next six months going to five AA meetings a week just to keep from diving into a bottle of booze to forget that I'd ever known what it was like to be happy."

"Did you forget?" I asked, my jaw clenched. Part of me wanted to rub salt in his wound, and the other part wanted to know if there was hope.

"Not for a second."

"Good," I ground out.

"My father is the one who brought me the job. Your father wanted someone to keep an eye on you and make sure you didn't do anything stupid. Who better than a soldier to keep you safe? I said okay to get my dad off my back. I thought it would be an easy job. Good money, free traveling, and maybe the chance to take my mind off my problems. But then I watched you falling into my old patterns. I watched you heading down the same road, and I just wanted to save you from it. I wanted to keep you from going through what I went through."

"So you pitied me? Fantastic. Please keep talking. You're making me feel so much better."

"I didn't pity you. I hated you."

"Keep it coming, Casanova."

"I hated you because you made me face my past. But once I did that . . . once I acknowledged it, I started to notice the ways you were different from me. I meant what I said in Germany, Kelsey. You burn so brightly and beautifully. You light up a room when you walk into it. I watched people flock to you city after city, bar after bar. You just . . . even at your most miserable, you had more life in your pinky than I had in my whole body. And when I stopped hating you, I started wanting you. And then I didn't stand a chance. I tried to stay away, but I just . . . I couldn't."

He looked at me with such longing that my heart seemed to turn, like his eyes were a magnet, trying to pull it from my chest.

I believed him. There was too much pain in his voice and shame in his body to not believe that he hadn't meant for this to happen. But that didn't take my pain away or my shame at being fooled.

I waited to make sure he was done talking, and then I said, "Okay."

I turned to walk away and he yelled at my back, "Okay? That's it?"

"Yes, okay. I understand. Thank you for explaining. Goodbye Hunt."

"Don't go, Kelsey. Please. I'm sorry. I've never been more sorry. I was going to tell you everything as soon as I thought you were strong enough to handle it."

I stopped, but didn't turn around as I said, "Of course, I can handle it. It's nothing, really. Just another thing that wasn't real." I could feel myself falling back into that familiar pit, that place where I'd wasted so many years. "It was just another thing that doesn't count."

29

A month later, and I still couldn't run fast enough to get away.

I tried Greece.

The ruins reminded me of Rome.

The islands reminded me of Capri.

It all reminded me of Hunt.

So, I moved on.

Germany had too many castles.

Austria, too.

Every river bisecting a city sent me running.
Every playground played my heart, and I lost.

You don't realize how many bridges there are until the
sight of one collapses something inside of you.

I came close to giving up hope, to believing that I would never
find a place that could ever feel like home. I couldn't return
to the place I grew up. That house was a graveyard, a memorial to things lost and problems gained. And some part of me
ached in every new place, like old wounds that protested at
every shift in the weather.

But then I realized when no *place* felt like home, I had
one other option. In Madrid, I found a quiet spot in my
hostel, which translated to a maintenance closet full of
cleaning supplies that itself probably hadn't been cleaned
in decades.

I settled my laptop on my knees, and Bliss answered my
Skype call in seconds with a banshee scream.

"Oh my God. Never wait that long to call me again. My
crazy has reached embarrassingly new heights in your absence."

My voice choked over the words, "You? Crazier than you
were? Impossible."

"Kelsey? Are you there? It sounds like you're breaking up."

Breaking apart was more like it.

I pressed my fist against my lips, hard. Bones pushed
against teeth, both as strong as I wanted to be.

"I'm here," I said. "Can you hear me now?"

"Now I can. Loud and clear, love."

"Oh, honey. Stop talking like your boyfriend. It's just creepy without the accent."

"Jetting around the world made you judgmental."

"All that sex you're having must have damaged your brain because I've always been judgmental."

Bliss laughed and then sighed on the other line, and I wondered if I would have sounded like that if I'd ever gotten around to telling her about Jackson before all this.

"Oh my God, Kels. I can't even. I think I might actually be addicted to him."

I made a sound that fell somewhere between a laugh and a groan because I *knew* what that felt like. And withdrawals were a bitch.

"Just enjoy it," I said. *While it lasts.*

"What's the matter?" Bliss asked.

"What do you mean?"

I thought I'd been hiding it well. God, was I such a mess that it just seeped out of me and across international phone connections?

"You've got that sound," she said. "Your acting voice."

"I don't *have* an acting voice."

"Oh, honey. You do. You know . . . it's that thing where your voice gets deeper, and you suddenly have very good enunciation. You get louder too, projecting like having a deafening volume makes you more believable. It's an actor tick. We all have one. Now fess up and tell me what's wrong."

I thumped my head back against the wall and sighed. "Everything. It's *all* wrong."

"Well . . . start at the beginning. Tell me what went wrong first."

That much was easy. *"Me."*

Telling Bliss about my childhood was both shockingly easy and incredibly difficult.

Over the years, I'd learned how to twist the truth about my past, so that I could participate when friends told childhood stories without giving up my secrets. Like any other role I played, I took liberties. I painted a picture of the cool, rebellious girl with an appetite for adventure. Now I had to break that illusion to reveal the real girl, not cool or rebellious . . . just lost.

And though it was a hard story to start, it was easy to keep going. I told her about Mr. Ames and my parents. And I told her about how I'd learned to cope and that that only ruined me more in the end.

I told her everything.

Except for Hunt.

I opened my mouth to say something, but the words just wouldn't come. I didn't know how to talk about him without disintegrating into despair. I couldn't explain what he'd done to me without explaining how different he'd been, how different I'd been *with him*. I wasn't a relationship kind of girl. And maybe Hunt and I hadn't had a real relationship, but it was the realest thing I'd ever had. Which only served to make me realize even more how twisted I'd let myself get. If I tried to talk about him . . . I'm not sure what would happen, but the clenching in my stomach told me that I was scared. Scared of falling for him all over again in my mind, only to have to relive hitting bottom.

I kept quiet. Maybe I was ashamed of being fooled. I hoped that was it.

But an inkling in the back of my mind told me that there was something else. Despite being hurt and furious, I didn't want Bliss to think badly of him.

Man, how fucking crazy was that?

I should tear him to pieces, rake him over the coals, and let Bliss join in. That's what I *should* have done.

Bliss said, "You know what you need to do, don't you Kelsey?"

"Try to outrun my troubles through a dozen different countries?"

It hadn't been working so far, but maybe twelve was the magic number.

"I think you know how well that's been working."

It's one thing to know something for yourself. It's worse when everyone else knows it, too.

"Abysmally. What's your point?"

"You've got to face your parents."

"No. No, Bliss." The laptop suddenly burned too hot against my legs, and the closet felt too small. "I can't. I can't go back there. Not now. Things are . . . complicated."

I didn't know who I was more angry with . . . Hunt or my father. But I couldn't stomach the thought of seeing either of them.

"You don't have to go back. But you spent too long accepting their lies as truth. You need to tell them how wrong they were."

My heart was beating too fast. I hated that I was so scared of this.

"It won't change anything. You don't know my parents."

"You're not doing it to change *them*."

Damn it. *Goddamn it.* When the fuck did Bliss's ramblings start making so much sense?

"I'll think about it," I said.

"Kelsey, you have to. You can't hide from it anymore."

I banged my head against the wall behind me a few more times, furious that she was so right.

"Fine. I guess I don't have anything to lose anyway. At the very least, it will feel *really* good to tell them off."

"You don't have *anything* to lose?"

"Not really. I, uh, went a little crazy a few weeks back. Might have given my credit card to a stranger and told him to have at it."

"Oh my God, Kels. Your dad is going to go ballistic."

Good. At least then, we could both be pissed.

"I'm sure Dad had the account frozen in no time."

"But what are you doing for money? Where are you staying?"

"Chillax, babe. I'm fine. Don't worry about me. I got a decent chunk of change before ditching all daddy-related items. And my Eurail pass is good through the end of the month."

Don't ask me what I was doing at the end of the month. No. Fucking. Clue.

"Then what?" She just *had* to ask. "How will you get home?"

I'd really grown to despise that word, but for a language as vast and repetitive as English, I'd yet to find a synonym that held the same immeasurable meaning.

"I'm staying here, Bliss. At least for now. I've been looking for jobs—"

290

"You don't have to do that. Let me talk to Garrick. Between the two of us, we could probably manage to cover a decent portion of your ticket."

"I can't—"

"You can stay with us here in Philly for as long as you need. Our apartment is small, but we have a couch that folds out into a bed. It might smell a little mothy. We got it from a used furniture place, but it—"

"Thank you, but no." I could almost picture her jaw snapping shut to form a frown. "Money isn't why I'm staying. You were right. There are some things I need to work out, including talking to my parents. Until I do, it won't matter where I go. My issues will follow. Spain seems like as good a place as any to put my life back together. All matadors and bulls and red capes. Should be good inspiration to face things head-on."

I sounded twice as confident as I actually felt. I wondered if I would ever be able to stop pretending. This was how it started last time. First, you pretend for others, then you pretend for yourself. Then you pretend because everything is a lie, and you have to keep the cycle going.

Bliss said, "Speaking of matadors . . . any dangerously sexy Spanish men I should know about?"

"I'm taking a break from that, too."

I couldn't even think about sex right now. It just . . . it wasn't what it used to be for me, like a word with a new definition.

Silence took up the other end of the phone.

"I think that's smart, Kels. You're going to get through this. You're bold and brave and strong. You'll be fine."

"You're obligated as my best friend to say things like that."

"It's the truth. The only reason I'm as happy as I am now is because one night in a bar, I borrowed your bravery. Have I ever thanked you for that, by the way?"

"You have, and you're welcome. But I'm not nearly as brave as I pretend to be."

"Bull-massive-shit. Do you realize how much courage you had to have to tell me about all this? It took me until senior year to even admit to you that I was a virgin."

I gave an almost laugh. "Oh, those were the days."

"Feel free to relive my moments of awkwardness if it cheers you up."

I smiled, small but real. "Thanks for the pep talk. And for listening."

"Of course. I love you."

"Like family," I answered. The only one that mattered to me now.

"Call me again soon!"

"I will. Bye, Bliss."

Hunt was many things, many of them not good. But in this what instance, he'd been dead right.

Because even as the cold concrete floor kissed my skin, and the stringent smell of cleaner dulled my senses, I excavated a full smile. It had been brief—like a too-short touch—but I had felt it.

Just a whisper of home.

30

After months of wandering and wanting with no direction, it was good to finally have a tangible thing at which to direct my energies.

A job. Money. A place to stay.

I could handle that.

As it turned out, there was a high demand in Madrid for English-speakers to teach or assist in classrooms in bilingual programs. I'd never been a teacher, but I had a degree. And Hunt's mention of the career had stuck with me. After growing up in Texas, I had enough basic Spanish skills to get around. When I saw the ad in an English-language newspaper in my hostel, and it said no teaching experience was necessary, I knew it was perfect. Like when you find the perfect dress that somehow makes you feel *better* for having slipped it on.

I applied for a work visa and contacted the Ministry of Education. By the end of the month, I had a job as a Language and Culture Assistant. Well . . . two jobs, technically: one working part-time with teenagers and the other working with younger kids. Plus about four private lessons a week to help make ends meet.

New Life Realization #1:

Being an adult is hard work. I know people tell you this growing up, but it doesn't really sink in until you're *living* it, waist deep in the swamps of no-free-time and not-enough-money.

New Life Realization #2:

It's worth it.

It was a new kind of satisfaction, being on my own and being okay. More than okay, I was *good*.

I had a job. Okay, lots of them. I had an apartment, too. And I'd sent a letter to my parents.

I'd poured out every bitter hurt and vulnerable thought I'd ever suppressed and sealed a slice of my heart inside an envelope. It wasn't the bravest way to face them, but the words were brave, and that was enough for now.

Predictably, I didn't hear back. I hadn't expected to either. Answering would acknowledge that there was a problem, and they much preferred to pretend those didn't exist. Even now they were probably telling some atrocious lie about why I wasn't around.

I was surprised by how little that bothered me. I wondered if everyone experienced a moment like this—a moment where you realize you've outgrown your own parents. Not just because I didn't need them anymore, but because I'd finally realized that they were as stuck as I had been. I saw them with a kind of clarity that it's impossible to see when you're a kid, and when you're parents are the end all and be all of your life.

A reply did come eventually, but not from my parents.

"Carlos? What is this?"

Carlos was nine, and had the biggest attitude in class by far. That's probably why I adored him.

"My homework, Miss Summers."

"Not that, I mean this." I held up the sealed envelope he'd turned in with his work.

He smiled, a heartbreaker smirk in the making. "That's for you, Miss."

"And what is it?"

He shrugged in that way that kids do when they don't know or care about the answer.

"Where did you get it?"

"A man."

"What man?"

"I don't know. *Americano.*"

Señora Alvez, the lead teacher, shushed him. "English only, Carlos."

I didn't ask any more questions because I didn't want to get him in trouble. But when Señora Alvez began her lesson, I slipped my finger under the lip of the envelope and pried it open as quietly as possible.

I'd never really seen Hunt's handwriting, but I recognized it anyway. It just . . . looked like him. Strong. Meticulous. Aggravating.

I couldn't read the words. I wouldn't. But I counted one, two, three pages, and a sketch. The playground. The one from Prague.

My heart seized up, ice cold, frost spreading over the prison of my rib cage and piercing my lungs. My hands trembling, I shoved the papers back in the envelope and stood. Señora Alvez stared at me, and my blood roared in my ears.

"I have to—I need to—" God. All I wanted to do was scream obscenities, but I was in a classroom full of children. "I have to go."

I didn't give an explanation as I bolted for the door. Let them think I was sick. Because I was. To my very bones.

I signed out in the office, this time lying about not feeling well. Then I left for home. I had the strangest instinct to run as I walked the blocks to my apartment. I wasn't ready for this. I'd pieced together the other parts of my life, but this . . . this was still so raw. And the body's instinct when wounded was to jerk away when touched, to run to prevent more injury.

Running wouldn't have done any good, though, because there was another letter waiting at my apartment. I picked it up from where it had been dropped outside my door. I didn't know whether to crush it or tear it or hold it tight.

I settled for ignoring it.

But they kept coming. There was another slid under the classroom door when I arrived on Wednesday morning. They came through the mail. My landlord brought me another.

I threw them on my desk unopened, but every time I entered my apartment, they called to me.

A week after the first letter appeared, I came home from work to find the tenth letter on my doorstep. Rather than adding it to a pile, I fished a marker out of my purse. (My God, I kept markers in my purse. I was such a *teacher*.)

Across the back I wrote, "Still following me? Still not okay."

Then I left it on my porch where he would presumably find it the next day.

The next letter came from Carlos. He dropped it off at my desk the one day without the pretext of homework this time.

"The American man said to read them, and he'll stop following you."

"Carlos, I don't want you to talk to that man again, okay? If he comes up to you, just walk away. Don't take any more letters from him."

I thought maybe that had worked, that he'd finally taken the hint because I didn't see another letter for a week.

I was relieved for the first day or two. But then I started to look for them. I started to wonder why they were missing, why he'd stopped now. And more than anything . . . I wondered what they said.

But I couldn't read them. I *wanted* to stay mad. It was safer to stay mad. But considering the way the absence of the letters made me feel, there was no way I could actually read their contents and stay strong.

The following week, though, I realized he hadn't stopped

writing the letters—he'd just been waiting. I walked through the school courtyard on Monday, and saw a group of my kids gathered outside the doors, Carlos in the middle.

He was handing something out, and when I got closer, they all switched to whispers and not-so-subtly stared at me as I passed. When the students took their seats that morning, every desk in the room had an envelope, all for me.

I was angry and relieved, and a giant mess of wants.

I trekked home that day with my arms full of envelopes and a head full of frustration.

I thought about doing something to prove a point. I could throw all the letters out where he would find them. I could burn them. I could tear them up.

Or I could open them.

Maybe if I showed that I had opened them, he would stop.

So, I plucked one out of the pile, my skin suddenly buzzing. I tried to swallow, but something knotted in my throat.

It's just a letter. Just words. Probably words that you've already heard.

The shaking spread from my fingers to the rest of my body as I tore open the letter.

A sketch tumbled out first.

Even without having been there, I knew it was Venice. There was a gondola passing by a home that seemed to sit directly on the water. There were balconies with roses, and it looked so impossible and beautiful that I felt myself tearing up.

The letter with this one was short.

I can't go anywhere beautiful without thinking of you. Hell, who am I kidding, I can't go anywhere period without thinking of you. I wanted to take you here. I know there's no excuse for what I did. I could explain the ways I reasoned with myself. I could explain that I needed the money, the job. I could explain that I waited because I was worried about you. But the real truth is that I just didn't want it to end. I knew you'd leave when you found out. And I just kept telling myself . . . one more day. But if there's anything I learned with you, it's that one more day was never enough.

I sunk down to the floor at the edge of my bed, a noise pulling from my chest that I couldn't even put a word to. It wasn't crying. It was something deeper. It unraveled from my lungs, low and keening and hollow. If I had to guess . . . I'd say it was what it sounds like to miss someone. To feel their absence like a second skin.

I picked up another letter.

This time, the sketch wasn't of a beautiful sight or a grand city. It was four men in military fatigues. Their faces were detailed, realistic, alive. So either he sketched them from a picture or they were burned into his memory.

I remembered what he'd told me about his unit, and how he'd lost them, and I gave up trying to wipe away the tears that rolled down my cheeks.

I'm sorry I didn't tell you more about me. That I didn't open up. It's just . . . I thought I lost all the parts of me that meant something when I lost these guys. They were family. That's why I liked to jump off bridges and climb cliffs and do whatever other crazy stunt that could make me feel something. But even that had stopped working . . . until I met you. You made me feel more with a look than I felt jumping out of a plane. I felt more adrenaline from your touch than when I was moving into enemy territory or taking fire. I know how crazy I sound. I know how crazy this all is. And I'm probably doing it all wrong. But my only excuse is that I'm crazy about you. And life is not living unless I'm with you. You're my adventure. The only one I want to have. So, if this doesn't work, I'll try something else. If the military taught me anything, it was to be persistent. To weather the storms. So, that's what I'll do.

I opened every letter.

My bedroom was a sea of paper, words with the depth of an ocean and sketches with all the power of the tide. When I had read them all, when the words had filled the empty spaces he'd left behind, I wrote a letter of my own and put it outside my door.

31

sat on the swing, my heart hurdling back and forth even though I was still. What if he didn't come? The letter disappeared while I was at work, so unless there was a mail thief in the neighborhood, he'd gotten it.

I'd given him directions to get here, but what if they weren't good enough? Or what if I'd waited too long?

I squeezed the chain links of the swing until they imprinted on my palms. I ducked my head, and closed my eyes, trying to stay calm. This situation was mine to control. Nothing had to happen unless I said so. This was my choice.

"I'm glad you gave me directions. I'm afraid the picture wasn't very . . . ah, informative."

My head popped up, and Hunt was there, his tall frame blocking out the sun and casting me in shadow. It took a few long moments for me to focus, for me to do anything other than stare at him.

It sounds cliché, but I'd forgotten how gorgeous he was. I'd forgotten the way that smile was magnetic enough to pull the sun across the sky.

He was holding one of the pages from my letter, my attempt to sketch the playground where I'd set for us to meet.

I shrugged, the weight on my shoulders almost too heavy to lift.

"I'm not an artist," I said. "Stick figures and squiggles were about the best I could do."

His smiled widened, and his eyes skipped across my face like he couldn't quite believe I was there.

"I like the stick figures. I'm guessing the tall one is me?"

God, he couldn't even tell which one was the girl. How embarrassing.

I didn't know what to say. I'd called this meeting. I should be the one to say something, the one to take control. But when I looked at him, my mind was full with all the things that had happened and all the things that hadn't. And he looked at me like a man that had been starved. Of food and light and attention and everything.

"Have you been here before?" he asked.

I cleared my throat. "Not the playground, but I come to the park sometimes. It's nice. Relaxing."

Silence settled again, loud and uncomfortable.

I said, "I read your letters," at the same time that he said, "I'm sorry."

"You did?" he said. "I'm sorry if I went overboard. In my defense, the whole classroom thing was Carlos's idea."

Of course. Carlos wasn't just a messenger. My favorite student was a co-conspirator.

"No." I cleared my throat again. My mouth was dry, and words kept tangling on my tongue. "The letters were . . . good. I mean, excessive, yes. But they were good."

His hands were shoved into his pockets, and I could see the way his firsts were clenched tight beneath the fabric.

"You hurt me," I said.

His expression contorted, pain and shame written in his features.

"I know." His voice was thick, deep. "The biggest mistake I've ever made. And I've made a lot."

I didn't know what the right answer was here. I didn't know what I was supposed to do.

My heart and every romantic comedy ever made told me I was supposed to leap into his arms and forget it all ever happened.

My head told me to run. To close myself off. To never let him close, never let anyone close.

And me . . . the me that was neither my head, nor my heart, but something else . . . it told me that there was no right answer. Forgiving him would be hard and painful, but so would living without him. I didn't know if I could ever trust him again. But I knew I wanted to.

I wanted to be able to leap into his arms, and believe that he would catch me. I wanted the confidence I'd had when we toppled over the side of that bridge in Prague.

I said, "What I felt for you"—he stood up straighter, and I watched his mouth purse and straighten, riddled with tension—"it's never been like that. Not with anyone. But you have to understand, my whole life was built on lies. And I'd felt that way for you because you were the one thing that felt true. *Real*."

I didn't know how to make it work, how to make it hurt less. All I knew was that I was done living out of fear. Afraid of everything. Of growing up and growing old. Of living and of love.

I was happy here in Madrid. It was a different kind of happy than what I'd been with Hunt, less incendiary, but it was stable. It didn't burn me up, but it filled some of the empty spaces.

I looked into his gray eyes. I could forget a hundred things looking into his eyes, but could I forget this? He must have seen my walls weakening, because slowly, he approached me. He knelt before me on the swing, and ever so slowly, his hand touched my cheek.

"Every day. I will prove *every day* how much you mean to me. How real this is. You told me once that history matters, but it's frozen, set in stone. This is part of our history. I can't change it or undo it. But it doesn't have to dictate our future."

Our future.

Those two simple words hooked into my heart, and it felt almost like we'd never been apart. Like I'd just been sleeping.

I'd known I wanted to see him when I came here today,

and I had thought about the possibility of us being together, but I hadn't honestly known if I could handle it.

But now, I was making the decision. I *could*.

Because every time, every single time, I would choose *our* future over *my* future. Because in my wildest imagination, I couldn't imagine how the best future without him could even compare to the worst future with him. Because even though the life I'd made here in Madrid filled the empty spaces, I didn't *burn* without him. Of all the things I'd wanted in life—the places I wanted to see and the things I want to accomplish—the thing I'd always wanted most was to be the kind of person that *burned*.

I leaned into his hand, and said, "Jackson?"

His breaths were shallow, and I could imagine the way his heart was beating. As fast as mine, I guessed.

"Yes?"

"Do I have another dare left?"

His lips pulled into a smile, the faintest dimple showing in one cheek.

"You can have as many dares as you want."

"Good. I dare you to kiss—"

I didn't even finish the sentence before his mouth was on mine. He stood bent over me, his hands cradling my face, and he worshiped my lips like it was the first time we'd touched in a thousand years.

His tongue swept across my lip, and my belly tightened just at the memory of how he tasted. His lips pushed harder, and on the second sweep of his tongue, I opened to him. Our tongues touched, and he groaned, his fingers pushing back into my hair.

I shivered, and released the death grip I had on the swing to reach for him. With him standing and me sitting, I couldn't wrap my arms around him the way I wanted. Before I could order my legs to stand, he took hold of the swing chains, and pushed me back and up, like he was about to set me swinging. Instead, he pushed me just high enough that my mouth was level with his and nudged my knees apart to settle between them.

It was my turn to moan into his mouth, as his body was brought in line with mine. His hands slid from the chains to my back, and he tugged until my chest smashed against his. I wrapped my arms around him, and the familiar feel of his muscles beneath my fingertips made me ache with want.

"God, I've missed you," he murmured against my lips.

Missed didn't even begin to describe the feeling that simmered through my bloodstream. With his lips on mine, and his hips pressing intimately against my center, I couldn't even understand how I'd lasted as long as I had.

He leaned harder into me, pushing back against the swing. His hardness pressed against the zipper of my jeans, and I saw stars just from the friction.

I whimpered. "Maybe we should move this off the playground."

"No one's around."

I'd have to take his word for it because his lips didn't leave mine long enough to look around. His tongue curled around mine, and I was shaking against him. My hands, my arms, my legs—all of them trembling and weak with desire. I wound my hands together at his neck, afraid I wouldn't be able to keep them up if I didn't.

He pulled back to release a breath, and I tasted him on the air. He kissed me again, softly, teasing and nipping at my swollen lips. He hummed, and I felt the vibrations slink their way beneath my skin. His hands sank into my hair, like fingers sinking into the sand, into my soul. He rested his forehead against mine, and gave a chagrined smile.

"Okay, so there might be people around. But in my defense, I was too preoccupied to really see them."

I probably should have been embarrassed. But in truth, I didn't even care enough to look around and find the, no doubt, scandalized family who'd witnessed our reunion.

Gradually, he backed away until my swing lowered back into place. My legs were still shaking when I stood in front of him. Immediately, he reached out to touch me again, his hand curling around my neck and tilting my head back.

His gaze tore through me just like the first night we'd met. I wanted nothing more than to take him back to my apartment and continue our reunion.

I said, "Let's go home."

He kissed me again with the same detail, the same intricacy I saw in his sketches. Fire raged everywhere our skin met, and he said, "I'm already there."

ACKNOWLEDGMENTS

Wow. The release of this book coincides almost exactly with the day I published *Losing It* in October of 2012. *Dramatically* doesn't seem like a strong enough word to describe all the ways my life has changed. You'd think after a year it would feel less surreal, but it doesn't. I want to pinch myself because this is all more than I could have ever dreamed. I am so very grateful to God and luck and family and friends and every minuscule happening that brought me to this moment. These two words will never be enough, but thank you.

To my fans: You. Are. Incredible. I cannot even begin to express how awesome you are and how much I adore you. Thanks for all your messages and tweets and e-mails. Thanks for telling me how much you love my characters, and for drawing awesome pictures for me and making gorgeous icons. Thanks for spreading the word to your friends and family and complete strangers. Thanks for coming to see me at signings and for making what I do so much fun. Please don't stop. Tweet me. Facebook me. Attend signings. Sometimes I get busy writing and am a little slow on the replies, but I promise I read and love everything you say.

To my family: You keep me sane. Thanks for watching my cat while I fly off to amazing places (and have a bazillion flight problems that cause me to have to spend the night in some not-so-amazing places). Thanks for reading my things when I need help, and thanks for understanding when I hole up in my apartment for weeks and don't call or visit. Thanks for always being supportive and cheering me on. Thanks for making me who I am. Without your love and care and criticism (and that time my sisters locked me outside in the Texas heat), I wouldn't have become this person who gets to do what she loves for a living. Mom, thanks for listening to me prattle on about plots and publishing for hours even when what I'm saying makes no sense and there's no solution to be had.

To my friends: Thanks for being my second family, and for being my home. Much like Kelsey, it kills me that you're all scattered so far and wide across this world, but I'm so thankful to have you in my past, present, and future. You guys helped teach me who I was, and I always feel like I'm at home when I'm with you. Kristin—you know all the reasons I love you. Stop letting me go so long without visiting. I miss you. P.S. Let's go back to Europe. Lindsay—thanks for the stories and the texts that make me laugh (and make everything better). Thanks for always being my first reader, and for introducing me to *Doctor Who*. Patrick—gah. I cannot even begin to describe all the things I need to thank you for. You're amazing, and anytime I forget to tell you, feel free to punch me (just not in the face). To Ana, most of my books are written to you in some way. I just hope you always know you're not alone. And because Bethany would kill me if I didn't do a full list: Thanks, Bethany, Joey, Shelly, Sam, Murmur, Daniel, Matt, Karina, Tyler, and gah . . . I know I'm missing people. Thank you all. Especially my BUT family. HSFAC will always be home to me.

And to "my" people: Suzie—you are a rockstar. You don't know how grateful I am I didn't read your newest blog post before querying you. And there must be something in the water over at New Leaf because Kathleen, Pouya, Joanna, Danielle—you're all rockstars. Thank you. Amanda—you were my cheerleader and my lifesaver in this book. Thanks for being so flexible and so kind and so generally awesome. Best. Editor. Ever. Jessie—I love you like Draco loves Hermione (in my imagination, anyway). To everyone at Harper: I couldn't have wished for a better home. Thanks for all the support. To Kelly—thanks for dealing with my mess and for being the sweetest, most talented lady ever. To Jennifer—I hope you enjoy Jenny's character that I wrote for you. You're an awesome fan. To Sophie, Jennifer, Monica, and Kathleen—thanks for the blurbs. You guys are the best. And to all of my author friends that I've met over the past year . . . your amazingness could fill a whole book.

And finally, thank you for reading. I hope you enjoyed Kelsey and Hunt's story. I hope it will encourage you to go after what you want, to take a leap. As a brilliant author once said (and an amazing class at VCFA will tell you) . . . Jump off the cliff, and build your wings on the way down.

If you've missed any of Cora Carmack's Losing It series, read on for a look at where it all began . . .

Losing It

Virginity.

Bliss Edwards is about to graduate from college and still has hers. Sick of being the only virgin among her friends, she decides the best way to deal with the problem is to lose it as quickly and simply as possible—a one-night stand. But her plan turns out to be anything but simple when she freaks out and leaves a gorgeous guy alone and naked in her bed with an excuse that no one with half a brain would ever believe.

And as if that weren't embarrassing enough, when she arrives for her first class of her last college semester, she recognizes her new theatre professor.

She'd left him naked in her bed about eight hours earlier. . . .

Faking It

Mackenzie "Max" Miller has a problem. Her parents have arrived in town for a surprise visit, and if they see her dyed hair, tattoos, and piercings, they just might disown her. Even worse, they're expecting to meet a nice wholesome boyfriend, not a guy named Mace who has a neck tattoo and plays in a band. All her lies are about to come crashing down around her, but then she meets Cade.

Cade moved to Philadelphia to act and to leave his problems behind in Texas. So far, though, he's kept the problems and had very little opportunity to take the stage. When Max approaches him in a coffee shop with a crazy request to pretend to be her boyfriend, he agrees to play the part. But when Cade plays the role a little too well, they're forced to keep the ruse going. And the more they fake the relationship, the more real it begins to feel.

Keeping Her

A Losing It Novella

Garrick Taylor and Bliss Edwards managed to find their happily-ever-after despite a rather . . . ahem . . . complicated start. By comparison, meeting the parents should be an absolute breeze, right?

But from the moment the pair lands in London, new snags just keep cropping up: a disapproving mother-in-law-to-be, more than one (mostly) minor mishap, and the realization that perhaps they aren't quite as ready for their future as they thought.

As it turns out, the only thing harder than finding love is keeping it.

Hello Readers!

I hoped you enjoyed Kelsey's story! And if you are
dying for more, I have good news! First, in
January, Jackson Hunt is getting a novella all to
himself! It will start before *Finding It* and overlap
with the events at the beginning of this book. It
will be a great chance to see inside his head now
that you know his big secret.

Additionally, I have a very special treat just
for my Target readers. This is a deleted scene
from when Kelsey goes to the Night of Baths in
Budapest. This scene was a blast to write. It was
fun and sexy, and I was so sad to see it go. You
might ask: Why cut it if you loved it? Well, scenes
get cut for all kinds of reasons. In my first draft
of *Finding It,* the first, oh, one hundred pages were
about Kelsey just partying in Europe. It was
realistic (and fun to write), but after a hundred
pages it all started to blur together (much like it
does for Kelsey). So we decided to jump-start her
journey and her character arc a bit faster. That
resulted in a near-total rewrite of the Night of
Baths scenes. And try as I might to fit this
moment into the new version, it didn't fit the new
tone and just seemed out of place.

To refresh your memory, Kelsey is in
Budapest and met Hunt a few days earlier in the
ruin bars and made a bit of an ass of herself. She

meets Jenny, Tau, and John at her hostel, and together they go out for one crazy night of partying at the Turkish baths. There are fire dances and acrobats and general awesomeness. She runs into Hunt again and despite his rejecting her before, he seems plenty interested in getting to know her. So, without further ado, I give you "The Chicken Scene."

Cora

"Hey Jen!"

Her head snapped toward me, but her hand stayed on Tau's arm.

"What do you say we make this a little more interesting?"

She grinned. "What did you have in mind?"

I turned and pointed toward the corner of the pool where a group of people was playing chicken—girls sat atop guys' shoulders battling to see which duo could knock the other down. The perfect excuse to get all touchy-feely.

Jenny sidled closer to Tau and said, "Oh, Tau and I could take you and Hunt, easy." Somehow I had just stumbled into the best wingwoman ever. Match made in heaven, really. The grin playing about Hunt's mouth told me he thought it was a pretty great idea, too.

I waded back toward him and asked, "What do you say? Think you can handle me?"

His eyes fell to my lips. "I think I would love to."

There were fireworks going off low in my belly in celebration of the awesome night that was most definitely unfolding.

I smiled. "It's settled, then."

The bodies were packed on the side of the pool playing chicken. Some were waiting to play, and others were just watching. Judging by the disproportionate number of guys, I'd say most of them were waiting for a wardrobe malfunction. Hunt and Tau swam away to figure out who was coordinating the chicken matches, leaving me and Jen alone.

"Brilliant idea, by the way," she said. "I love hearing Tau talk. With that accent, who wouldn't? But any excuse to touch him trumps talking any day."

"Where is he from?"

"Australia now, but he grew up in South Africa."

I nodded. "Accents do get major bonus points."

"As does having an amazing body."

"Yeah, Tau looks pretty fit. Good choice."

"Oh, I know. But I wasn't talking about Tau. I was talking about the man you seemed determined to avoid ten minutes ago. What changed?"

"Magic memory-erasing pectoral muscles?"

"Ah, many a woman has been slain by magic pecs. We'll take a moment of silence to remember the fallen." I splashed her, laughing. She said, "But seriously . . . what memory could be bad enough to make you want to give *that* up?"

"Nothing. It doesn't matter. I was just blowing something out of proportion." Another habit I seemed to have picked up from Bliss.

"What are you blowing?" Hunt's hand grazed the small of my back for a few brief seconds, and my muscles practically writhed in joy.

Damn, he was a sneaky one. My original military suspicions had to be spot-on.

"Your mind," I answered. "But that's later. After we win."

His eyes swept across my face, and his chest brushed against my arm as he leaned closer.

"I guess we'll have to win, then."

"I wouldn't count on that," Jenny said.

I smiled. "Oh, honey. Fair warning: I play dirty."

"Do you, now?" Hunt said at my back.

"What can I say? I like winning. So you better hold on to me tightly."

He smirked. "With pleasure."

We moved out of the crowd into the circle. A large man in his forties was running the games. The hair on his head seemed to have fled for the forest on his chest.

He said something in Hungarian, and I just blinked in response. Over my shoulder Hunt said, "Igen."

The man nodded and gestured toward us in a way I could only assume meant go.

"You speak Hungarian?" I asked Hunt. "Who are you? James Bond?"

He smiled, and without warning his head disappeared beneath the water. His hands brushed down my thighs and pushed my knees apart. And holy aneurysm, Batman, his head was between my legs.

Before I could even gauge whether I was more shocked or excited, he was lifting me out of the pool. Water poured down my body and onto his. His hands clamped over my thighs just above the knees, and I tucked my feet behind his back. I braced myself with both hands on his head and said, "Jesus. Warn a girl before you go sticking your head between her legs."

Hunt barked a laugh. "Where's the fun in that?"

I looked up and made eye contact with Jen, who was already situated on Tau's shoulders. Simultaneously we mouthed, "Oh. My. God."

His short hair tickled my palms. I could feel the sloping muscles of his shoulders beneath me. I didn't remember chicken being so sexual the last time I played it. Maybe it was because I'd been like ten and naive then. Or maybe Hunt just made everything sexual. I was leaning toward the latter.

I tried to lean down to talk to him, but all it did was

press my chest into the back of his head. "What's a girl gotta do to get her trusty steed to charge?"

"I'm kind of tempted to toss you in the water right now."

I ran my hands down his neck to his chest, as if I was soothing his ruffled feathers.

"I'll make it up to you."

Jen held her hands out and said, "What are you waiting for, Kelsey? I could have beat you and composed a haiku about my victory in the time you've been stalling and flirting with Hunt."

"You can compose all the Haikus you want." I ran my fingers back up Hunt's chest and said, "This is more fun."

Jen cleared her throat and with a flourish said, "Kelsey, my soul mate / I fear our friendship may end / when you I destroy."

I nearly toppled off Hunt's shoulders, laughing. "Did you actually just haiku me, bitch?"

"You bet I did. What are you going to do about it?"

"Hunt and I are going to hai-kick your ass, that's what."

Out of the corner of my eye, I saw Tau mouthing something. Hunt's shoulders bounced in a chuckle, and that was all the warning I got before I started tipping sideways. I saw Jen's face go slack with shock a second before I hit the surface of the pool.

The warm water swallowed me, rushing into my

mouth and nose. My hair turned against me like Medusa's snakes, covering my face and choking out the neon lights refracting off the water's surface.

Something hooked around my elbows and then the suffocating water gave way to burning air. I pushed back the sopping hair from my face and fixed my glare on a grinning Hunt.

I coughed and tried not to think of how much I must look like a drowned rat. I thumped his chest and said, "Remember that promise I made you? Totally off the table."

"Oh come on, princess. You can't blame us. You and your wonder twin were never going to shut up otherwise."

"Hey, douceface," I thumped him again. "I was waiting on *you* to move."

He smirked and said, "Oops. My bad."

"You should work on your apologetic tone. It sucks."

I wrung out my hair and threw it over my shoulder. I beamed the sweetest smile I could manage (which was only slightly less bitter than a cup of black coffee and my soul). Then I flung myself at him. My legs wrapped around his waist, and his hands gripped my hips. I tried to push him under the water, but we only ended up toppling backward together.

He was still smiling when we submerged, tiny bubbles streaming from his nose and mouth. My hair haloed around us, and time seemed to slow. Beneath the water, the neon lights blurred and the music faded. The water washed away my annoyance, and I became acutely aware of the way our hips were pressed together. His gray eyes turned molten, and my heart might have actually skipped a beat. My lungs burned, but I didn't want to break this moment, to leave this underwater sanctuary. The world outside disappeared. The bodies surrounding us became pieces of the scenery just like the columns and archways. It was so silent that I couldn't even hear my own thoughts. There was heat in his gaze, but also something deeper, something that made my head spin with want.

One of his hands cupped my jaw, and his thumb ran across my bottom lip. My ribcage felt too constricting, and my lungs too empty. And his lips . . . those were too far away.

I wasn't going to make the same mistake of waiting for him again. I reached out and took his strong jaw in my hands. Then I did what I'd been wanting to do since I first saw his smug smile across the bar the night before.

I drew his lips toward mine, and the last of my breath rushed from my lungs as our mouths met. His hands circled around my waist, fingertips pressing into my lower back. My wet chest slid against his, and his tongue met mine.

I saw stars. Like . . . actual spots of light dancing behind my closed eyes. Blood roared in my ears. I tried to clutch him tighter to me, but my fingers felt suddenly weak.

Maybe it wasn't Hunt making my head spin. Maybe it was the whole about-to-die-due-to-a-total-lack-of-oxygen-in-my-lungs thing.

I pushed against his chest and dragged my head above the water. The stars behind my eyes were fireworks now, and my lungs felt like the fiery pits of Mordor. It hurt like a motherfucker, but when Hunt emerged from the water all glistening and romance-novel-y, I only had one thought.

Worth it.

I was still gasping when Jen said, "I literally thought you guys weren't going to come for air."

Still staring at me, Hunt said, "You didn't seem worried enough to try and save us from drowning."

I was more worried about the fact that I almost committed suicide via kissing. Not that that wouldn't be a great way to go . . . but still.

Jen shrugged. "I figured I'd let you die happy."

Hunt shot me a boyish grin that was different than every smolder and smirk I'd seen so far. A giggle rose in my throat before I could bitch slap it down.

I knew it the moment I saw him, but Hunt was dangerous. Not just because he had biceps like pythons. He was a different kind of dangerous . . . the heartbreaking kind.

Sophie Jordan

FOREPLAY A Novel
Available in Paperback and eBook Fall 2013

J Lynn

WAIT FOR YOU A Novel
Available in eBook
Available in Paperback Fall 2013

BE WITH ME A Novel
Available in Paperback Winter 2014

TRUST ME A Novella
Available in eBook Fall 2013

Molly McAdams

FROM ASHES A Novel
Available in Paperback and eBook

TAKING CHANCES A Novel
Available in Paperback and eBook

STEALING HARPER An Original eNovella
Available in eBook

FORGIVING LIES A Novel
Available in Paperback and eBook Fall 2013

DECEIVING LIES A Novel
Available in Paperback and eBook Winter 2014

Shannon Stoker

THE REGISTRY A Novel
Available in Paperback and eBook

THE COLLECTION A Novel
Available in Paperback and eBook Winter 2014